CRISS CROSS

by

CARON ALLAN

COPYRIGHT 2012 © CARON ALLAN - SECOND EDITION

The author asserts the moral right to be identified as the owner of this work.

No part of this book may be reproduced or transmitted in any form or by any means, including but not limited to: graphic, electronic, or mechanical, including photocopying, recording, taping, or by any informational storage retrieval system without advanced prior permission in writing from the publisher.

This is a work of fiction, and is not based on a true story or on real characters.

For Alan, with all my love

CRISS CROSS

Sun 24 June
To my darling Cressida
Happy Birthday, Sweetheart! Have fun writing down all your thoughts and plans and dreams, then when we're old and grey we can sit together on that terrace in Capri and watch the sun go down, drink a glass of wine and you can read me the spicy bits from this journal and we will have a good laugh and talk about the old days!
    With all my love forever and ever
    Thomas xx

Same day - 10.35pm
She must die!!!! I hate her!!! I refuse to put up with her a moment longer, she is an evil, conniving old bitch without a grain of family feeling and it's time she was dead!!!!

Mon 25 June – 2.35pm
Have you noticed how some people just never seem to realise they've gone too far?
I was going to start off my new journal with something terribly erudite and wise. Like a new school notebook, I particularly wanted the first page to look lovely. But I suppose it really doesn't matter if the first page isn't perfectly neat and everything – the whole purpose of a journal is to pour out one's innermost thoughts and give vent to all the frustrations that, as a nicely brought-up person, one can't give full reign to in 'real' life, and so obviously even the first page can get a bit messy. And now just look at it!

But I digress. I must explain from the beginning…

It was my birthday yesterday. 32 already. God, I'm old! I looked at myself in the bathroom mirror this morning and even in the flattering south-facing light and all steamy and fresh from the shower, I'm absolutely certain I could see the tiniest line down the left side of my face from my nose to the corner of my mouth – I'm convinced it wasn't there yesterday. Wonder if I've left it too late for Botox?

Among a number of very extravagant birthday gifts, my Darling Thomas gave me this sweet little journal. I'd mentioned weeks ago that I used to keep a journal when I was a melodramatic teenager, and how nice it was just to write down everything that happened and to really get it out of my system and add in lots of 'grrr' faces and heavy underlining, and lo and behold, the dear man, he surprised me with this journal for my birthday. So here I am.

It's an absolutely beautiful book. It has a hard cover with a weird kind of gothicky design in the most gorgeous shades of black and purple and gold, with a magneticky bit in the front flap to keep it closed, and the pages, somewhere between A5 and American letter-size, are edged in gold too, so it feels very glamorous to write in – in fact I was a bit afraid to begin the first page, hence all the fuss about it looking nice and neat, I almost got a kind of writer's block!

But all my good intentions and deep thoughts and years of accumulated adult wisdom and the desire to create something really special went out the window when my cow of a mother-in-law turned up on a 'surprise' visit and now my first page – well second really, under that really sweet little message from Thomas – is absolutely ruined! I only hope to God Thomas doesn't read it!

Not that she'd remembered it was my birthday any more than my own mother had – oh no! One can't expect her (or the other one!) to keep track of trivial little details like that. No, she needed Thomas' advice about some financial matters, and thought she'd pop over. After all what's an hour and a half's chauffeured drive here or there? Of course she didn't bother to ring first, see if we were in or free or anything. Clarice is used to everyone falling in with her plans.

'I knew you wouldn't be doing anything important,' she says as she breezes in, dropping her coat in the middle of the hall, frowning around at the décor before settling herself in the drawing room, demanding tea. Not just the drink! By 'tea' she means that Victorian/Edwardian meal between Luncheon as she calls it and Dinner. She expected crustless sandwiches, crumpets, cakes (large and small), scones, jam and cream, the works. And copious amounts, of course, of tea-the-drink. China, not Indian. With lemon slices in a dainty little crystal dish, not 2 litres of semi-skimmed in a huge plastic container.

Thomas reminded her that it was my birthday and that consequently we had plans for the evening. She waved a negligent hand. Her hair, a shade too brave, was salon-perfectly waved if somewhat stiff-looking, and her clothes were at least one generation too young for her, but hideously expensive as well as just – well, hideous. Did I mention I hate her?

'Oh that can be set aside. You can easily go out some other evening. My financial affairs are of the first import.'

Thomas looked at me. He didn't want to fight with his mother and I knew there would be no point in trying to push him to resist the onslaught, so for poor Thomas' sake, I sighed and shrugged and he sat down next to the old dragon and asked what she wanted to know. Meanwhile I dashed off to ring Monica Pearson-Jones and a few others, to let them know that we would either be horribly late for the theatre party, or quite possibly not turn up at all. I have to admit I was feeling quite cross and rather sorry for myself. However, Huw and Monica's machine had to take the terrible news, as they were out. I hoped to God they weren't already on their way.

When I got back to the drawing room, Clarice was banging on about her bloody cats, and Thomas was all glazed over and away-with-the-fairies-looking. Clarice just looked up and taking in my flat tummy and slender waist (which take me hours to maintain, btw) glared at me and said 'so, still not knocked up yet then?' And before I could respond with a frosty, well-constructed rebuttal, she turned to Thomas and said, 'I told you she wouldn't be any good. Why you couldn't marry that Filipino girl the Honourable Addison-Marksburys brought back with them, I'll never understand. Very good child-bearing, the Filipinos. And it's not as though she would have expected you to take her anywhere.'

Thomas said nothing helpful, of course, just sat there like a rabbit in the headlights. And then, before I could recover my breath enough to pick my jaw up off the floor, at that moment, Huw and Monica arrived. I raced out into the hall, thinking I might be able to head them off, but just as I was discreetly mumbling to them just inside the front door, Thomas dashed out looking frazzled and dragged them in for a cuppa. Huw, only too glad to wade into a fight, immediately went in with Thomas, whilst Monica exchanged a 'families, what can you do!' eye-roll with me and we followed on at a more sedate pace, I with the awful sense that things were about to go even more horribly wrongerer!

How right I was. I could see Clarice eyeing them up and down. I knew she wouldn't like Huw, because he can seem a tad brash on first meeting. He might have the breeding she prefers, but he doesn't always act like a gentleman. Plus he takes great delight in saying exactly the wrong thing. Loves to shake things up a bit, does our Huw. But Monica – well, she's lovely! Clarice couldn't possibly find anything objectionable in Monica.

She found something.

After eyeing them very obtrusively for several full minutes and barely murmuring even the merest of pleasantries when Thomas made the introductions, Clarice said to me, quite loudly enough for them to hear, though it was supposed to be a whisper,

'Married his secretary, did he? She looks that type. Coarse. Rather Cheap. Eye to the main chance, one would imagine.'

Monica turned to glare, but before she could say anything, and as Huw was about to stroll to her defence, Thomas got their attention by forcing cake on them, but to no avail as, inspired once more, Clarice leaned towards me with another little gem.

'**He's** obviously a drinker. And looks like a bit of a lech, too. Just like Millicent Huntingdon's first husband. Thoroughgoing bastard, that one. No back-bone, morally speaking.'

Our friends left just seconds later, Huw saying something over his shoulder about a 'vile old bag.' In fact the duration between Clarice's comment and their car careering off down the drive was less than thirty seconds. I think that's probably a record. I say 'our friends' but after the insults from Clarice, we'll probably never see them again. Then of course, on being reprimanded for her poor manners, Clarice sulked and kept going on about how she didn't know what the younger generation were coming to and blaming Thomas for not executing better judgment.
'In more ways than one,' she said, and eyed me with malice once more.

So as I was saying to begin with, some people just never seem to realise they've gone too far!

I mean, the vast majority of normal people, people like you and I, we just instinctively know the correct way to behave. We apologise when someone else bumps into us, we begin every complaint with 'terribly sorry to be a nuisance, but…' We're nice. Pleasant. We have a kind of in-built mechanism, straight as a line in damp sand, an invisible barrier which prevents us stepping beyond the realm of reasonable and acceptable behaviour.

Some people do not.

Some people never read the signs, they ignore all warnings and plough doggedly on, intent only on saying what they want to say and doing what they want to do. They don't care about your feelings. They turn up unannounced and uninvited, they change your plans without considering your wishes. They don't notice the look on your face, the halting of your phrase, they are oblivious to the cooling of the atmosphere around them. They never notice that infinitesimal pause before you continue to hand around the petit-fours, a fixed smile plastered on your face, inane pleasantries tripping off your tongue. Some people remain completely and utterly ignorant of all the signs.

Everyone else, metaphorically speaking, has grabbed their handbags and jackets, collected their madeleine-tins from your kitchen, tossed the keys to the Range Rover to their husbands, dashed out of the door leaving kisses still hanging in the air, and are already on the slip road to the motorway whilst **That Person** is still looking vaguely around as a few motes of dust drift gently down to the Axminster. They are wearing that idiotic expression that says, 'who me? What could I have possibly said?' or even worse, 'well I only said what everyone else was thinking'.

And they are always, always, always completely unaware when they have outstayed their welcome.

There's only one way to deal with people like that.

One way and only one way.

You have to kill them.

They never take the hint, you see. They fail to detect the slight frost in your demeanour as they witter on, insulting your loved ones, criticising your friends, your home, your life. Such people cannot be taught, changed or reasoned with. In the end, it's just easier for all concerned if you get rid of them before they truly become a Nuisance and make everyone with whom they come into contact completely and utterly miserable.

And if that seems a little harsh, just think for a moment about what these people do to your self-esteem, to your inner calm, to your peace of mind. When the phone rings, these are the people whose voice one dreads to hear. One begins to dread all family occasions and holidays because of That Person. Frankly, it's just not worth the emotional and psychological trauma of putting up with them. Life is quite challenging enough. And that is the stage I've now reached with Clarice.

So.

That said, it's one thing to say to oneself, Monday, water plants, collect dry-cleaning, go to library, bake fairy cakes for the One-to-One drop-in day-centre fundraiser, and quite another thing to just sort of slip onto the bottom of your to-do list, 'oh and kill mother-in-law and get everything tidied up because dinner will be on the table at seven o'clock sharp due to drinks at eight-thirty at the Pearson-Jones'.

Things – unfortunately – just aren't quite that simple.

The Grandes Dames of the murder mystery genre, practising their art in the early and middle parts of the twentieth century – what one might term the 'Golden Age' of detective fiction – espoused the pleasures of poisoning. Fly-papers were meticulously soaked to extract their lethal properties, berries and toadstools were carefully gathered and sliced and diced and surreptitiously introduced into steaming casseroles and tempting omelettes. On every domestic shelf such things as sleeping draughts and rat poison and eye drops sat unnoticed and unremarked, and a home was not a home without at least a few jars of cyanide or arsenic sulking forgotten in garden sheds and garages.

But, sadly, these items are notoriously tricky to come by nowadays in our 'Nanny state'.

Of course, one watches these TV programmes that explain all about the forensic process, so that one is pre-armed with useful information. Knives wielded by the left-handed protagonist cut quite differently to those employed by a right-handed person. Equally so the short protagonist and the weak slash feeble protagonist.

In addition the actual wound inflicted by a classic blunt weapon can yield so much information about not just the weapon itself but also the attacker – the approximate height, stance, and even weight and probable gender, for example, and the ferocity of attack is sometimes a gauge as to motive and psychology. Firing a gun leaves residue on one's clothes, gloves, and skin, and, contrary to popular belief, it can be quite a job laying one's hands on a firearm.

According to the Daily Tabloid, a gun may readily be obtained at certain pubs in our larger cities for as little as £30, usually from a gentleman going by the name of Baz or Tel, but the problem is, these tend to be the kind of establishments one would hesitate to enter in broad daylight, let alone late in the evening.

Remember, it's very difficult to get a decent glass of Merlot in this kind of hostelry, and one can't just go in and hang about without making a purchase of some kind. If you do just go into the bar and stand or sit in a corner, the other patrons are likely to stare and nudge one another. They may even whisper to one another, 'wot jer fink er game is thin?' or possibly, 'Oi Tel, woss up wiv er – she too good fer us or summink?'

This is especially the case when one gentleman approaches and states that he and his friend, Gaz or Stevo or even 'Arrison would like to buy you a beverage of some description, usually a Mojito or similar, and you are forced to politely but firmly decline. They are apt to be offended.

And if you do order a nice glass of Merlot, there's always a momentary look of confusion on the face of the Landlord as he tries to recollect whether he has a corkscrew within easy reach, or how long ago he opened the half-empty bottle on the back counter - was it recently enough to avoid the expense of opening a brand new bottle?

Then he'll ask if you'd like ice and lemon. Might as well add a cherry-on-a-stick and a little umbrella! And there's no point in trying to charge it to your Diamond Visa or Platinum Amex - they much prefer to deal with cash. It's altogether a rather unpleasant experience.

In any case, Baz or Tel are always surprisingly suspicious when one asks them if it would be possible to purchase a small Eastern-European revolver, something with a fairly hefty slug but small enough to slip into a small Louis Vuitton clutch-purse, or at a pinch into a Mulberry shoulder bag, or even, and here I may be straying into the realms of fantasy or James Bond (same thing, I suppose), even into the top of one's stocking.

The gentleman invariably looks a bit puzzled and says something along the lines of, ' 'ere that sounds a bit dodgy Darlin'. I don't do nuffin like that.' Well, of course it's a bit dodgy, one points out, one is illegally attempting to buy a gun in a corner of the car park of a fleabag pub at eleven o'clock at night, and paying cash into the bargain. How could one possibly see it in any other light than dodgy? It doesn't matter if you offer them £100, £200 or even £500 at this point, they just walk away shaking their heads and saying, 'screw that, I don't wanna get cort up in nuffin dodgy.'

I ask you.

The criminal classes aren't what they once were. But what other choices does one have?

A pillow over the face in the dead of night is liable to leave a filament of goose-down in the lungs of your chosen recipient. This will immediately be detected by any half-decent forensic examiner and blabbed all over the Car Crash Telly channel in a late-night special called **Toffs Who Kill** or something or the kind.

A bit of a bump with the car in a quiet part of town on a wet Wednesday afternoon may lead to eyewitnesses or CCTV footage recording your number plate for posterity. For goodness sake, tiny fragments of paint from the wing of your vehicle may embed themselves in the depths of the wound you inflict, and these same may be delicately reclaimed by a steady-handed science-nerd in a lab coat wielding a pair of sterile tweezers.

Murder is a difficult road to travel. But one must bear in mind the old maxim that nothing worthwhile is ever attained without a struggle. Therefore it is imperative to be utterly committed, to be dedicated in one's approach, to persevere in the face of adversity and to make copious notes so that one may learn from one's mistakes. And of course, it goes almost without saying, each stage must be planned in intricate, even tedious, detail.

Today I went to my local stationer's – it's so vital, I feel, that one supports local businesses wherever possible - and bought two notebooks, a small index card box, a set of ruled index cards, and a rather nice fountain pen. My husband seems to be under the impression that I require these items to catalogue my shoe collection. Sweet! And not a bad idea…but first things first.

Now, I've worked out I have approximately six weeks in which to plan and carry out my little project, and still have time for a decent mourning period before we have to be in Scotland for the 'glorious twelfth' – my Thomas's cousin Jessica (lovely woman!) always has a house party. Actually this year it's the glorious thirteenth as the twelfth falls on the Sabbath, and one never shoots in Scotland on the Sabbath. Der! Thomas loves his shooting, so although I'm not a lover of messy pastimes, I always like to encourage him to relax and have a bit of fun, stockbrokers work so hard don't they, and such high stress levels, one obviously doesn't want them to crack up under the pressure!

Not, of course, that we would need a mourning period as such, as Thomas hates his mother almost as much as I do, but one must maintain appearances, and I'd need a good week, I'm absolutely certain, to sort out the contents of Highgates – she has so much accumulated old tat, although most of it is stored in boxes in the disused bedrooms, and has been sitting there untouched for simply decades. But it will take me a full day just to sort through the Spode and other china and porcelain in case there are any little gems lurking amongst the dross.

There are also two rather elderly and smelly cats that will have to have put to sleep, and of course the whole legal side of things to sort out. Thomas will have to see to that.

Then there'll be the funeral to arrange.

Now one thing I do think is really important, and that is to ensure a really beautiful casket is purchased. And of course, it's no good skimping when it comes to fittings, not if you want to do the job properly. Brass, highly polished, is the only thing that will do. Not that horrid plated stuff that rubs off as soon as you touch it. That's what happened to Thomas' colleague Miranda Kettle (she's got the biggest nose I have ever seen, and the smallest chin! Nothing grows in the shade, does it?). She skimped on her mother's coffin. We all noticed the green stain on the pall-bearers' gloves, of course. No one said anything obviously, and in any case, Miranda herself didn't notice. She had her nose buried in an extra-large gentlemen's handkerchief most of the time, she was so inconsolably upset. Poor woman. Absolutely distraught throughout the entire funeral. Thought the mortgage had been paid off years ago! Such a beastly shock.

Same day - 5.45pm
I've just had a bit of a break to think about this a little longer. So I went to sit out on the terrace with a cup of tea. Then it came to me, and I had to dash indoors and fetch this journal.

Of course, the very thing!

The scourge of society nowadays - the house-breaker. Or, more precisely, the drug addict, who, as the papers will no doubt report, desperate to gain some funds for another few grammes of white powder to snort, breaks into a nice house in an attractive part of Ely in the hope of some opportunistic gain. Then is surprised by a feisty, elderly lady with a bit of oomph about her, and during the course of a desperate struggle, the evil perp bludgeons the poor old dear and makes off with some loot.

Meanwhile, I could be enjoying a well-deserved break at a health spa in – ooh, let me think – Cambridgeshire, perhaps?

This might actually work!

Things to do:
Purchase rubber gloves, not those cheap ones, they make me itch.
Ditto black woollen ski mask or balaclava
Goggles
Also some black shoe polish (for face, obviously, so must make sure I purchase a 'gentle' formula) as I believe we're actually out of black shoe polish at the moment.
I think I already have a black (or navy would suffice at a push) pac-a-mac somewhere in the rear cloakroom from that ill-fated walking holiday of 2006 – Thomas had wanted to try something different – suffice to say, we went straight back to Antigua after that.
Oh, and black slacks.
Next, book visit to health spa. Tell Thomas am going away for a couple of days to a nice, reputable place in Cambridgeshire. Must buy a copy of 'The Lady' in case none of my pals can think of anything in that area.
Will need to purchase a cheap, disposable holdall for disguise. (Could use a plastic grocery bag, I suppose, but it's not really me. Also, this might scream homicidal housewife slash amateur-hour and want to look like I know what I'm doing, right tools for the right job etc etc but can't actually use one of my own in case it's traced back to me).
No need to buy a bludgeoning implement, as plenty of scope at Thomas' mother's house. Lots of beastly vases and figurines (some really quite large and heavy and ghastly but without any actual value) – and, as will obviously have gloves on, can leave figurine in situ once used, no need concern oneself about disposal of same. Actually leaving

the weapon behind looks better from a *not*-going equipped point of view. More impromptu.

You know, I'm so excited. I really think this might actually work. Must just go and fish my little filofax out of my bag to work out a timetable. Then I can start writing in the headings on my index cards. Ooh Goody!

Tues 26 June - 7.15 pm
I had to stop in order to prepare dinner – time had simply run away with me. You know how it is when you get your teeth into a really fabulous new project and you just can't bear to leave it for a moment! Today has just flown by, and I feel so alive! Fortunately Mrs Hopkins had left quite clear instructions about the best way to reheat her venison casserole and had left all the china and silverware and napkins ready, and the lychee and mango bombe just wants five minutes out of the freezer to soften slightly. Such a treasure, if a little rough around the edges. Mrs H. I mean, not her bombe. That is absolutely divine.

    But, blast! Had completely forgotten about the Menzies and the Pearson-Jones' coming over this evening for drinks. Did not even remember to confirm with Mrs Hopkins, so consequently I had no lemons or limes sliced, no crudités chopped, but fortunately there were some left-over dips from yesterday still in the fridge in mixing bowls and covered with cling-film so I just had to fling those into some china dishes. But damn! I had completely forgotten to do my signature borage-flower ice-cubes. I could tell Thomas was absolutely shocked to the core - he raised an eyebrow at me.

    And whilst I was flapping about, he was asking me if I could remember which of the Menzies' daughters is the concert pianist and which is the high class call-girl we never mention. He's so sweet, his attention to detail never fails to astonish me.

    One could hardly risk muddling the two girls up – imagine saying, is Georgia still banging the businessmen at Heathrow? Daphne could hardly turn around and say, oh no, it's Saskia that does that, Georgia still relies on her training at the Royal College of Music to pay her bills. Lovely to hear Thomas having a good old chuckle over that one. What a pet.

Wed 27 June - 9.20am
What a horrid summer! The spring was so hot and dry there was talk of a hosepipe ban and comparisons with the summer-long drought of 1976 and the next moment, when all I've got in my wardrobes are strappy tops and gorgeous little floaty skirts, it's peeing down with rain and freezing cold! We've had to put the heating on – in JUNE! What must the tourists think?

Thomas says if it doesn't improve by the time the Olympics begins, 'everyone' will lose a fortune and I think he's right – I mean, who goes to the Olympics to sit in the rain?

Pleasant evening last night with dear Huw and Monica. And the Menzies, of course. I asked Monica if she knew of a nice spa in Cambridgeshire and she told me about one just outside Basingstoke. I pointed out to her that Basingstoke is not and never has been within the county of Cambs, and that nothing short of a *very* big civil war would be capable of placing Basingstoke within the county of Cambridgeshire, and frankly I didn't see it being worth the hassle. She said, 'Oh? But what about when Rutland became part of the United Kingdom? I thought all the county borders got changed around?'

And this was before we had any alcohol. So much for a private education. Will have to fall back on a two month old copy of The Lady I thieved from my hairdresser's.

I finally have a few minutes to myself to try to put together a kind of draft schedule for killing my mother-in-law.

Yesterday, when I first started thinking about it, everything seemed so simple, so straightforward, so naïve, if you see what I mean.

But now…I don't know if its nerves or something – but now it all just seems so terribly complicated. I feel a little discouraged. Perhaps getting it all down on paper will give me a bit of a boost, and I'll be able to get a proper overview.

Wise to start at the end, so to speak. I'll need a few days to pack; so that means, must be back from cleaning up and sorting out at Thomas' mother's place by, say, August 7th, in order to be at Jessica's on the 11th.

Which means we must have the cleaning done that week, so the funeral would have to be between 28th July to 2nd August, say.

Hmm.

Will have to 'top' Clarice at least a week earlier, which gives us 21st July, to be on the safe side. What day of the week is that? Oh, a Saturday. Hmm. Not sure. Perhaps a Wednesday would be better? So the 18th then, it's always good to do things on a Wednesday, it breaks up the week a bit, and also if it's any later in the week, the funeral might get pushed back to after the weekend and upset the schedule, so you know, Wednesday is better all round. I'll pencil that in.

Added 'tennis shoes' to my list of things to buy, as realised will need to sneak about a bit, prior to the actual bludgeoning, and you can't do that in three inch Italian heels, not at Highgates with all that polished wood. Would it have killed the woman to buy in a decent bit of carpet?

So, Wednesday the 18th. Hmm. Will have to book a few days, perhaps the Monday to Wednesday. Three days at Chapleys Health Spa (top place for five years running out of a poll of twenty according to Harpers'. The Lady didn't offer much in Cambs although there is apparently someone there who dyes and knits the wool from her own rare-breed sheep. V. Interesting, I wonder if she sells her wares online?) So that's settled, Monday 16th, Tuesday 17th and Wednesday 18th. Lovely! Will arrange to come home in the evening and have a light supper with Thomas, just in time to receive terrible news. Although of course, am much cheered by the thought that it is theoretically possible I receive the terrible news earlier in the day when in the middle of a seaweed wrap for example – that would be Marvellous!

    I can imagine the shocked looks, the hushed tones of all the staff at Chapley's. Then me, quiet, dignified, getting into the police car with poor Thomas, handsome and pale but composed. People will say I'm very brave. I wonder how much a swooning couch would cost? It would be perfect for receiving visitors during those first few days following our tragic loss.

    Oops, must dash. Nearly time for Mrs Hopkins to arrive – today's her day for doing the floors. Well, well, plenty to think about anyway. V. exciting!

Same day - 12.15pm

Gosh, I'm just shaking with rage! In fact am really astonished at myself, can't believe I am so upset. Must calm down. Perhaps a small sherry?

Thomas' mother rang. Quelle surprise.

Mrs Hopkins had just been explaining to me that 'the bleedin' 'oover don' pick up proper an' it's not the bag, cos that's been emptid'. Dratted woman. Will ask Thomas if any suggestions or failing that, ring up and order a new vacuum cleaner. In fact that's probably the easiest thing to do anyway. I'm absolutely certain she sabotaged it in order to obtain one of those new all-singing, all-dancing bag-free brightly-coloured ones. Honestly! Surely that's why one has servants anyway, to save one all this faffing about with trivialities?

And just as all that was going on, Clarice rang. She didn't even wait for me to finish stating the number etc when I was forced to answer my own phone due to Mrs Hopkins preoccupation with the shortcomings of our cleaning equipment, she just jumped right in with 'I have decided that I could do with a break, so I'm going up to Jessica's for a few days. You will be going up as usual, I imagine, for Dear Tommy's Shooting, so you can easily give me a lift, there'll be oodles of room in your car. Make sure you're here promptly at nine to collect me. That will mean we will be able to stop for luncheon at twelve at The Bush Hotel. That will be quite adequate. Make sure you're not late. And don't pack the car up too much, I shall have a lot of luggage.'

She didn't even waste time on the accepted niceties such as, 'hello, dear, it's your mother-in-law, how are you?' She just started in the middle then put the phone down when she had finished.

And her tone! Really most peremptory. I began a really quite mild protestation, trying to point out something silly like I'd have to check with Thomas – just because I didn't want her to have it all her own way - and I do so hate it when she calls him Tommy – it sounds so childish and patronising. No one has called him Tommy for twenty years. But again, she just cut across me mid-sentence with all this heavy tutting and in quite a nasty tone said, 'oh for heaven's sake, child, it's not as though I ever ask either of you to do anything for me. Now I can't stand about chatting all day, the vet's coming to worm the cats.' And that was when she put the phone down.

Child? I felt like screaming 'I'm 32 for God's sake!' Really, such a feeling of sheer frustrated rage came over me. I actually think if she had been standing right there in front of me, I could have throttled the life out of her with my bare hands. I'm still shaking, and it happened almost ten minutes ago.

If she hadn't already been on my hit-list, she would be right there at the top after that!

It's not as though that's the first time something of this sort has happened.

How many times has Thomas told me she's said to him, 'I suppose you'll be bringing That Girl with you when you come?' To which he has variously replied, 'Yes, of course I shall, she's my girlfriend/fiancée/wife.'

And there have been numerous criticisms over the years relating to my hair, my fashion sense, my education, my background. My figure has been described alternately as too thin, too angular, and even, 'not a real woman at all', followed by such pronouncements as 'no wonder she's not managed to give you a child after all these years.'

And the last of these was, obviously, the worst of her sins. She took it upon herself, during one miserable visit to her home, to advise him to divorce me and marry someone who would be able to give him the children he so desperately wanted. After all, he'd given me almost ten years, time to give someone else a chance. She's even tried to persuade him to take a foreign mistress, (an illegal immigrant preferably, as according to her, the woman wouldn't be able to do anything from a legal standpoint and would be glad of the money) in order to take up the slack as it were. Clarice thinks that money is all anyone is interested in.

He tried to explain to her that he loved me and therefore takes his marriage vows seriously as to fidelity and neither did he want to divorce me, and in any case, it wasn't my fault alone that we had no children – he pointed out to her that both of us had difficulties in that direction. Upon which she turned her face away with a wrinkling of the nose, saying scornfully, 'Nonsense, the Barker-Powell men have always been renowned for their virility, and it would be scandalous to suggest otherwise.'

Miserable old bag.

Will definitely book Chapley's tomorrow.

Fri 29 June - 9.45am
OMG what bloody awful weather! To start with, we've had to have the heating on in the evenings and first thing in the morning – in JUNE – for a week now, it's so bloody cold. Then we had two (count them!) hot sunny days, and then yesterday we had the hugest storm – I think the last time I can remember a massive storm in the daytime must have been when I was a child and I was on the stairs at Lady Margaret's, and with it being all ghastly oak panelling the place was pitch black and Antoinettina Ferguson-Partridgley fell down the stairs and broke three ribs and her collar-bone.

    Yesterday we had thunder, lightning, torrential rain (with the inherent flash-flooding all over the country, thank God we live on a slight incline!) Really it was absolutely biblical, then, just as it started to roll away and the sun was peeping cautiously between the skirts of some clouds, Bam! There was another storm, even louder, wetter and rumblier with hail and everything! Much worse than the first. And if this ruins Wimbledon yet again, I will not be a happy bunny! The grass is six inches high all over the back lawn, and at the front of the house, our drive is rapidly disappearing behind a screen of long, drippy whip-cords of drunken forsythia and rambling roses that are utterly uncontrolled, and I haven't been able to cut any for the dinner table this year. With the weather the way it is our odd-jobby gardener-chappie hasn't been able to sort the place out properly. Our grounds are beginning to resemble a council estate. All we need is a set of pram wheels and a pile of bricks and some doggy-doo.

    Which reminds me, must book a trip to London, it's been ages since we popped into the

Tate Modern. We could do with a spot of culture. Or if Thomas doesn't fancy it, I can ask Monica along.

I asked Monica if she and Huw had tickets for any of the Olympic events and she didn't even know it was on! Honestly, that woman never knows what's going on in the world around her! Of course the reason I asked was because Thomas rang me from his office to say our tickets had arrived – women's gymnastics heats and finals – how wonderful! I love to watch the gymnastics events though I can barely do a forward roll myself. Such grace, such co-ordination, such composure - I wasn't going to give all that up just to fling myself about in a leotard.

Same day - 10.45 am

How disappointing! Chapley's are full on the date I wanted – some society girl's hen-party that week, and she's taking a large group of pals with her for a few days' frolics. So I've had to make the booking for next weekend, a whole ten days earlier than I'd anticipated, because that was all they had available until October. I can't possibly wait that long.

    It will mean some re-jigging, of course, but I don't foresee any serious difficulties. Although it is a bit of a worry – I do so hate to be rushed, I might forget something vital. Of course it will come a bit out of the blue for poor Thomas, but I doubt he'll mind too much – I should think if we have the slightest chance of any half-decent weather, even for an hour, he'll be straight out onto the golf course anyway, and naturally I shouldn't go with him, as I don't play. Beastly game, golf, completely pointless. I believe it was Mark Twain who said golf was an excellent way to spoil a nice walk and I must say I quite agree.

    I must stop now, I need to pop to the shops to buy a few…well, just a few items that might come in 'handy' on my little trip.

Same day 12.50pm

Gosh! Well I've just got back from shopping and I must say, it's awfully strange – you've absolutely no idea how difficult it is to buy a proper, traditional balaclava in the summer. In the end I had to go to a ski-wear specialist. I'm still not sure that what I've got is suitable or appropriate and it cost a great deal of money. Never mind, it'll probably be all right if I add a silk headsquare or something. I suspect my pashmina will be too long and flowing. And not very break-and-enter-like. Not with that long fringe around the edge and of course, all that silver embroidery and beading.

And tonight it's drinks at the Pearson-Jones's again. I do hope there's not too much of a crowd, I feel a bit done in. In fact I could have done without having to go out tonight, I need time to formulate an action-plan and double-check I've got everything I need. After all, my special weekend is only a week away. But we'd already promised to attend before I knew I was going to take on this new 'project' and I don't feel I can back out now.

Sun 1 July – 11.30 am
Friday night was a pleasant enough evening, actually. Very pleasant. Only three other couples, in addition to ourselves and the Pearson-Jones'. Some people called Maybury, quite nice. She was a teensy bit of a fuss-pot, but he was very charming. Then there were the Blairs, I think he is in the same sort of line as Thomas because they talked Portfolios and Hedge Funds all evening – so dull. She talked jam and HRT to Monica all night – so they must be a bit older than the rest of us. The third couple are not married, just 'life-partners' like almost everyone one meets these days. I'm so glad we're actually married, one feels as though one has a psychological advantage over those who won't commit. He, Jeremy Patterson, is in Law, but I can't quite remember what sort, and she, Nadina Cooper, is a primary school teacher. Little mousy person, quite timid. I couldn't quite picture her controlling a bunch of six year olds, I bet they make mincemeat of her. Well of course I put it a bit more tactfully than that.

'Yes,' she said, 'of course they can be quite a challenge at that age, but children are such precious little charges, aren't they? And of course one doesn't like to discourage them from expressing themselves ***really*** freely, I mean, they are Our Future, aren't they? And of course, one feels oneself to be so privileged to help them embark upon life's journey of discovery. Just watching them each day, like delicate little blossoms unfolding, it's really really special.'

Of course it is.

I had to hide a little smile. Really. She seems like a complete ninny to me. Monica caught my eye and it was all I could do not to giggle.

But I must admit, as Nadina wittered on in excruciating detail with anecdote after anecdote that illustrated just how challenging her precious little charges could be – she did impart one single nugget of useful information. And of course, she doesn't **teach** them, she guides them. Obviously. Silly me.

I had been smiling vaguely at something Thomas had just told one or other of the men, probably Maybury, when just behind me, I heard Nadina speaking to Monica.

I had been mentally sort of tuning her out for the last half hour or so – one can only take so much complacent wittering – and a little of her certainly goes a long way. She's not particularly bright, and her only interest in life seems to be those little monsters she teaches, so although every so often the conversation was diverted into another topic, no matter what efforts we others went to, somehow she managed to steer us back to school, usually with a phrase such as, 'well, in my experience at primary school…', or occasionally she varied it with, 'speaking as a primary education professional, I remember when…' or possibly even, 'as one of My Parents was telling me recently at Contact Evening…'

Stupid woman. She made it sound as if the 25 sets of children's parents were her own, in addition to the two fools who selfishly begat her. For a moment my mind wandered as I tried to imagine myself with 25 lots of Clarice to deal with. I shuddered and spilt Pinot Grigio down my Miu Miu blouse. Monica offered me a napkin to mop myself up with, then my teeth were set on edge by Nadina's jingly happy voice saying,

'Of course, My Parents find it so much easier to obtain the more traditional uniform items now that Holt's outfitters have opened up in town. They stock simply everything, and very reasonably priced, too.'

'I must make a note,' Mrs Maybury said, and she grabbed her bag and started rummaging for paper and a pencil so she could make a note of the name of the place. Her daughter needed a new blazer for her youngest for the autumn term. As she rummaged she told us the hilarious anecdote of how little Neville had ripped the entire right side of his blazer off. Not even Nadina was listening. Of course we all quickly realised that Mrs Maybury was never going to find any paper or pencil in that rather huge and over-full nylon and polyester handbag (from a chain-store, of all places, if I'm not mistaken). Thomas handed her his Mont Blanc, and I ripped out a page from my filofax. Mrs Maybury gushed and blushed and thanked us far more than was necessary and it all became horribly embarrassing.

But… The point is - I was able to memorise the address myself. I could picture the place. Formerly a knitting and needlework store, it had been empty for more than a year. How nice to know that it had reopened. And what a useful sort of shop to have in our area. I must pop in there tomorrow morning. It is, after all, one's duty to support local shops as far as possible. Use it or lose it, I always say. LOL.

Mon 2 July – 11.30 am
At the counter there was a short, stout woman hiding behind huge glasses. She was wearing a sensible, serviceable nylon house-coat of a type I haven't seen since I was a child. Even my Mrs H wouldn't be seen dead in one of those. The salesperson looked as though she had equipped several generations of youngsters for school. And hated all of them.

'Can I 'elp you?' She asked. The fingers of her right hand were yellow at the tips and she wheezed as she spoke.

'I would like a balaclava for my son.' I said.

'Ho yes? In this wevver?'

'Sorry? Oh, yes. You see, he's lost his, and I need to replace it before the new school term begins.' Why did I feel I needed to explain myself to her? Didn't she want to sell the bloody things? And anyway, we've had a crap summer so far, cold and wet. Today is yet another day of off-and-on-again rain – perfect for balaclava-wearing, one would think.

But she'd already lost interest in my explanation and had turned away to drag a small pair of steps out and she set them before the far end of the range of deep drawers behind the counter.

'Colour?' She said. It took me a moment to realise what she meant. I hesitated. Better not ask for black, it might seem suspicious.

'Navy blue, please.' I said with a bright smile.

'It would be bleedin' navy,' she grumbled, 'they're right at the top.' She creaked up another step and hauled open a drawer. I apologised and thanked her.

She flung a navy blue item wrapped in cellophane over her shoulder and it landed on the counter with a plop. She creaked back down the steps and turned back to me, wheezing alarmingly and leaning forward to rest her elbows on the counter, her face bright red.

'Tha' it?' She asked. Tempting though it was to spend a lot of money in her charming establishment, I confirmed that that was indeed it.

'Nine'een nine'y-five.' She said. She did not ring it up on a cash register. There was no cash register. I was surprised by the price, especially after what Nadina Cooper had said about reasonable prices. I raised an eyebrow.

'Nineteen pounds ninety-five?' I queried. It seemed rather a lot just for a balaclava. How do working-class mothers with large families manage?

'Of course it's pahnds, it wouldn't be bleedin' bananas, would it? That's the price, take it or leave it.' She snapped. For a moment I was tempted to leave it, if only for the pleasure of forcing her to climb back up again and put it away.

But I slapped down my twenty pounds with a smile and my gracious hostess supplied me with a shiny five pence piece from a drawer under the counter. She made no move to hand me my purchase, still less to put it in a bag or offer me a receipt.

'Don't I get a bag?' I asked, not very politely I regret to say, but I was feeling a little cheated out of my customer service quotient. I was more than a little irritated.

'Nope.' She said. 'That's 'ow I keeps me prices so low.'

As I left the shop in a huff she yelled after me, 'it's fer the inviroment yer selfish cow!'

Can't wait to hasten back.

Tues 3 July - 9.55am
I now have everything I need. I'm going to Chapley's on Friday. I've booked a few sessions to make the whole thing look like a genuine getaway-experience, but now I look at my programme, I'm wondering how I'm going to be able to fit in popping out to murder my mother-in-law. Hmm. Must think about this a bit more carefully. But the thing is, they have so many attractive treatments. I would hate to miss out and also, essential to maintain cover story, obviously.

I've got a slot Saturday afternoon. It's the post-lunch, pre-yoga relaxation period. But that only gives me an hour. Will that be enough, do you think? Let's think. According to the Wonderful World Wide Web, Highgates would be about a twenty to thirty minute drive from Chapley's, depending on the traffic. Of course, if it's closer to twenty minutes each way that would be perfect. But if there are some hold-ups on the roads, well, I could end up being late for yoga and that might be remarked upon at a later date. One never knows if one is going to be suspected of killing one's mother-in-law. I mean, it would be nice to think that a daughter-in-law would be above suspicion, wouldn't it? Yet sadly, I imagine that today's police officers are trained to suspect everyone. What with the declining moral standards of the country and everything. And they always say one is most likely to be murdered by one's nearest and dearest, so it could be a problem. Shall have to be really careful!

Same day - 11.25pm
I've been unable to think about anything else all evening. Thomas said I seemed very far away. And once, halfway through the evening, a sudden panic came over me and I almost reached for the phone to cancel. The more I think about it, it seems such a huge undertaking - am quite daunted.

     Poor Thomas, I haven't been very attentive. He wanted so much to tell me about his day at work, but I'm afraid my thoughts kept wandering. In the end he put on the television. I tried to make it up to him, so he was somewhat mollified, but it was a real struggle for me, and I had to watch golf with him for over an hour! Besides, poor lamb, it's not as if he does anything interesting at work. I mean, it's only money, isn't it?

Wed 4 July - 4.30pm
I suppose as a matter of course, the police would be bound to say something along the lines of, 'by the way Madam, where were you on the afternoon in question?' And of course one would respond, 'why, officer, I was relaxing in my room at Chapley's Spa', to which they would be sure to reply, 'and can anyone corroborate that statement?' which of course they wouldn't be able to, so I would immediately become Main Suspect.

Or, one might say, 'certainly Inspector, I was at my yoga session, with six other people'. Which would be good as far as that goes. But then the Inspector would pop in and see Amari Oman, and she would say, 'yes, Mrs Cressida Barker-Powell was in the yoga session, but she missed the first twenty minutes, arriving out of breath and very flustered and clutching a large holdall she wouldn't let anyone touch. Oh and there were splashes of what may have been blood on her boot-polished face'.

Hmm.

On reflection then, afternoon could be a bit of a washout. Must think about it a bit more over dinner at Le Pierrot.

Same day - 5.20pm
What about the Saturday evening? I suppose, if I'm honest, afternoon was not the best choice for committing a crime, especially not something likely to leave me perspiring and possibly even blood-spattered. I'd be bound to be noticed going into or coming out of Clarice's house, as it would be broad daylight, and I'd be all dressed up like a Goth bank robber. It would surely be not only more appropriate but more convenient to murder someone in the evening?

Still same day - 6.45pm
I could have dinner quite early, eating very quickly, and then spend, say, half an hour in the bar chatting and generally being noticed. Then I could either join the 'Twilight Walk Experience' at ten o'clock, or I could do the 'Our Universe' stargazing thingy in the Auditorium. Or...there's a barbecue slash mixer from nine o'clock until eleven weather permitting. That might be better, because of course, one can put in a brief appearance, slope off to do the dirty deed, then pop back three-quarters of an hour or an hour later, drink in hand, looking a bit tipsy and saying what a lovely time one is having.

Yes. The more I think about it, the more convinced I become that it is absolutely the best idea. And the beauty of it is, if anyone should wonder where I am, they'll simply assume I'm off chatting with someone else! Simple but effective.

Ooh I'm so excited! It's lovely to have something really fun to look forward to!

Argh! Look at the time. Must quickly fling on a gorgeous frock and some face-powder and pop downstairs, the Pearson-Joneses will be here any minute.

Same night later still, almost 1.30 am
Hmm. Well. Where to begin? What a peculiar evening. I'm just not quite sure what to make of it. Can't seem to get my thoughts straight. I'm either up the proverbial creek with no paddle or everything is okay. It's all a bit…

Well it all began with dinner, obviously, which was very pleasant but completely unremarkable.

After dinner, we came back here for a nightcap and almost immediately the boys went off to look at some fabulous new finance software Thomas has just put on the new computer in his study. I knew we wouldn't see them for hours, so Monica and I went out onto the terrace with our wine and coffee and a lovely big box of Belgian chocolates Monica had brought over.

We were just sitting and chatting, you know, nothing particularly earth-shattering, but pleasant, you know, just relaxing. I haven't known her for much more than a year, but the more we see of each other - the more I get to know her - the better I like her. She's gentle, caring, like me she's interested in the 'little' things, like gardening and cooking and family things. She's not just pearls and Prada and charity dinners like most of my other friends. I feel I can really relax with her and simply be myself.

As I say, we were sitting and chatting. It was already quite late and so the light was beginning to fade, and the solar fairy-lights came on all round the terrace, glowing softly and looking awfully pretty.

And then Twinkle emerged from the rhododendrons. Twinkle is the ginger tom from further down the lane. Once a dainty little kitten, the name Twinkle had initially seemed quite apt, but due to the good home life he leads at several local houses coupled with lashings of Whiskas he has grown into a hulking great beast, as if in spite of his name, like that boy named Sue. For some reason the horrid thing is always prowling around our garden, and he is definitely the most enormous cat I have ever seen. The size of the average corgi, but with longer legs, he's quite intimidating.

    'Oh my God!' said Monica, 'what a bloody great brute of a cat!'

    'I know,' I responded. 'And it makes me laugh to think they named him Twinkle.'

    We began to laugh until we realised Twinkle had deposited something on the lawn. Something large and feathery. Something that still moved, but not in a good way.

    Concerned, we both slapped our glasses down on the little table and ran towards the evil cat which fled at once, leaving his prey behind.

    Close up, the prey was larger than we realised and proved to be a horribly maimed Crow. I don't know how long Twinkle had been playing with it, but it was in a terrible state. One wing was hanging almost off, the few remaining feathers on the other were matted with blood, one leg lay at completely the wrong angle, and the whole of the back and breast of the bird was a mess of bloody bare patches. Its head was almost down on one shoulder.

    I know I gasped. It was such a bloody shock, an almost physical jolt. Instinctively I clapped my hand across my mouth, stifling a cry and I gaped at Monica. She looked every bit as horrified. The bird flopped about on the grass, refusing to simply lie still and die, but trampling on its own tattered wing and leg, the head flopping about all over the place, it was desperate for escape. There was a quick mess of blood on the grass.

'It's not going to recover from those injuries.' Monica said. I had to agree. It seemed clear that a slow, agonising death was ahead of the poor creature. I felt sick.

But in a part of my mind, the part that wanted to be released from the millstone that was Clarice, that part of my mind began to see this little episode as a useful learning experience. I turned to Monica, and in what I hoped was a calm, sensible voice, I said,

'We'll have to kill it. It would be a kindness, cutting short its suffering.'

Monica nodded.

'You're right,' she said, 'we need to put it out of its misery and much as I love animals, in the grand scheme of things, it's just one unfortunate bird. But I couldn't bring myself to wring its neck or anything like that. I'm a complete idiot about blood and so on. So what shall we do?'

'What about a quick whack over the head with something. All over quickly, no suffering, no mess.'

'Good idea.' She said, 'though perhaps we ought to cover it with a towel or something. I couldn't bear to see it actually die or get squashed.'

'Good point. Hang on a mo.' And I ran indoors to find what was needed, all the time muttering a prayer under my breath, 'let it be dead when I get back, let it be dead when I get back.'

It wasn't. When I got back just a minute later Monica and the bird were in a slightly different spot and she was almost hysterical with anguish over the poor thing, alternately wringing her hands and covering her face.

'Oh Cress! It's awful, it just won't give up. It just won't stay still and die!' She said, and a sob broke through her speech and her nose bubbled. The bird gathered enough strength to crash haphazardly into some empty plant pots, staggering yet crazily determined.

'Oh my God! I had hoped I'd come back and find it had died all on its own,' I told her, dithering. I was less sure now what was the right thing to do. It all just seemed so shocking, so raw. Unable to rip my eyes from the terrible sight, I watched it for another second, still uncertain. I said, 'perhaps we shouldn't.'

Monica shook her head, surprisingly firm.

'No, we have to kill it, it won't be able to fend for itself now. It'll be prey to anything that comes along, won't even make it through the night, I should think. But a night can seem like an awful long time.'

She was right, of course. But still reluctant, I continued to prevaricate. 'But – well - what about a vet or an animal welfare organisation?'

'There's no vet near here, and anyway I doubt they'd come out in the middle of the night just for a crow. Same with the welfare people. And we'd still have to catch it. Cressida, we can't leave it in this state any longer. We need to do something now!'

'Oh God.' I said.

But she was right. I took a deep breath. Straightened my shoulders.

'There's nothing for it, then.' I said. And I handed her the towel as I reached for the hefty marble rolling-pin. As the bird, after a few seconds' rest, began to drag itself round in a drunken circle again, Monica quickly plopped the towel over it. For a second there was no movement at all, and I began to think it had just quietly died of shock, but then there were a series of fluttering movements and the towel began to jerk along on the bloodied ground. It was freakish, insane.

    I hesitated still, trembling, sickened. Out of the corner of my eye I could see Monica's white face. I hadn't been brought up to do unpleasant things, and no matter how posh we were, I had certainly never hunted. This was altogether too gruesome and horrid for me, but in an odd way it made me feel a little better to see Monica was not finding it any easier.

    I gripped the rolling pin with both hands and uttering a banzai-type shriek to gird up my loins, I whacked the towel twice with all my might, guilt-racked and sobbing prayers of repentance.

    I was dimly aware of Monica's hand clutching at me, and she was gasping, 'oh my God, oh my God, oh my God.'

    But the towel was still moving. How could there still be life in that bloody bird? And now I wasn't sure which end was the head but having steeled myself to do the deed, I couldn't give up. With a trembling hand I twitched the towel back to see that the tail was now where the head had been and vice-versa. As the crow tried to scramble clear of the towel, feebly flapping its one half-useful wing and dragging itself along the ground, I flicked the towel back in position and harnessing a sudden inexplicable rage, whacked the head-end of the towel another three or four times with all my strength, before collapsing onto the grass, weeping and guilty. I dimly registered the sharp crackling sound the rolling pin made as it rolled away across our stepping stones. This no longer felt like a mercy killing.

With the towel still flailing and undulating, the bizarre rage I had momentarily felt had left me and I was cold and empty except for an incredible sense of failure. Defeated, I hardly knew what I was saying when I wailed,

'If I can't kill one pathetic bird, how can I kill my mother-in-law?'

The movement under the towel began to subside and finally stilled, and Monica sank down next to me on the grass and hugged me. We sat for a short time watching the towel. After a few minutes I felt calmer, more rational, and more than a little embarrassed at the jolly peculiar outburst of emotion. Monica was pulling wodges of tissues out of her bag and flinging them at me. We scrubbed our cheeks and blew our noses, and straightened our hair and skirts. We got up and went back and sat down again on the terrace, and took long swigs of our wine, our hands shaking as we reached for our glasses. It was just like when soldiers in the movies come back from Vietnam or Iraq and say, 'you weren't there, Man, you don't know what it was like.' We were veterans together, survivors, bonded.

And that was when, looking at me strangely, Monica said in a quiet voice,

'What did you mean when you said, 'if I can't kill one pathetic bird, how can I kill my mother-in-law'?'

I know I gaped at her like an idiot. Eventually, and a bit unsteadily, I did a little laugh and said I'd only been kidding, trying to lighten the tension a bit. A bit of gallows humour, sadly ill-timed.

Obviously, I said, I didn't want to actually kill my mother-in-law. She's a lovely woman, I said, I adore her. It didn't sound the least bit convincing, even to myself. I mean, Monica's met Clarice, been personally insulted by the woman, so she knows no one under any circs could possibly refer to Clarice as a 'lovely woman'. I don't know what she thought, I expected her to look puzzled, or maybe to laugh disbelievingly. But there was just this weird sort of closed-in expression on her face, and she didn't really say anything and all I could think, childishly, was that she wouldn't like me anymore and she wouldn't be my friend.

    And then the men came back.

    I could have hugged them both, it was as if the cavalry had finally ridden into sight over the brow of a hill. Of course they immediately took charge, fussed us back into the house where Monica's hubby Huw poured us both fresh drinks whilst Thomas cleared up outside. Monica made a point of asking Huw about the software they had been playing with. I sensed she wanted to give us both a bit of a chance to pull ourselves together. I shot her a grateful glance and downed my drink in one, and although we chatted on, more or less normally, I noticed that every so often, she would glance back at me and her expression seemed somehow rather - speculative.

    They left about an hour later. Thomas reminded them both I am off to Chapley's the day after tomorrow. We said our goodnights and stood at the front door waving them off. I wasn't sure if Monica would ever invite us to dinner again, but I was nevertheless relieved the bloody evening was over.

Fri 6 July - 3.30pm
I'm so fed up, and I just don't know what to do.

 I had been so looking forward to this lovely weekend away, and all my plans and everything. It was a lovely drive down, the sun was shining (finally), there were little fluffy white clouds dotted across the sky, which was a gorgeous deep blue. It was divine, and here and there were occasional snatches of birdsong above the traffic and the honking of the usual Friday afternoon road-ragers' horns, and every time I was stuck in a traffic jam all I had to do was just think of my heavenly weekend away with my seaweed wraps and my yoga etc etc.

 And then, what do you think, I parked my car in the car park, wandered into Reception with my handbag, thinking I'd send someone out to get my suitcase a bit later, and there she was in the foyer, sipping a Martini and nosing through the weekend newspapers. I ask you. Not that I wouldn't be absolutely thrilled to see her at any other time, but after the affair with the bird the night before last, and what I stupidly said, and the way she looked at me and everything, it just seems so – ODD – somehow. I actually just don't know what to think.

 So I just stood there like an organic unwaxed lemon and said something completely moronic like, 'Oh Monica, I didn't expect to see you here.'

 And she just did this tinkly little Nadina-laugh and said,

 'Cress Darling! Just on the spur of the moment I thought it would be bloody brilliant if I popped down and joined you!'

 She clattered over to me on ridiculous heels and gave me a peck on the cheek and when she stepped back she gave me this look as if she was challenging me to react, then she said, 'what a lovely spot. You know, this may become my new fave haunt.'

So what could I say apart from, how exciting, shall we celebrate with some champagne. And so we did, and I've just been lying down because it's almost dinner-time and I'm still a bit squiffy from too much champagne on an empty stomach – I'm not much of a drinker, I'm afraid, and instead of a peaceful wander around the complex this evening to get the lie of the land, so to speak, and maybe a light stroll to give me the opportunity to check the night-time security arrangements, or a quick bludgeon to death of my mother in-law or something, she's making me meet her in the bar for a drink before dinner, and then she said, 'let's plan something really radical for this evening!' Then off she went, all air kisses and flouncing hips.

I feel horribly dampened somehow.

I don't understand it. Two days ago, I thought she was my best pal, and now I can't stand her, can't stand the thought of her company. But I hate myself for it. I must be such a horrid, horrid person to be anything other than thrilled to see her. How could I? And it's all because of that colossal gaffe I made about killing my mother in law. It's so true what they say about one's tendency to blurt out the truth in stressful situations. I wish to God I'd kept my fat mouth shut.

And yet, realistically speaking, to how many of one's friends could one say something like that, and still be able to call them friends? I'm a total cow. I should make more of an effort. Monica's one in a million – she's standing by me no matter what, warts and all, and still liking the deep-down person that is the essential Cressida. So, obviously, after all she is my bestest gal-pal.

In which case, why do I wish she was miles away?

Same day – 7.00pm

At least I might be able to somehow use her as an alibi – and I suppose it might look less suspicious from a purely legal point of view, if I came away to a health spa with a girlfriend, than it would if I just went somewhere on my own, at precisely the moment that my mother-in-law just happens to be brutally bludgeoned to death. At least, I hope it's brutal.

    Thinking it through, it seems to me this could still work. There is a possibility that this turn of events could work out for the best. Must keep telling myself that. Mustn't lose hope. All is not lost!

Later still - 11.45 pm
A simply lovely evening, I can't think what I was worrying about! Monica was witty, amusing and certainly not the slightest bit odd. It's obvious now that my mind was just playing tricks on me. Clearly I must have needed this break more than I realised! I feel so relaxed already and definitely looking forward to tomorrow – seaweed wrap, lymphatic drainage, mud bath, yoga, lunch in the Garden Room, colour therapy then an holistic massage slash reiki then a spot of aquarobics slash swimming, followed by a nice sauna late afternoon with time for a lie down before dinner, then after-dinner coffee on the terrace, followed by the Twilight Walk Experience, as already mentioned, and then off to bed for a well-earned sleep.

    This really is a wonderful spot, surrounded by trees and with massive shrubberies and flowers all over the place, and the air is so fresh, it makes one terribly drowsy. I shall sleep like a top tonight.

Sat 7 July - 6.30 pm
Marvellous day! Really I can't remember when I've had so much fun. I'm exhausted of course, and I've only got a few minutes before I go down to dinner, but in case there's no time later, just wanted to record that today was absolutely beyond words, magnificent, enchanting and I feel absolutely incredible – like a new woman in fact - Monica and I were both agreeing earlier that we feel ten years younger already.

    I should just mention I was a teeny bit disappointed that she wanted to join me on the Twilight Walk Experience, for obvious reasons. I'm not quite sure how I'm going to manage to slip away without her noticing, but she was so eager I felt it would be mean to put her off. Perhaps I'll be able to slip out again after we've said goodnight this evening. But I have to admit that I'm a bit worried about how I'm going to fit in my little jaunt over to Clarice's with Monica by my side at every turn. I'm desperately hoping something will just sort of 'turn up' – otherwise I'll have to try to sneak out in the middle of the night to do the dirty deed. But if I must, I suppose it will work out okay.

    In any case, I've suddenly realised that I can't wear the all-black jogging outfit I had planned – it's a bit too noticeably black and untrendy and I'm afraid the black face paint and balaclava will have to remain stashed in my luggage because I don't want to wear anything so out of place that it is likely to stick in the minds of other people. So I'm going to put on some dark jeans and a lovely little black silk camisole, with a nice embroidered, dark purple over-wrap thingy, and I'm hoping that with black pumps and a nice little shawl-type whatnot in

case it's chilly later, I'll look the part for dinner,
Twilight Walk Experience and bludgeoning Clarice.

Sun 8 July - 4.30pm
Oh my God Oh my God Oh my God!!!!!
I'm back at home. I don't know if last night was a total fiasco, a disaster, or if it's worked out perfectly or what the hell has happened. I can't get my brain to work properly and my head is killing me.

To start with, Monica didn't turn up for the Twilight Walk Experience doodah.

We had a lovely dinner, followed by a very pleasant coffee on the Terrace during which she flirted like mad with a waiter with a gorgeous bum. Then, seeing that she was wearing a floaty little top and a skirt that was almost floor-length (but it really was the most divine sheer fabric, and whichever way she moved, it just swirled about her the whole time, I was so envious, and I'm not sure who the designer was, though I must find out, it might not be too late to get one myself, though obviously I'd never be able to wear it somewhere if I knew Monica was going to be there too) - well anyway…Monica popped up to get changed - we'd stayed a bit longer on the Terrace than we meant to, so I waited in the foyer with the other Twilighters, holding her bag like a loon. She said she'd be just a jiffy but in the end the woman running it (most officious, like a girl guide leader or something) said it had been 20 minutes and we couldn't wait any longer, and Monica would just have to catch us up, which left me feeling rather awful. I felt like I was abandoning her or something – so guilty! But then a light kind of went on in my brain and I realised she was probably getting to know that waiter a little better, and then I was a bit cross with her for dumping me without warning.

Our girl guide leader warned to watch our step as it was a 'bit jolly tricky' in places - it was quite dark in some parts in the woods as it was well after half past ten by then and not just very overgrown but the sky was overcast. I was already watching for my moment, and the perfect opportunity arose about twenty minutes after we set off when our path doubled back on itself a bit. This meant we were only a hundred metres or so from the edge of the back part of the car park, and it was the simplest thing in the world to just drop back a bit and slip away behind some gigantic rhubarb without anyone noticing, which if Monica had been with me, I wouldn't have been able to do.

Well, obviously I had my keys etc in my tiny little evening bag, so in just a couple of moments I was in the car and driving out of the gate slowly. No one was around. Really I'm a bit cross at the Absolute lack of security in the place. I mean, if I can drive away unnoticed, so could countless car-jackers, obviously. The car park is simply groaning with jags and mercs and all manner of high-end merchandise. So anyway once I reached the main road I put on the headlights and tried to act normally.

Anyway, got to Clarice's in only 18 minutes. No traffic whatsoever. Incredible!

Then…

…It really was awful, I don't know what to make of it. I feel like I've had the tables well and truly turned on me.

I parked the car down the lane a little, a short walk from Clarice's front gates. Fortunately her house is on a sharpish bend in the road, and it can be quite dangerous, so it shouldn't look too suspicious my doing that, though there's not usually a lot of passing traffic, so I really doubt anyone would have noticed me or the car.

The lane was very quiet, no one was about and no vehicles anywhere nearby. And Clarice's drive was terribly dark as usual, so again, I had nothing to fear with regard to being seen by casual observers, and I reached the front door without incident. The house was in total darkness, which didn't seem especially odd as she never keeps late hours, she's far too mean to pay for unnecessary electricity. I stood there for a moment deliberating – would it be best after all to go round to the side door? And as I stood there, I heard a sort of tinkling sound from inside and a faint cry. Then I noticed the front door was standing very slightly open, and suddenly I realised that a robbery or something of the sort was taking place.

I pushed open the door carefully with just the tip of my fingernail, stepped inside, and was just reaching for the light switch on the opposite side of the hall when I felt a terrific whack on the back of my head, and I just crumpled onto the floor.

It felt like years later when I came to, and it seemed like hours that I lay there trying to pluck up the courage to move, because I knew purely instinctively that my head would fall off and roll away if I did anything too quickly. I had this deafening roaring sound in my ears, my head was pounding more than I've ever known, and I felt so, so sick and disoriented. The back of my head felt like it was the size of a bus - and the pain!

Eventually I did manage to open my eyes, and the brightness of the light made me cry out with pain, and the sound of my voice also jarred not just my nerves but my whole head. The hall light was on, and the last thing I could remember before the attack was reaching out towards the switch, so obviously someone other than myself had actually turned it on. But although I wasn't really afraid, I was aware of a vague sense of anxiety, and I felt as though a lengthy amount of time had passed by since I lost consciousness.

There were no other sounds about me. The house was eerily still, the front door closed. I fumbled in my bag for my phone. The screen told me it was now four minutes past eleven. I'd been out for about two minutes, three at the most, but this just didn't make sense to me – I felt as though I'd been out for hours.

I felt so sick from the pain in my head all I wanted to do was to curl up in a little ball and die, but I forced myself focus on the glaring screen of my phone and to ring the emergency services and requested police and an ambulance. I told them I had been attacked coming into my mother-in-law's house.

Then they asked me if Clarice was all right, and I realised that I'd completely forgotten about her, and at the same time I recalled the slight cry I had heard when I was outside the front door.

The thought of having to search the whole house filled me with dread – I don't think I could have managed it, in fact I really only wanted to get to the nearest loo to chuck my guts up – but I mumbled into the phone something about checking in the drawing room first as it was the closest. I dragged myself to my feet, and bit by bit, holding my head with one hand and trying to use the wall for support and hold on to my phone with the other, I made my way to the drawing room. The room was in darkness, so with a slight sense of déjà vu, I reached out and put on the light, and there she was, lying face down on the floor next to her favourite chair, head turned towards me, eyes staring into nothingness and a pool of dark, sticky-looking blood around her head like a halo tipped awry. My mother-in-law. Dead.

The shock I felt, probably coupled with my own injuries, caused me to quite involuntarily to give the performance of a lifetime to the woman on the other end of the line. I went completely to pieces, and looking back, I'm quite proud of my hysteria. Of course, at the time, it wasn't so much fun, but I don't think anyone will ever now suspect my true reason for being in Clarice's house. And since then I've been questioned twice more and I've fallen apart each time, perfectly spontaneously and serendipitously hysterical. The police have been so kind, so sweet to me. Who'd have thought these rugged detective types could be so gentle and considerate? As I said, I'm quite proud, because really I had no idea I was such a fab little actress!

I had two missed calls from Monica in my phone, where was I, did I want to meet up etc. Thomas called her for me after he'd collected me from the hospital, and he told her what had happened, asked her to pack up my stuff. She doesn't appear to have said anything to contradict the idea that my visit was planned in advance and perfectly ordinary in every way. Nor has anyone made any suggestion that I did not adore my dear old mother-in-law. Luckily for me.

And my head aches too much even to watch Andy in the Wimbledon finals – Thomas is taping it for me on the tv-top-box, so I can watch it later if I feel like it.

Poor Thomas. He's not distraught over the loss of his mother – they were never close – but he's very upset. It's not a nice way to lose even the most hated of parents. And he seems particularly touched that I'd made time to go and visit Clarice whilst in the area. The police summed it up beautifully. As they told the press conference this lunchtime, 'an elderly lady was brutally and fatally attacked in her own home on the outskirts of Ely sometime between the hours of nine and eleven o'clock last night. The attacker or attackers were interrupted by the arrival of the lady's daughter-in-law who herself was attacked and knocked unconscious, sustaining head injuries. The daughter-in-law, who is now recovering in hospital, was able to alert emergency services once she regained consciousness, although sadly it was too late to help the elderly lady. A motive for this ferocious and inhuman attack has not yet been established, although we are not ruling out the possibility of a burglary gone wrong. We believe the perpetrators of this terrible and callous crime may attempt to sell the proceeds of the break-in to obtain drugs.'

Flowers have arrived from absolutely everyone. And a reporter. Thomas keeps making me cups of tea and arranging my pillows, he's horribly upset. He fusses constantly.

The only fly in my ointment of self-satisfaction is the imminent arrival of his beastly sister, no doubt in full mourning and dragging her profane betting-shop-owning husband with her, with his eternal sniffing and belching and hearty laugh.

And my head aches abominably.

And I still feel a bit sick and dizzy.

But in spite of all that, it's all quite exciting.

Mon 9 July - 10.15am
Feeling much better today, apart from hideously aching head, obviously.

A number of well-wishers called to offer their condolences. Feel a bit guilty telling all and sundry how awful it is and keep catching myself telling everyone what a wonderful, feisty old lady she was, an individual, a character etc etc, and how an Englishwoman's home is no longer her castle and how, to the great detriment of society, we won't see her like again. Well, you have to say these things, don't you? You can't exactly tell people what you really thought of the miserable old bag.

Thomas and his sister went off to see the funeral director to fix a date, and to the police to sign some papers and get the body released later this week (don't see why they can't keep her, really) and to sort out a whole host of other things. We're going down to the house in a few days, assuming I'm feeling a bit better.

I was relieved that when Monica popped round, it was when Thomas and Cecily (Cess! I ask you!) were out.

Mrs Hopkins let Monica in, moaning about how she was obviously a bleedin' butler now what wiv me convaleskin' and all, but don't get her wrong, she don't give a monkey's, but them barfrooms won't clean 'emselves.

'Cressida! You look terrible! So pale! What shocking news! How are you holding up?' Monica came rushing across to me and enveloping me in a hug, surrounded me with air kisses. Mrs H just sniffed and disappeared.

'Not too bad,' I said, on a bit of a croak, feeling suddenly emotional. We sat down, then I remembered my manners and offered Monica some coffee, which to my relief she declined.

'How's the head? And have the police got any leads yet?'

'My head's better than it was, thanks. Still feel a bit sick and dizzy, which is absolutely horrid. No, the police don't seem to have any news. They think it might have been a robbery gone wrong, but I suppose it's still early days.'

'That's good.' She said cryptically, adding less cryptically, 'let's hope it stays that way. Fingers crossed, you should get away with it completely.' She said it with a bright smile.

I gaped at her. She smiled even more brightly as if she couldn't believe I didn't get the joke.

'What?' She asked.

I said nothing, just couldn't think of anything to say, couldn't take my eyes off her. She rolled her eyes.

'Oh come on Cress,' she said gently, 'surely you don't think I haven't figured it out? I mean it wasn't exactly the most elaborate scheme.'

'But…but…Monica!' I blustered. Completely stunned. For the second time in two days.

'Sorry Darling, but we are friends, and you know, cards on the table and all that. I'll never forget what you said the other night after that whole bloody bird fiasco. And then to slip away during the Twilight walk thingy, well…It was just obvious. By the way, Sweetie, you've still got my evening bag.'

I blustered a bit more, completely thrown off track. I couldn't think for a minute. I couldn't decide what was for the best, to deny it all or give in to the urge to confide in her, and tell her everything, and ease my burden of guilt.

So I was silent. She leaned back on the sofa and gave me an appraising look. We looked at each other, both of us now a little wary. Then the door was thrown open and in came Mrs H with an enormous tray.

'Tea.' She snapped. She made it sound as though it were my idea, adding to her already over-burdened working day.

But I was really thrown. Due to my feeble, post-attack fragility, I came over all emotional. Choking back tears, I thanked her, astonishment on top of my infirmity making me warmer than I normally would be with Mrs H. She glared at me on her way out as if to warn me it was a one-off, and not to go getting ideas. But she removed herself slowly from our presence, giving me a few precious seconds to recompose myself. And now, with something to do, a prop to aid my role, I began to feel once more in control.

I scooched forward and took up the teapot, hefted it in the air, and waved it vaguely in Monica's direction.

'Shall I be mother?'

'Oh do, Darling, I'd love a cup. And a bickie, if there is one. Ooh scones! How lovely!' She sounded light and airy, and more Monica-like than ever but her eyes still watched me closely.

A thought came to me. Relieved to have something normal to say, I said,

'Monica, I'm so sorry about your bag, I completely forgot about it. I hope you didn't need it for anything? It's still in the car, I'd better just pop and get it…'

'No, no need, Cress,' she stopped me getting to my feet with a wave, and she hesitated for two seconds, then fixing me with her dark eyes she leaned forward and said in a very quiet voice, 'Cress, as I was just saying, I know what you did.'

Of course, I should have known she wouldn't let it go. I stopped what I was doing, setting down the teapot, flustered again. How on earth was I going to convince her that I was innocent?

'Monica, no! I – I don't know what you...'

'Yes, you do. Like I said, it was the other evening, with the bird thing. And you'd planned to do it Saturday night all along. That's why you were so upset about me arriving at Chapley's. Don't bother denying it – I could see it in your face as soon as you caught sight of me in the foyer. You were horrified to see me sitting there. Then, you obviously pulled yourself together a bit and decided to make the best of it, but at first – no, Cressida, you were not pleased to see me. You thought I'd get in the way or stop you or something. You killed your mother-in-law, I know you did.'

'No!' I said loudly, and suddenly I was on my feet, head swimming madly. Then, remembering Mrs H just down the hall, I took a deep, calming breath and sat myself back down again. I leaned forward and spoke quietly, carefully. 'No, that's not...I wasn't...I certainly didn't...'

'But of course you did, Cress!' And Monica sat back in the chair with her new fake, tinkly laugh. She looked around as she leant back as if asking an imaginary audience how I expected to get away with saying something like that. And suddenly I was on-stage on Car Crash Telly's live episode of Toffs Who Kill. I could almost hear the audience calling out 'shame!' and see them shaking their heads.

'Now look,' I growled through gritted teeth. (Even if she was my best friend, I wasn't standing for any of this.) 'I did not k – I did not do whatever it is you think I did. Nor was I upset about you coming to Chapley's. We had a whale of a time! And whatever stupid emotional thing I blurted out a few nights ago was – well I was simply affected by the emotion at the time – the stress of the situation. I've never had to take a life before, however small and insignificant.'

'Oh please!' Monica began, but I got there first. The invisible audience leaned forwards in their seats, waiting to see where all this was going before nailing their collective colours to any masts.

'No! Listen to me! I went there on Saturday night to visit my mother-in-law purely because I happened to have a free evening and I was in the area. I – If nothing else, it would have been rude to go all that way and not visit, frankly.'

'You did not have a free evening, you ditched me!'

Gasps of shock from the audience. And me.

'You ditched me! You left me literally holding the bag and you buggered off 'to change' and that was the last I saw of you – the tour got fed up with waiting for you and left you behind, and I admit I bailed out shortly afterwards, but that was because I just didn't fancy doing the Walk without you. I bet you were you with that waiter with the bum!'

I sat back, my work here was done. I had had the last word and won both the argument and the sympathy of the fictitious audience. Game, set and match. Go me. Unlike poor old Andy Murray.

'And so you just 'happened' ' and she did air-quotes at this point just to annoy me even more, 'to decide on the spur of the moment to visit your mother-in-law at eleven o'clock at night, without letting her know in advance.' Monica continued, her voice heavy with sarcasm. 'Because of course, we all know how terribly fond of her you were.' Put like that, it sounded pretty bad, but I wasn't throwing in the towel. But her argument no longer carried any true conviction. I had my answer ready.

'It's not a question of being fond of anyone – its family duty and – and human compassion, just wanting to be sure the old girl was all right!'

'Well that worked out beautifully!' Monica bellowed. I lost it.

'She was dead when I got there! I didn't kill her!' I yelled back, on my feet now, reason ditched in favour of emphasis, and Mrs H, from the doorway, made a little throat-clearing noise and said,

'Well, I'll be off now, Mrs Powell.' But she looked as though she wished she'd kept her mouth shut. Fancy having to leave just as it was getting interesting! Her eyes were practically on stalks as she turned very, very slowly and began the long, slow walk to the front door, slowly, slowly putting on her coat, first one arm and then the other, moving down the hall and looking over her shoulder all the while and fumbling for the buttons.

I swore to myself. It would be all over town by tomorrow morning. In fact, I'd probably be arrested in the middle of the night and smuggled in and out of courtrooms with some old policeman's anorak over my head whilst women in Primark jeggings and Porn Star t-shirts shouted 'shame!' and threw empty designer-cider bottles at me. I felt sure the invisible audience would no longer be impressed.

Finally the door closed on Mrs H and I dragged my attention back to the drawing room and Monica, my nerves in tatters. I was wondering where to go from here. I looked at Monica. She was staring back at me, warily, eyes fixed on me, tense. She licked her lips.

What was that look all about? Why on earth should she be so wary? Did she think now Mrs H had gone I was going to batter her over the head with the tea tray? I sat down on the ottoman opposite her.

'Now look,' I said in a calmer voice, 'I promise you, on Thomas' life, Clarice was dead when I got there. I was at the front door, about to knock when not only did I notice the door was open just a crack, but I heard a sound from inside. And so I went in, really quietly, or so I thought, and then I got a massive whack on the head. I was knocked out cold. When I came to, the attacker or attackers had gone and Clarice was well and truly dead. And that's the gospel truth.'

Sort of.

She looked at me. I had won. I could see it in her eyes, her slumping shoulders.

'Sorry,' she said softly, and looked at her hands, almost guiltily, 'I do believe you. I didn't mean what I said – call it an off-colour joke. I really do believe you. And it must have been terrifying, not to mention super painful.'

I was a bit thrown off guard by her sudden turn-around.

'Definitely,' I said, 'look I've even got a little dent and a bit of hair has come out. I don't know if it'll grow back. I might have to keep my hair brushed over this side. And my head is killing me, I don't know how long it takes to recover from concussion, even if it's just the mild sort.'

She took a closer look, made concerned tsks.

'It looks jolly painful. I'm really so, so sorry.'

I felt bad then, felt sad about arguing with my friend.

'Oh never mind. I said, 'it was a weird situation. How about some more tea?'

'No, sorry Cress, I've got to get back. D'you know when the funeral is going to be?'

'Not yet,' I told her, 'Thomas is hoping to get all that sorted out today. With his beastly sister, Cess.' I added with emphasis. She smirked.

'Cess? Oh dear! Right. Anyway. Well let me know,' she said, grabbing her bag and jacket, 'and obviously if you need anything, don't hesitate. I'll give you a ring Wednesday or so. Give my love to Thomas, say how sorry we both are...'

And I saw her out, stopping to retrieve her 'other' bag from my car, where it had spilled out stuff all over the footwell at the back and I had to grovel around stuffing her make-up and woolly mittens and tissues back in and assuring her if I found anything else I'd let her have it back next time.

It was a relief to get back inside and have a bit of a rest, I can tell you, my head was throbbing. I was glad of the peace and quiet but still, it struck me as a bit odd she left so quickly. And that odd look after Mrs H had left. Maybe she really didn't believe me after all and really was too afraid to be alone with me?

I wonder if I ought to give Mrs H a bit of a pay rise, to encourage her to be loyal and to feel like a valued member of the household? That should ensure she keeps anything she heard to herself, especially if I add a bit of back pay. I don't like to think of her chatting to people about me, one never knows who might be listening.

I wonder why there were woolly mittens in Monica's evening bag? It couldn't have been a wrap – too small – or, well, what else could it have been? And why now, I mean, it's been glorious weather for weeks now. And they're not very pretty and eveningy, just big, woolly, wintery, dog-walking gloves.

I suppose she might have thought the evening would cool when we were out doing the Twilight thingy. But you'd think she'd just grab a jacket or a wrap when she went up to her room to change? It just doesn't make sense. Oh I don't know. Why does anyone do anything?

Tues 10 July – the middle of the night!
It's almost four in the morning. I have just woken up with such a start, and I'm so shocked by the truth that's finally dawned on me, I know I'll never get back to sleep now, it's all going round and round in my head. It can't be true. It just can't. Can it? I'm raving. I must be making it up, I'm tired, and what with my head and everything. What I'm thinking can't possibly be true.

So I've come downstairs and I'm wearing a pair of Thomas' socks, his dressing gown, and a waxed jacket over the top of that, a woolly scarf around me and still my teeth are chattering, I can't get warm.

I've made some cocoa, it's still too hot to drink but I'm clutching at the mug like a lifeline, feeling the heat going in through my fingers and travelling up my arms and into my body, and the steam is rising up to soothe my face. My thoughts keep going round and round and round in my head and I can't seem to make them stop.

And I can't phone her, it's far too early, but I can't bear to wait. I'm just beside myself. I'm convinced I've realised the truth.

Monica killed Clarice.

She must have.

It's a crazy notion, but it's the only one that makes sense.

Why would burglars strike at exactly the time they did? Perfectly in time with my plan, though admittedly I didn't tell anyone – not even, in fact especially not, Monica. But it' a bit of a coincidence otherwise, isn't it?

That's why she went upstairs to change, and didn't come down, didn't come on the Twilight bark. She was probably already there at Clarice's when I was just pulling out of Chapley's car park.

Oh - My - God! That means it was her that hit me – no wonder she was so apologetic when I showed her my head – it wasn't guilt over accusing me - it was guilt guilt – guilt over almost killing me guilt! She bludgeoned her best mate!

That's why she came to Chapley's to begin with! Oh! My! God! I can't believe it – but it must be true! Oh! I'm such an idiot, I can't think of anything else to say – suddenly everything makes sense.

I bet that was a balaclava she had in her bag! That would make a lot more sense than woolly mittens in summer. If only I'd paid more attention, there might have been other stuff in there – medical gloves or – well I don't know exactly what there might have been in there, but it's the principle!

Oh my God! My best friend is a murderer!

Fri 13 July - 9pm
Well that's the funeral out of the way. It was all right, I suppose. Quite a good turnout, although of course a lot of people were only there to find out the gruesome details of what happened that night – vultures! Was it really less than a week ago?

    Monica was there, hovering in the background, but I haven't seen her for long enough to do more than exchange air kisses and the briefest of pleasantries. But in a day or two, when everything has settled down a bit, I need to have a heart to heart talk with her – I don't see I can put it off much longer. I mean, it's all I can think about. I absolutely have to speak to her about it, I need to make her tell me all about that night and see if she can come up with even one good reason why she nearly killed me.

    Fortunately Thomas' beastly sister and her hideous husband have hoofed it home again. They popped back to the house along with everyone else after the funeral, but by mid-afternoon they'd made their half-arsed excuses and we'd waved them off, fixed smiles firmly in place. I blush to remember I said something along the lines of 'and don't leave it so long next time'. I put it down to the excitement of the moment, seeing them leave. And of course I had my fingers crossed behind my back the whole time, so it clearly doesn't count. Have nasty suspicion, though, that one day I shall have to answer for my sins to a higher power!

    On her way out Nadina came over with Jeremy in tow. She had her sad face on, her bottom lip was even sticking out a little bit – I could have happily slapped her, she looked like one of her own six year olds when told they can't play in the home corner! She took both my hands in hers, to my surprise slash horror, and gazed into my face with more close-up sincerity than a Televangelist. Nodding slowly as she said it, as if speaking some deep and eternal truth, she said,

'The Lord giveth, Cressida, and the Lord taketh away.'

I bit my lip to keep from laughing and nodded back in what I hoped was a grateful and comforted way. Then she had moved on, Jeremy dutifully in tow. Thomas laughed unfortunately rather loudly, and Monica leaned in close between the two of us to say in my ear,

'And if by any chance the Lord dothn't taketh awayeth, Thou hatheth to putteth up with people.'

Bizarrely Thomas also laughed at this, which isn't his type of humour at all usually, but he had put away several glasses of sherry by this time, so that probably explains it. I turned to Monica to reply,

'Or one canth maketh awayeth with people onethelf ath nethethary.'

She laughed merrily at this, and then I had to help Thomas mop himself down with about thirty napkins after he had spluttered sherry all down his tie and waistcoat.

I was pleasantly surprised to find everyone else had drifted off by about fiveish. There were no maudlin drunks to dispose of, no need to snatch china ornaments out of the trembling hands of elderly busybodies before shoving the old dears out the front door. Everyone was really very nicely behaved. Really a most enjoyable day, I do love a good funeral! Monica was the last to leave and gave me air kisses at the front door, shouting toodle-oo merrily over her shoulder as she waved goodbye and got into her car.

Now all I've got to worry about is sorting out all Clarice's bloody old tat.

Cess did ask me, this morning when I was in a terrific flap to get ready for the funeral (really that woman has no sense of suitable timing!), if I needed any help sorting out Clarice's house and effects. She said it in that negative way, you don't need any help, do you? The tone of her voice indicating she expected a negative response, so obviously I felt had to say no. Frankly I was a bit surprised. One usually hears of relatives descending like so many locusts to pick clean the bones of the deceased person's property. They don't usually rush off in the opposite direction, terrified of being left alone with the silver.

Thomas says she's superstitious, but that surely can't be it? She is really reluctant to go to the house. I don't get it. I mean, the only reason I used to be reluctant to go to Clarice's house was because Clarice herself was there. Now she's gone, well, I can't wait to drop by.

Must make a note to ring Cess tomorrow and ask her if there's anything she wants – any small item to remember her mother by (surely she can't have always hated her, can she?) – anything at all, no matter how small or insignificant or cheap, any tiny little low-value item I could fit in a small jiffy bag to send on to her once I've had a chance to look over the place.

Thomas was all for getting a firm in to clear the house, and no doubt we shall, but not until I've had a chance to have a really good look round, those people only ever give you a fraction of what the contents are truly worth, and goodness only knows what Clarice has stashed away over the years.

Have pencilled in tomorrow for general sort of relaxing and recuperation as head still iffy. Poor Thomas is going to squeeze in a few holes at his club, fitting it around the weather obviously, and frankly I'm looking forward to the break from his constant fussing and caring. Then I thought we'd drive down on Sunday to look over the house and make up some sort of inventory, and then Thomas can ring up a few house clearance firms on Monday.

Bish bosh sorted, as Mrs H would say. I feel so light and happy. It's an enormous relief to have all this out of the way at long last. A huge weight off my shoulders. After all these years of misery and humiliation, she's finally gone. Ahh!

Blast! Damn and Blast, in fact. Thomas has just popped his head around the door and said, 'Cats!' And of course, he's absolutely right. I'd completely forgotten about the little buggers, even though one of Clarice's dottier neighbours made a point of 'reassuring' us about Clarice's cats just as we were about to go into the funeral home for the service.

'Now don't you go worrying about Dear Clarice's cats,' she said, 'I've been popping in to feed them twice a day, and they seem all right, though a bit lost, which is only to be expected now that they've lost their Mummy. I feel so sorry for them. And they're dear little things. But I couldn't keep them, my Trixie wouldn't like it.'

And as soon as I heard this woman say the words 'Dear' and 'Clarice' in the same sentence, I should have known that she obviously wasn't sane. Completely batty!

Thomas had assured her we hadn't forgotten about the cats for a single moment, which isn't really a fib, because we'd forgotten about them completely and utterly and permanently. I couldn't resist a slight curl of the lip at her reference to Clarice as the animals' 'Mummy'. Can't think of anyone less maternal than Clarice. She's maternal in the same way that there are some creatures in nature that enjoy eating their children. That kind of maternal.

Very well, we will have to acquire a couple of cat baskets from a local pet supplies warehouse. And I'll find the name and address of the nearest veterinary practice, so that whilst I'm looking around the house and making lists and so on, Thomas can cart the cats off to their eternal reward.

Sun 15 July - 10.30pm
Absolutely bloody terrible bloody day!

We got to Highgates without incident – a really very pleasant run down, stopped for coffee somewhere on the way – so nice to just sit and chat for 20 minutes or so. Thomas was looking very handsome in casual clothing for once, I know it's hard to believe but sometimes I get fed-up with seeing him in bespoke suits all the time. Fortunately he's the sort of man who looks gorgeous no matter what he wears.

Got everything sorted at the house without any real difficulties. We walked over the whole house making a note of the main items in each room, along with approximate value and anything else that seemed remotely noteworthy. It wasn't too difficult as there was a lot of old crap I wouldn't dream of having in my shed, let alone the house. And her jewellery was a bit of a disappointment, I have to say. No delightfully unexpected little windfalls there. What she did with all the good stuff, I haven't a clue - perhaps Thomas will get more info from her solicitor when he sees him on Tuesday. But we selected and packed up the few items either we or Cess wanted to keep.

Next, obviously, we had to settle up with Clarice's cleaning woman. She seemed very pleasant – obviously she must be an angel, to have put up with Clarice all these years. (I wonder if she'd be willing to come to us? Mrs H is such an old dragon.) Once the house has been completely emptied, she has promised to give it a thorough clean from top to bottom, and we are leaving a set of keys with her so that the agent can show people around once the place is on the market so he won't need to bother us every five minutes. In fact, she'll have to let the agent himself in for the initial appraisal next week, but she is so obliging, she's happy to do anything of that sort. And of course we'll make it worth her while.

Then we came to the question of the cats.

Thomas brought in the cat baskets and we went in search of the little…creatures.

It was almost half an hour later that we found them outside. One – the tabby - was asleep in the summerhouse at the far end of the main lawn, curled up in a neat little ball in an old garden chair; the other was snoozing on a sunny patch of flattened flowers on the edge of the shrubbery.

I had no idea they would be so reluctant to get into the baskets. I had fondly imagined – never having had an animal myself – that one simply called to them and over they trotted, obedient, loyal, brimming with animal affection and eager to please. But no. I mean, admittedly cat owners are always banging on about how difficult it is to get little Muffin or Fido to the vets, or to take tablets or whatever, but I had always assumed that was a gross exaggeration, much like the way women go on and on about the pain of childbirth.

The fluffy grey one, particularly, put up quite a struggle as we managed to grab it and shove it into one of the baskets and it howled the place down when we jammed the door shut on its tail. The creatures were surprisingly strong considering they are supposed to be in their dotage. And then of course, the two of them just had to wail all the way to the vets. It's almost as if they knew what was going to happen.

So it was quite a relief when Thomas popped them into the vets, paid the bill and dashed out again, and we were at last able to head for home.

Finally I was able to relax! It felt wonderful, knowing all the hard work and the aggravation was behind us. Thomas said he felt wonderfully free, and I had to agree. I was so happy, so light – so unburdened! No more nasty visits from Clarice, no more dancing attendance on her or pandering to her inflated ego, no more insults being hurled down the phone line at me. No more miserable Christmasses and Birthdays. Bliss! Thomas was humming and tapping along in time with the radio on the steering wheel, I was looking at the scenery, it was just lovely!

And then we got home.

To my surprise, Mrs H was still there, for some reason. She gave us an odd look and handed over an urgent message from Clarice's neighbour. We called the woman back.

'You appear to have left one of Clarice's cats behind,' she immediately told Thomas. He said she sounded really quite cross. Poor old biddy, we thought. Speaking loudly and slowly in case she was deaf, Thomas reassured her with a broad smile for my benefit that we had taken both cats away with us, a tabby and a smoky grey one. And then, even before any more was said, I knew, I intuited the problem.

Oh! My! God!

Well of course it was too late by then. Thomas rang up immediately but the vet was quite terse with him.

'You were very specific about wanting both animals euthanized due to your wife's allergies and not having time to find new homes for your mother's two cats.'

Thomas explained that yes, but one of them hadn't been the cat we thought it was. The vet was not very helpful.

'Too late.' He said and slammed the phone down.

Clarice's neighbour was not only upset, she was horrified, disgusted, appalled, bereaved and desolated, one emotion chasing after another down the phone to Thomas' ear. Threat succeeded threat as she vented her outraged grief. Trixie, her pedigree Blue Persian, had, it transpired, been more than just a cat, she had been a precious little bundle of love and Clarice's neighbour was going to call the police. Then she was going to write to the Times, her MP and the RSPCA.

Poor Thomas had to listen to her rant on for fifteen minutes about what should happen to people who kill other people's pets – no, not just pets, practically family members, and of noble blood at that. She recalled all the Persian's little foibles, most of which sounded utterly and disgustingly revolting to Thomas.

I ask you!

So I got Thomas a Scotch and water, and he offered her some money. But money was not what she wanted, apparently. What she wanted was revenge, but finally they settled on £5,000.

And in addition Thomas now has to drive back down to Highgates again tomorrow to collect the other cat that eluded us today, another tabby mongrel. We weren't particularly surprised to hear that the super-efficient, feline-doting neighbour had managed to corner it and catch it and had shut it in one of the rooms downstairs.

I must remind him to get that key off the woman when he gives her the money.
God, what a disaster.

Mon 16 July - 8.20pm
Poor Thomas was simply exhausted when he got back from Clarice's today. I must say, I was a teensy bit cross when he brought the 'other' tabby back here. But I suppose he couldn't help it. What else could he do? The neighbour didn't want it, the cleaning lady didn't want it, and as soon as Thomas put a toe inside the door of the vet's, the vet started shouting at him and threatening to call the police.

  I looked through the bars of the basket's door. I'm absolutely certain that cat gave me a smug look. Of course, I immediately rang round all of my friends, and although I told them it's quite a pretty colour and more than likely house-trained, no one I knew wanted a tabby cat of uncertain vintage and even more uncertain pedigree.

Tues 17 July - 11.15pm
That bloody cat howled all night. We'd left it in the basket in the kitchen – that being the furthest point from both the drawing-room and our bedroom, but I could still hear the little git. It literally howled for the best part of the night. We hardly slept. At one point I offered Thomas my body if he would just pop downstairs and sort it out with a brick. He simply said he had done his bit with regard to his mother's cats. He put his headphones on and went to sleep. Men can be so selfish sometimes, even though we love them. I laid awake all night only dozing off when the sun came up and the cat finally fell silent, no doubt having lost its voice.

Consequently I overslept this morning. When I awoke, Mrs H was already here. As I was dressing, I remembered I'd forgotten to leave a note or anything to explain about the cat to tell her she wasn't to worry, it would going on a little visit to the vet – any vet – later in the morning. I rushed downstairs without even waiting to put my make-up on. I could hear Mrs H banging about in the kitchen.

When I entered the kitchen, I was already saying 'by the way, Mrs Hopkins, I'm afraid I forgot to mention about my mother-in-law's…'

'…your mother-in-law's cat, yes I know.' She said. She was wiping a champagne glass and placing it in the cabinet. She turned and gave me a huge smile, which was a bit of a worry in itself. She's never done that before.

Now I finally looked around me and for the first time I took in the shallow Wedgwood bowl on the floor, still containing the remains of some mashed sardines and beyond the kitchen, through the open garden door, a small tabby cat smugly washing its paws in the sunshine. Of the cat basket there was no sign.

'I fort there was two cats?' Mrs H said anxiously. Feeling somewhat backed into a corner, I smiled rather stiffly and said the only thing that immediately came to mind.

'Unfortunately the other wasn't very well. The vet told my husband there was nothing he could do to help it. It seemed best to ease its suffering.'

'Poor little bugger.' Mrs H said with a sniff. She turned away and rummaged in the pocket of her overalls for a tissue. 'At least we've given one of 'em a lovin' 'ome. What's its name?'

I gaped at her floral-encased rear. Was Mrs H crying? Could it be she had a weakness? Was she truly Mortal? And what was I going to say? I couldn't recall whether or not anyone had ever mentioned the names of the cats. Although – Trixie? But no, that was the neighbour's cat, or should I say, late cat. But I had never seen Mrs H so human, so malleable, so weak. I was not going to risk losing all that now.

I looked around the kitchen, desperately trying to gain inspiration for a name that would be suited to a brown tabby cat, whilst maintaining the appearance of someone who has it on the tip of her tongue, a mere momentary aberration.

Mrs H turned to me with a querying look.

'Tetley.' I said. Mrs H looked a bit surprised and then smiled.

'Ah that's quite sweet, innit? Unusual. Er, Mrs Powell, about the 'oover.'

'Oh Mrs Hopkins, I'm afraid I haven't…'

'I'll get my Sid to have a look at it, if you don't mind. 'E might be able to fix it. Save you splashin' out on a noo one. Ah look at little Tetley, washing 'er arse on the driveway. Ain't she a pretty little fing? It'll be luvly, 'aving a cat about the place.'

OMG I have been outmanoeuvred by a small tabby cat saved from the gallows by a mere quirk of fate!

All day I worried about breaking the news to Thomas.

I told him over dinner. He was surprisingly accepting of the situation. In fact, sensing that he was in the mood to be entertained, I told him the whole story in detail, everything Mrs H said, how I frantically tried to think of a name. Lovely to hear him laughing like that. He leaned across the table and took my hand in his. Gazing into my eyes, he said,

'Darling, I love you so much.'

And at that point our beautiful interlude was shattered as the dining room door was thrown open and Mrs H slammed a couple of plates down on the table in front of us, said 'cheesecake!' and left again. The spell was broken, but the remaining sense of warmth and happiness enveloped us.

Thomas told me about his visit to Clarice's solicitor this morning. As soon as he started, I interrupted him excitedly with 'ooh, did he tell you where the rest of her cash was stashed?'

He shook his head sadly. I was a bit surprised.

'Really?'

He shook his head again. 'There's no stash.' I gawped at him.

'No stash?'

He shook his head again. His face showed his disappointment.

'Apparently there were gambling debts.'

'Gambling debts?' He nodded soberly. This was getting worse and worse!

'Apparently she used to get the milkman to put on bets for her, and she wasn't very good at picking winners. Mr Stroudly was a bit embarrassed to tell me that his firm had to settle what he termed as a 'substantial' account at a whole string of betting shops within about a thirty mile radius of High Trees.'

'How substantial?' I asked, my eyes narrowing at the thought of that hideous old bag frivolling away our – I mean - Thomas' inheritance.

'That's what I wanted to know. He reluctantly told me that she owed £470,000 on bets placed over the last two years.

OMG! This time I had nothing to say. I just stared at him. He looked as if he wanted to cry. I knew just how he felt. But after a moment, I came over all philosophical, and shrugged my shoulders, and put my best foot forward and whatnot, reaching out to take his hand across the table and giving it a squeeze of wifely encouragement and support.

'Never mind, Darling. We don't need the money. And if it brought her a bit of pleasure, then it doesn't really matter, does it?'

'I suppose not. All the same it's a hell of a lot of money. Wish I'd have known, I could have bought shares in RiteBet.'

He sipped his wine then pushed his glass away. Sighing heavily, he got to his feet and drew me over to the sofa.

He dropped a kiss on my hair and we sat back and gazed into the fire.

Later in the evening I had a call from Monica.

It took me a bit by surprise, and due to my new suspicion of her, I found it difficult to think of something to say. I know I sounded a bit stilted and awkward and unnatural, but I just couldn't help it. I couldn't remember how to talk to her normally. She asked me how I was and I made the excuse that I was a bit tired following the funeral and going down to the house and everything.

She invited me to coffee the following morning. Any other time I would have been keen to go, and I accepted, purely because I didn't have the wit to think of an excuse. So I said I'd love to, and accepted her best wishes for a good night's sleep.

But again and again throughout this evening I've found myself returning to the same thought.

What am I going to say to my friend the murderer?

Wed 18 July - 6.30pm

Just when I think life can't get any more peculiar, I spend some time with Monica.

Huw was out when I got there. Obviously. He is something important in a large corporation – may even be right at the top, I'm not sure. I mean, who knows what one's friends' husbands do for a living? It's as much as I can do to manage to listen my own husband banging on about work, let alone other people's.

So when Monica and I sat down to coffee and cake in the little summerhouse behind their nicely lavish home, we were alone. I was immediately struck by how tense Monica appeared. I mean, if anyone ought to have been tense it ought to have been me – I was the one taking coffee alone with a murderer just yards away from who knew what variety of implements and gadgets and poisons in a remote part of the garden about fifty metres from any kind of useful assistance.

I sat back in my chair, cup in hand, and glancing up, I caught her watching me, apparently appraising me. Again! It was as if we were strangers, meeting for the first time and sneakily trying to size one another up, but at the same time it was more than that. It was almost as if we knew each other too well, like old lovers, and knowing far too much about each other, as if we were somehow trying to find a way back. I set my cup down, biting my lip, wondering if I should invent an excuse to leave. Our friendship was surely over, I didn't see how it could work anymore. Then she said:

'I didn't think you would come.'

Surprised, I just gaped at her.

'Why did you?' She asked. I tried to make light of it.

'When have I ever turned down a free coffee?' I tried a little laugh but her expression silenced me. So I simply sat back in the chair and looked at her. Time to be honest.

'Nothing's changed,' I said, 'not really. We're still friends – you're still my best friend. You haven't changed.'

She didn't speak. Just sat there, looking at me. But she seemed in some inexplicable way softer. I felt bolder.

'I know that you did what you did for my sake, to make life easier for me. You knew I was having problems with Thomas' mother. Let's face it, how could you have not known, after the way she spoke to the two of you. And I'm so grateful to you. It's wonderful to feel so free again.'

There was still a palpable tension. So I picked up my cup, saluted her with it and said, 'thank you!' Then I drank deeply and set down the cup. I grinned at her.

'At least I got a cat out of it. My cleaning lady slash housekeeper adores me now.'

She smiled at this and immediately I felt at ease. We looked out at the garden, hollyhocks and penstemons nodding bright heads in the sunshine.

'Do you like old films?' Monica asked a moment later. I was thrown for a moment. If I had given any thought to what she might say next, I would have expected her to say something a bit more on-topic. So after a slight double-take I said yes, I loved old films.

'Hitchcock?' She asked. I nodded.

'There's a special showing at that new arty cinema in town, The Cube. I wondered if you fancied going? Huw's not interested so I thought a girls' night out might be nice? I mean, if you want to, it might be fun. But it's okay if you're not really into that.'

'I might. What are they showing?'

'They're double-bills, so there's a pick of **Vertigo** and **The Lady Vanishes**, **Dial M for Murder** and **Strangers on a Train**, or **North by Northwest** and **Rear Window**. Take your pick.'

'What do you fancy?' I asked, 'I love all of those but **Dial M for Murde**r is my favourite. 'Mark – I think I'm going to have that breakdown now.' ' I said in my best BBC English, then burst out laughing.

'Sure you wouldn't rather stay in and paste some press cuttings into a scrapbook? Or darn a few stockings?' Quoting from the film, Monica was laughing too, and as she sat forward on her chair, she seemed suddenly relaxed and animated. 'Though I like the modern remake too. 'I always think bludgeon has a spur of the moment sound...' She said in an exaggerated American accent à là Michael Douglas in **A Perfect Murder**.

'What about the other Hitchcock film, **Strangers** – there was a spin-off of that too. A comedy. **Throw Momma From the Train**? I loved that film when I was a teenager.'

'So long as you're Danny DeVito!'

I laughed, and went on,

'But I've never read the original book, though I've always intended to.'

'I'm not a huge fan of Agatha Christie myself,' Monica said, wrinkling her nose. I gaped at her, not sure if she was joking or whether she really thought Christie had written **Strangers on a Train**. But then she made another comment, and I replied to that and then the moment was gone, though the discrepancy still nagged at the back of my mind. Poor Patricia Highsmith! This is not the first time I've had cause to be concerned about Monica's pitiful lack in the education department. Made a mental note to order the book, asap.

We laughed together and chatted, suddenly at ease, thinking of all our favourite scenes in our favourite Hitchcock films, reminding each other of all the places where he cropped up in his famous cameos – in pictures on the wall, wrestling with a cello case, simply walking along a street, that kind of thing. With that and drinking coffee and eating cake, it was all very pleasant. It was lovely to feel like we had got back on that old, friendly footing again, all that strange tension between us gone as quickly as it came.

The films are showing tomorrow evening, so we have arranged to grab a bite to eat beforehand. We're going to meet at around five thirty at Fat Nigel's for a pub dinner and a couple of drinks, then it's only a short walk and we're at The Cube. It'll be fun. I'll leave the car at home and get a taxi in, then I won't need to worry if we have some wine.

Same Day – 10.15pm
This evening over dinner, Thomas said, 'Mrs Hopkins seems to be spending more and more time here. Have you given her more hours?'

'No.' I said. And I thought for a moment. 'Hmm. You're right, she's supposed to do 2 hours a day, but even allowing for the fact that I said she could choose which two hours a day she does, to suit herself, just recently she's always here.' I bit my lip, pondering. 'I'd better have a word with her.'

'It's not that I mind, or anything,' Thomas said, 'I was just curious, that's all. It might be a good idea to give her more hours if she can't get everything done in the original two per day we agreed. I mean, this is a big house. And she does quite a few things that are not technically cleaning.'

'She's taken over the cooking now,' I said thinking about it, 'in fact she does seem to be practically living here at the moment,' I said, and I paused, thinking, puzzling it over. 'I hadn't really thought about it until now, but I definitely saw her going out to the dustbin this morning, first thing, as I was leaving to go into town before going to Monica's. And yet she was still here to get dinner out of the oven for me half an hour ago. I mean, she might have popped home first thing this morning and not come back again until an hour or so ago, but I'm not sure, that wouldn't make much sense, would it? I'll speak to her tomorrow.' I shook my head, puzzled now about what was going on. We ate in silence for a few minutes.

'She just adores that cat,' I added. He smiled.

'If it keeps her happy, it's worth it.'

Then I told him about Monica's suggestion of the cinema. He was keen for me to go. Old films weren't really his thing, but he knew how much I enjoyed them.

'She'll probably lean quite heavily on you over the next few weeks and months,' he said next. Weird, I thought. A bit cryptic. What did he mean?

'What do you mean?' I asked. He bit his lip, pondering.

'Don't let on you know, but Huw told me the other evening – more like a confession really – he's been having it off with his secretary – bloody horrible cliché – but he's decided to actually leave Monica for this woman. He wants a divorce!'

'No!' My knife clattered on my plate. Huw had always seemed such a nice chap. A bit dull, like Thomas, but surely that's an ideal quality in a husband? Who'd have thought he was up to no good with, of all people, his secretary.

'Does Monica know?' I asked. Thomas nodded, taking a good swig of his Merlot.

'Yes, apparently she'd suspected for some time, then she confronted him and he admitted it. They had the most enormous row, Huw said. He's been sleeping in one of the guest rooms, and she's told him to move out by the end of the week. He says she's devastated.'

'He might be kidding himself there,' I said, 'she seemed very calm and relaxed with me today. Not as if anything was on her mind. Although…' my thoughts drifted off.

Had she been, though? I took a moment to think about that. Her manner had been rather odd. There had been something wrong, but of course, I'd assumed it was something to do with that other little matter, Clarice's murder. When she asked me to go to the pictures with her, she'd said Huw wouldn't be interested, but now I could see why. I couldn't believe he could betray her so horribly.

We ate on in silence. I brought in Mrs H's lemon sorbet from the kitchen. Thomas, dabbing his chin with his napkin, said,

'Perhaps Monica's got someone on the side too. Perhaps she's glad to get out of the marriage?'

'If she has got anyone, she's never so much as given me a hint of it, and I think – I hope – she'd confide in me, we are best friends, after all. But she always seems so happy, so contented although possibly a bit lonely. I'm just so shocked. I can't believe it.'

He nodded.

'It's very sad,' he said. 'I told Huw I thought he was a total wanker.'

'He certainly is.' I said. And we got up from the table.

Thurs 19 July - 10.35am

Feeling very dull today. Horrid dreams last night ruined my sleep and left me in that tense state of fear that they might come true.

Dreamed Huw was found with his head bashed in, and that Monica had done it and that she was coming after our cat Tetley next. It was all very weird and stupid and nonsensical as dreams often are, and the only weapon I had to defend my home and family with was that rolling pin except it wasn't glass but some sort of floppy plastic.

I woke a couple of times and tried to get the dream out of my head, but when I drifted back to sleep again, there I was, right back in the middle of the same damned dream. And it was not so much the actual events of the dream that scared me but more an overwhelming presence, an atmosphere of malice that seemed to cling about me, penetrating my clothes, my skin, unnerving me. I was so glad to wake up properly and find it was a sunny morning, although the nice weather didn't last long.

I've just had a rather unsatisfactory interview with Mrs H a few minutes ago. I taxed her with the fact that she seemed to be doing a lot more hours than I paid her for, but she just kept saying that she didn't mind, she didn't feel right taking so much of my money for so few hours and in the end, she said it was because she wanted to keep an eye on the cat. What is going on with that woman? The house gleams and shines – there's not a speck of dust anywhere. The fridge, the freezer, the larder are all stocked up – I haven't had to do any food shopping or cooking for ages now, she's taken over everything. I mean, it's not as if I mind. But it is a bit odd. Although I have to admit, she really is the most exquisite cook. At the end of the day, however, I only pay her for cleaning and a little light cooking, 12 hours a week. She's here more like fifty hours a week, surely? I mean, I know I pay well, but not that well!

    She seemed a bit furtive too. Something is definitely going on, but I'm obviously not going to be able to get to the bottom of it right away, and in any case, I'm far too busy. I nearly ran out of time to get ready for my yoga class and then tonight is my evening out with Monica. I feel a small sense of doom.

Fri 20 July - 8.00am
I must admit to a certain amount of apprehension before I met up with Monica last night. Why do I always feel so much anxiety before the two of us meet? I mean, I felt this way even before I knew she was a brutal murderer.

    Though on reflection that was probably because I was planning a murder myself and I was afraid she would find me out. Hmm. I suppose that could explain it. But surely if it was just guilt I was feeling, it would have gone now the crisis is over and my hands are still lily-white? Anyway. Somehow my nerves are always taut before I meet up with her. But then once I'm there, I'm fine, and we have a great time. Strange.

    I'm writing this over breakfast and remembering how this time yesterday I was fretting about my evening ahead with Monica, and the fact that I had so much to squeeze in before I met her – yoga first, then hair, manicure, pedicure, waxing and massage – in fact barely a moment to myself all day, but I have to keep breaking off as Thomas keeps banging on and on about some meeting he is addressing and saying how tired he is and how worried he is that he won't be absolutely on the ball what with waking up several times during the night. He apparently kept hearing noises or something that disturbed him, I don't know what, I must confess I wasn't really listening. Coming back to yesterday, I had wondered if it would be best to cancel something, the massage for example. But then that would have given me almost an extra hour to kill between the end of my waxing and meeting Monica, and I hadn't fancied wandering the streets just as all the school children are piling into the pubs. So in the end I'd decided I'd be better to keep all the appointments after all.

Mrs H has just been in to clear the breakfast things. I looked up in surprise.

'You're in a bit early again Mrs Hopkins.' I commented. She seemed a bit shifty again. Something is definitely up. She muttered something about needing to get on with something in the kitchen so she'd come in early to make a start.

All very peculiar. Surely this isn't just about that flaming cat? If I'd known it was going to mean my daily woman had to reorganise her schedule, I would have got rid of it. But who knows what goes on the minds of these people? Probably her house hasn't got any electricity or something.

Thomas gave me a peck on the cheek and grabbed his briefcase and I waved him off from the front door like the good little hausfrau I am. Poor lamb, he looks absolutely shattered.

Anyway, to come back to last night - by the time I met Monica at Fat Nigel's, I felt fabulously primped and pampered. She air-kissed me with loud mwah, mwahs and said I looked wonderful, which was lovely, and she waved at the waiter for drinks.

I took a look at her and said, in a quiet voice obviously, but with some concern,

'Monica, you look awful, if you don't mind me saying.'

And as soon as I said it, I was cross with myself, because I remembered what Thomas had told me about Huw and how it was all very hush-hush and then I know I blushed. She looked at me, saying nothing.

'Oh Darling, I'm so sorry, how thoughtless of me!' I said, all contrition.

'You know, don't you?' And the way she said it made me feel so uncomfortable. After all Thomas hadn't been supposed to tell me.

'Well, I…'

She slumped down in a heap on her elbows.

'Oh! Thank God! You have no idea how I've dreaded telling you. It's such a relief not to have to keep carrying on this charade of cheerfulness and being normal. And trying to keep it all in like this. Oh Cress my life is over!' And her voice tailed away into a whiny little screech as she covered her face with her hands for a moment.

Dashing tears from her eyes she enveloped me in a tight brief hug and then out came the whole story of Huw's betrayal with, horrific cliché, his secretary. There was precious little for me to say or do, apart from the odd 'what a bastard' now and again and to keep handing her clean tissues and vodka.

It sounds awful, I know, but we actually had a really good time – we ate, we talked and then it was a mad dash to The Cube for the movie-marathon. (Do two films make a marathon? I think not!) (Not that I would have wanted to sit through all of them in one go - who would? – my bum would have well and truly gone to sleep.)

Monica had booked us excellent seats in the studio showing **Dial M for Murder** and **Strangers on a Train**. Not that she'd really needed to book, if you ask me, the place was half empty but still, it was nice of her.

As the house lights went down, and as the room was caught in that brief, throbbing darkness before the film began, Monica murmured to me,

'Pop quiz – what sport is featured in both these films?'

I shook my head. **Dial M** I knew quite well, but I'd only seen **Strangers** once, years ago, and all I could remember about it was a night-time scene in a fairground. But in **Dial M**, I remembered the husband, Ray Milland's character, had been a retired tennis player.

'Tennis?' I therefore guessed, my eyes glued to the screen. I felt Monica nod in response. 'I don't remember **Strangers** very well, is there anything to do with tennis in that?'

'Wait and see,' said Monica, and then there was Grace Kelly, looking heartbreakingly beautiful at the breakfast table and Ray Milland, the debonaire husband with whom she exchanges an unsatisfyingly chaste kiss.

Lost in the story, the fresh yet dated look of the film, taking it all in, I forgot about my popcorn, Monica, Mrs Hopkins, Thomas, Clarice, everything and everyone, until we reached that climactic moment when Grace turned her face away from her husband and towards her lover.

I kept my eyes fixed on the screen until that scene. This has always been my favourite moment, the moment where the heroine and her lover and the Inspector are waiting tensely for the heroine's husband to come back to the flat, just before he lets himself in with the key he had hidden for the would-be murderer, and that only he knows about and thereby exposes himself for the villain he truly is. (Spoiler alert! Lol!)

And turning to Monica with a huge grin, I and she and all the rest of the rapt audience said those famous words with Grace,

'Mark, I think I'm going to have that breakdown now!' Then we all cheered and clapped and wolf-whistled, laughing at our own silliness.

Glancing about the studio, I could see the absorbed faces, the glistening eyes of the other people, and Monica was smiling at the screen, and I felt warm and happy and wryly aware of the way the film had drawn us into its vanished world and all of us loving every second of it, suspending belief very, very willingly.

Then the house lights came up for the intermission. I stretched and yawned luxuriously and turned to Monica. Her eyes were still spacey, unfocussed. She was still half lost in the film.

'That was amazing, wasn't it?' I said, and she smiled and nodded but was still miles away. With a little shake she pulled herself together, and getting to her feet, ushered me out.

'Let's grab a choc-ice or something,' she suggested, 'we've got twenty minutes or so.'

'Okay.'

In the foyer there was quite a hubbub, as film-buffs from one of the other studios were also having their intermission, and everyone crowded in the direction of the bar.

We found ourselves in a laughing, chattering queue with two other ladies from our screening, and they were enthusiastic in their praise of the film, drawing us quickly into their conversation.

'I'm always a bit sad,' the woman in a burnt orange silk jacket said, 'that Ray Milland doesn't get away with it. He's such a polite, well-bred and cold murderer.'

'Yes, I know!' Monica chimed in, 'you do almost want him to get away with it!' We all laughed.

'After all, his wife is having an affair, she deserves to die like the harlot she is.' Orange Silk's companion Black Velvet Headband said.

'And murder is definitely cheaper than a messy divorce!' I added with a laugh, then hearing myself say the D-word, I faltered, but Monica was laughing too, and did not seem the least bit upset by what I'd said. We got our ice-creams and fizzy wine and made our way back to our seats, still chatting to the other two film-goers. We continued to enlarge upon the theme of how much easier it would be to kill someone than put oneself through the cost and emotional turmoil of a divorce.

'Wish I'd thought of murder myself,' said Orange Silk, 'instead of letting the bastard get my dog and my car and worst of all, his bottle-blonde hussy got my new kitchen!' We all laughed gaily at her heartbreak.

'Especially as you can't be hanged for it!' Monica said, her eyes staring at me fixedly, still spacy.

Orange Silk agreed vigorously, slurping her G and T. She added, 'I mean, what's ten or even twenty years in a cosy prison doing an Open University degree or an apprenticeship in floristry and talking about your feelings, compared to the mess and misery and financial chaos of a divorce?'

'And that's only if you get caught!' I pointed out with a laugh, and she called back with a cackle,

'Knowing my luck, I probably would!'

We settled into our seats, wriggling to get comfortable, unwrapping our ice-creams and turning expectantly towards the screen as the house lights once more faded, and the chattering and laughter died away, and the opening credits of **Strangers** began to roll, accompanied by lots of shots of walking feet.

'I wouldn't...' Monica said in my ear, under cover of the opening dialogue. She didn't add a laugh. She didn't elaborate. She didn't need to - I knew exactly what she was saying. She wouldn't get caught. My mouth dropping open, I turned to look at her but she was staring straight ahead. I could see the square movie screen small and shining in the depths of her eyes. It gave her a detached, alien look.

And then I watched the film.

When we came out I was vaguely surprised to find it was still light – though only just. I felt as if I had been miles away in time and space, but it seemed the world had gone on with its evening routine without me.

My mind was buzzing with notions, crazy notions, thoughts and images whirling and persistent. Robert Walker's face as he says 'criss cross' which came to be his catch-phrase to explain the way the two main characters were to carry out each other's murder.

We chatted and laughed with Orange Silk and Black Velvet Headband as we left the venue and walked slowly towards the taxi rank.

I felt as though I were outside myself, watching the other Cressida talking, making conversation, walking along the road, when all the time, the real Cressida was here inside, watching scattered images of Clarice and of yet another Cressida: Clarice dead on her floor, blood in a little pool around her head, Cressida waiting in the foyer at Chapley's, waiting for Monica who didn't come. Cressida driving, getting out of her car, walking towards the house, pushing open the already open door at Highgates. Clarice dead on her floor, blood in a little pool around her head. The crow bloody and refusing to die. Cats in the baskets, going to the vets, eyes watching me through the little doors. Clarice's peremptory voice on the phone, 'well really, Child.'

'Are you okay?' Monica asked, 'you seem awfully far away.'

We were in the taxi, driving through the streets and already it seemed darker than it had been when we had first left The Cube.

'Yes. Yes, I'm fine, Mon.'

'Wasn't it a great evening? It's been years since I had so much fun. Apart from the bit when I was crying buckets and pouring my heart out like a fourteen-year-old of course. Sorry about that, I feel such an idiot now, but it did me the world of good.'

I laughed a little as she seemed to expect it, told her it was all okay, nothing to worry about and yet she seemed to still be looking for reassurance, for an answer, she watched my face carefully, but I didn't really feel like laughing. I felt a strange tension hanging in the air around us.

'Are you going home?' I asked.

'Yes,' she said in a questioning voice.

'I just wondered – I mean, you'd be very welcome to stay with us for a while, if you wanted to, if you felt you couldn't face him, or well - whatever, just 'if'.'

'Oh Cress, you are a Sweetheart! But no, it's fine. He's hardly ever home anyway, he mainly stays with Her. In fact he's been relatively considerate. I can't help wondering if there will be a big wrangle at some point over the house and everything – I suppose that's inevitable. We'll probably have to sell the house and split the money. Such a shame, I love that house. It's practically a part of me – or the other way round. We've been there fifteen years now. It's the only real home I've ever known. I've never lived anywhere else that long, we moved around so much when I was growing up, what with my father being in the army.' She sighed.

'I'm so sorry, Monica, I really am. If there's anything we can do, anything at all, you know you can…'

'I know I can. Thanks Cress. I don't know if it's just the wine talking, but I feel a bit soppy. I want you to know how nice it is to have someone I can pour my heart out to and not feel an absolute idiot. It's so nice to know there's someone I don't have to keep up the pretence with. Thanks, Sweetie-pie.'

'Any time, yer daft cow!' I said, trying to make it all light and fluffy again. 'And I do mean any time.' I added just to make absolutely sure.

'I know.' She said and patted my hand.

And then we were pulling up outside her house, and the taxi door was opening and she was getting out. She passed me some money through the window.

'My share of the fare.' She said across my protests and blew a kiss at me before heading for her front door.

I was deep in thought for the remainder of the journey home.

Thomas was already asleep when I got into bed. In spite of the warm night I shivered and I snuggled in beside him, so glad he was there.

I knew now what I had to do.

Mon 23 July - 11.30am
Haven't heard from Monica for a few days, not since we said goodnight on Thursday when the taxi dropped her off, so I thought I'd better give her a ring, make sure she's all right.

    The conversation was a bit one-sided. She told me Huw had actually packed up some of his things in a couple of suitcases and moved out! She wasn't teary though, as she had cried herself out this morning. But she seemed rather morose, didn't really seem to have much to say, and when I tried to invite her over for drinks, or for dinner or just for morning coffee, she kept making excuses, excuses so thin a five year old could see through them.

    The only time she seemed to perk up was when I mentioned our trip to the Hitchcock 'movie marathon', and thanked her once again for suggesting it. Just for a moment she seemed to come to life – she talked about the films, the ladies we met and our nice chat with them about how much easier it was to kill someone than divorce them, and her voice held real warmth and enthusiasm, but then she sank back and was again distant, indifferent, colourless, her voice coming slowly down the line to me, saying Huw had just come in for some more stuff and she'd have to go. Then, just as she was about to ring off, she said in quick, frantic voice, 'Cress! Thanks for ringing – you're such a lifeline, it means so much to know you're on my side. You're all that's keeping me going at the moment. Thank you, Sweetie.' And then the line went dead, leaving me listening to emptiness.

    I sat thinking.

    I knew what I had to do.

I just didn't know quite how to do it.

Same day – 10.30pm
Standing by the window with my cup of tea this afternoon, looking out into the garden, half day-dreaming, I spied Tetley prowling in the shade of the shrubbery, and not far off, a young blackbird was pecking carelessly at a windfall. It seemed likely there was going to be a repeat of the traumatic crow-killing melodrama again - different cat, different bird, same tediously messy outcome.

    I stood there day-dreaming for a few minutes, and then quite suddenly I had an idea. A brilliant audacious brainwave!

Tues 24 July - 4.15pm
Thomas is very tired and irritable. He's still not sleeping properly, and I think this whole Huw and Monica thing is upsetting him more than he's willing to admit, men like to pretend to be so macho, don't they? Poor Sweetie-pie, at least it's only another three weeks or so until we go away for his shooting. That'll pick him up no end.

    That film keeps preying on my mind. I feel that I've got to do something. Of course, there's only one thing that I can do, just one course of action that will be of any use, but it seems so incredibly drastic, and I just don't know if I can pull it off. I've got the germ of an idea, a massive, crazy, audacious idea, but this is really a job for a Professional, for someone who knows what they're doing, not just an enthusiastic amateur. There are so many things that could go wrong, just thinking about it makes me want to run away and hide. But Monica has been so good to me, and she is so miserable, and after all, she is my best friend.

    What was it the woman at The Cube said? 'At least they can't hang you for it.'

    That's not much of a consolation at this point.

    This is just crazy. It's completely nuts. No, I can't do this. I've got to put it out of my mind completely. Even to be giving it house-room in my mind, to even contemplate it is utterly ridiculous.

Wed 25 July - 9.20pm
I can't believe how Mrs H dotes on that stupid cat. There are about ten different types of cat food in my kitchen, and the smaller the tin, the higher the price, it seems. And, indeed, the higher the scent. And the little git eats off my finest Wedgwood.

But it's very odd. I just popped into the kitchen for a moment before breakfast this morning – it must have been about a quarter to eight – hideously early! I meant to leave a note for Mrs H about the vacuum cleaner, just to make sure Her Sid does indeed manage to sort it out permanently and just in case there had been any further problems and so on.

And there, in the middle of the kitchen was the most enormous man in a scruffy shirt, baggy jeans and some ancient, dog-eared slippers. He had clearly just entered from the garden and seemed to have been about to say something to Mrs H who was standing there with a daft expression on her face, watching that cat eating when I walked in, still in my dressing gown.

She looked at him, he looked at me, I looked at him, he looked at her, and she looked from me back to him. They couldn't have looked more shocked. True, I don't usually wander into the kitchen at that time of day, and certainly not in my nightwear, but there was more to it than that.

Then, in an attempt to collect herself, Mrs H said, still sounding a bit flustered,

'Oh, er, this 'ere's my Sid, Mrs Powell.'

'Oh indeed? How nice to make your acquaintance, Mr Hopkins, and many thanks for offering to repair the vacuum cleaner, too, that was very thoughtful.'

He seemed a bit shifty. He didn't seem too sure if he should shake my proffered hand or not. In the end, he did just give it a brief clasp in his gnarly bear paw. He seemed a bit uncomfortable, and if I hadn't been there, I'm fairly sure he would have wiped his nose on the back of his hand. He looked like the sort of chap who does that.

'Snuffink, I'm sure, Mrs, er –'

'Well, 'op it then,' Mrs H scolded him, flapping her hands at him. He didn't immediately seem to realise what she meant but then with a sudden nod, and apparent clarity, he stepped back towards the door. He waved his hand in a half-salute and said carefully in a much louder voice,

'Well, I'll - er – I'll be off, then, I 'ave now told you what it was that I had to come over and – er – and tell you, and so now I can go and – er – I shall see you at 'ome later. Bye me duck.'

And in one smooth motion he had opened the door and gone through it, and the door was already closing behind him when Mrs H called out to him somewhat belatedly,

'Bye, Ducks, see you this afternoon.' She turned back to me, a little flustered.

'Has he got a day off?' I asked.

'A day…? Oh, er, yes, Mrs Powell, he's having a day off today. That's right. A day…just doing a few odd jobs at home, like.'

'You should have said,' I told her, 'you could have quite easily had today off - you haven't used any of your holiday yet. In fact why don't you go now? It's still early, you'd have virtually a full day together. You really have arrived very early this morning once again. There's no need to get here quite so early, you know.'

She looked at me with something like dismay. What on earth was wrong with the woman? Generally one's staff are all too eager to have some time off on full pay. But not my Mrs H, it would seem. She shook her head vehemently.

'Ooh, er, well, that's very generous of you, Mrs Powell, it is really, but you know, I think I'd just be in his way, you know how men are when they've got their jobs to do, tools everywhere and everything. Thanks all the same, you know but well…'

'Well, if you're sure.' I said doubtfully. 'Just let me know if you change your mind, it's really not a problem, I can manage without you for one day.'

I drifted off to the sitting-room again, totally baffled. But in the end though, I stopped worrying. I mean, I know I shouldn't say it, as it's not very PC, but everyone knows the working classes are not like Us. There's no point in working one's fingers to the bone trying to understand them.

Sat 28 July - 7pm

So, to dish the dirt on last night's fiasco! To think that Huw could have the gall go to a dinner party with 'our set' and, before the dust has even settled following his abrupt departure from the marital home, he is carting his secretary slash mistress about with him as brazenly as anything!

I could tell Cherub Bryston-Harrison was horribly embarrassed. It was all Garrison's idea, of course, he has simply no idea about good taste. Well the man does work in advertising, so one is hardly surprised.

'Don't know if all of you have already met Mandi Morgan, Huw's new – er – well, er – Ladyfriend.' He said once we made our way into the drawing room before dinner.

'It's wiv two Ds,' she said with a giggle and a slight lisp that made me want to smack her. I assumed she meant Manddi not Laddyfriend. Huw at least had the grace to look a little uncomfortable. He couldn't meet my accusing eyes. Good! The Bastard! It's literally just been a few days. How could he? Fortunately I didn't have to sit anywhere near either of them during dinner – Cherub's good taste coming to the fore there, I should think.

When we left the men to their port and cigars (all very Edwardian), and She nipped off to the ladies, wiggling her pert yet massive backside as she went, Cherub grabbed my arm and hissed in my ear,

'Oh Cressida, I'm so sorry. I'm truly mortified! I had absolutely no idea they were coming – and I know Monica is your best pal – I just don't know what to say…it's all Garrison's fault. Men are completely useless, aren't they?'

But then She came back in. We were all handing round coffees and talking about holiday plans and Cherub's new baby daughter's christening gown. It's antique lace – and Cherub needs recipes for bleaching it as it's gone a bit of a horrid yellow in her great aunt's attic. Naturally Cherub doesn't want to upset all the old biddies in the family but at the same time without some serious renovation, that lace will look really ghastly on her gorgeous little baby girl and obviously the christening photos will be utterly ruined.

She sat at the other end of the room, but she didn't appear the slightest bit self-conscious or uncomfortable. She just chatted away in her little corner with Nadina (That turncoat! I definitely hate her now, if I didn't already!) and another girl whom I'm sure I heard Nadina call Weasel. I do hate these big dinner parties, one never gets the chance to really interrogate people.

Later, I made the mistake of popping to the loo. And when I returned to the drawing room, I caught the tail-end of something Manddi with two double Ds was saying, which a few people sniggered at then broke off guiltily when they saw me standing there. Now there is nothing worse than that awful feeling of being the only one not in on a joke, or rather, of feeling a horrid sense that one has become the joke.

So it was evident she had been talking about me.

I remember when I came into the room she was saying,

'…lookth ethactly like a huge big giant overgrown Barbie doll, innit?'

But I was on fine form. For once I had a comeback, not especially witty but a comeback nonetheless and I was quite pleased that I sounded rather cool as I said in a bright happy voice,

'Speaking of Barbies, don't you think it's time, in our modern world, the manufacturers brought out a transgender Barbie? They could take a Ken doll, give him tiny little pink plastic boobs, and long hair, five o'clock shadow and high heels? They could call him slash her Kelly.'

No one laughed. It was all so horrid. I so wished Monica had been there to take the edge off the situation. Eventually someone asked if anyone had seen a television show called **Made in Chelsea**. It seems they all had.

Once everyone was talking again, Nadina snuck over to earnestly whisper to me,

'Darling Cressie, I'm so sorry you had to hear that, obviously it was a perfectly hideous thing for her to say and she's far too new to our set to have a right…I just wanted to say that I for one made a point of not laughing, and I don't think you look anything like a Barbie doll. I'm on your side, Cressie.'

I smiled and said something polite that I can't even remember now. In my mind I was pounding her face into the top of the nearby glass coffee table. Cressie!

When we got home, Thomas told me he had actually felt physically ill to hear Huw banging on over the vintage port about how great the sex was, and he said even Giles Smytherton-Netherbury seemed a bit embarrassed, and everyone knows him as one of the filthiest old goats that ever prowled the earth in search of a guilt-free quickie.

I'm not anything like a Barbie. Well, I'm not all that tall, and my boobs are not even slightly plastic! They're all nature's own fine work, I'm proud to say (and Thomas would agree!) and that's more than Manddi would be able to boast! Cow.

We talked about the situation when we were in bed last night, even though we were late getting back and poor Thomas had to be up early for golf this morning. It was just like when we first got married - talking really seriously into the wee hours about how sad we were about our friends' upcoming divorce. Thomas is quite angry about the way Huw is carrying on and it's so nice to know he has such strong, firm morals. He is wonderful. I'm so lucky to have him.

Only thing is, it makes me feel so ashamed of the things I've planned and thought about and plotted towards. I mean, Clarice, you know, and well, that sort of thing because obviously if he knew – well, I don't think he'd love me anymore. He'd be so shocked, so disappointed in me. I would have let him down so completely and utterly. I know I wouldn't be able to bear the look on his face. And realising that has really made me think about other things I'd been thinking about a bit more. I mean the other aspects of the Huw slash Monica situation. If you see what I mean.

Just before he dropped off to sleep, Thomas said, 'Can you ring up a pest control firm on Monday? I'm absolutely convinced we've got mice or rats or something in the attic, I keep hearing little noises. I can't take any more broken nights.'

I promised I would and gave him one last peck on the cheek and off he drifted, from wide awake to softly snoring in less than thirty seconds. Typical chap.

But I lay awake for ages. All I could think about was Huw's betrayal and what I, as Monica's best friend, ought to do about it. And yet, there's Thomas to consider, and how he would feel if he found out what sort of woman I really am. If anything happened, if he found out and left me because of it, I would just die, I know I would. There wouldn't be anything worth living for. To know that he was alive in the world and thinking ill of me.

I suppose the main thing is, not to let him find out. I don't see how I have any choice about what I've got to do? Or have I? Should I do it? I mean, obviously, you know, it's wrong, but she's my friend. If I don't look after her interests, take her side, then who will? Oh God, I'm so confused.

There were definitely quite a lot of odd little sounds from above our heads. Thomas is quite right. And, poor lamb, he tossed and turned restlessly, he's such a light sleeper. Suppose it's Clarice's ghost come back to haunt us? That's just the malicious sort of beastly thing she would do.

Must get Mrs H to ring the Rat Man on Monday. And if he can't help, might have to turn to **Britain's Most Wanted Ghost Walk Investigator Paranormal Cops**. That's one of my favourite TV shows. I wonder if they have a helpline one can contact? Second thoughts, they've probably just got a Ouija board. I woke Thomas up a little bit with my giggling. Made a firmer effort to try to forget about everything and just go to sleep, such a big day ahead tomorrow!

Sun 29 July - 11.50pm
Absolutely exhausted after the most amazing day at the Olympics – the gymnastics was truly wonderful – such a talented lot – and it was lovely to see all the girls hugging one another and chatting and encouraging one another – not just their own team-mates, but, on occasion, other teams too. Such wonderful community spirit. I mean, I know one bangs on about uniting the world through sport and non-violent competition, but it really is amazing to see rivals truly happy for one another, and truly commiserating with one another.

    We had the most perfect seats, positioned so we could see the asymmetric bars and the floor routines, and the whole thing was such a spectacle, the arena was just electric, the atmosphere indescribable. I will never, ever forget today. And Beth Tweddle, and the other girls of course, was brilliant. She didn't win, but she certainly deserved to have done so.

    It was utterly magnificent from beginning to teary end.

Mon 30 July - 11.45am

The rat man – Ern – came out almost immediately Mrs H called him, and after two hours of poking about with all kinds of gadgets and looking very Ghostbusters, with a torch held together with sticky tape and a pair of steps not much better, he has now given us a completely clean bill of health, rodent-wise, much to Thomas' amazement. I rang him at work just now to tell him the good news.

I queried it with Mrs H as soon as she presented me with the bill.

'He found nothing?'

'Nuffink at all, Mrs Powell, not so much as a sniff of a mouse or rat. He were 'ere a good two hours. Very furrow, I must say.'

'Yes, I know, I heard him banging about upstairs. And twice I bumped into him coming out of the first floor bathroom.'

'Ah, yes, erm, I suspect 'e 'as a bit of a problem in the plumbing department.'

As I suspected she meant his own personal plumbing department, I decided to leave that whole topic well alone.

'Well, I'm very pleased to hear we don't have any kind of infestation. Though I think Thomas is going to be a bit surprised to hear it.' Which he was, as it turned out!

'Really Mrs Powell?' Mrs H was looking a bit puzzled.

'Yes, he keeps hearing noises at night, coming from the attic. At first I thought he must be imagining things, but now I know he's not, I've heard noises myself the last couple of nights. Sort of banging and scraping and quiet little noises, going on for at least two hours in the middle of the night. Whatever it is, we need to get to the bottom of it, the poor lamb isn't getting a wink of sleep.'

She looked a bit worried. I hastened to reassure her.

'Oh please don't let it bother you, Mrs Hopkins, I'm sure it's nothing to worry about.'

She hastily agreed, saying,

'I mean if it's not rats, what else could it be? It must be rats. Anyway, our clever little Tetley will catch anyfink what comes into the 'ouse.'

Looking at the steadily fattening, complacent tabby lying in a pool of sunshine just inside the garden door, I wasn't convinced. I seriously doubt she could move, let alone run fast enough to catch any pests. Sardines maybe, roast chicken definitely, rats – I seriously doubt it.

Same day – 10.10pm

'Birds.' Thomas said earlier this evening. 'Bloody great big crows or some damned thing, probably trying to nest in the chimney pots. I'll have to look into it next weekend, I can't just leave it, its driving me daft, all the aggravation of the tiny little stealthy noises in the wee hours of the night. I know it's only little creaks and slight sorts of rustling noises but once I start to hear them I can't relax, and then I can't get back to sleep. After four or five disturbed nights in a row, I feel like I'm going to crack up or something.'

I tried to remonstrate with him, pointing out that everything seems worse in the middle of the night and that I hardly ever heard anything, so perhaps he was letting his imagination run away with him.

I didn't really want him to know I'd heard the sounds too. What if it was really Clarice? I know the house isn't very old, but there could still be something other-worldly going on, and if a human or spirit-being was to blame it would definitely be Clarice, she loved to make our lives a misery when she was alive, I don't see that she'd let a little thing like death put a stop to that. And anyway, aren't murdered people always restless spirits? How could she rest in peace knowing someone had done her to death? Mind you, by that reasoning, technically she should be haunting Monica. And Monica has enough on her plate at the moment without being haunted too. And of course, Clarice, even if she had got a look at her killer, wouldn't know where Monica lived, and she could hardly look her up in the phone book, could she?

Thomas grumbled on a bit more, poor old pet, then we settled down in front of the television with some champagne and strawberries to watch ***Midsomer Murders***.

'D'you know,' I said, 'it's quite humbling to think that we're just like ordinary people sitting here watching TV together, with no shoes on, and with our drinks and snacks.'

He dropped a kiss on my hair.

'I know, Darling, it's the simple things in life that count. Relaxing in front of the old box with one's loved ones. Letting all one's troubles ease away. I bet even Our Sid and Mrs 'Opkins are doing just this very thing.'

'I'll ask her tomorrow.' I said.

Tues 31 July - 1.15am (so technically Wednesday!)
Went to relaxation class and reflexology. Had a quick massage. And I certainly felt like I needed it, with the stressful few days I've just had!

Sent a few texts to Monica asking how she is and suggesting we meet up. She just texted back to say she didn't really feel like going anywhere, didn't really feel like facing anyone, but thanked me for thinking of her.

So I grabbed some champers and some vodka (after all I wouldn't know until I actually got there and assessed the situation, which of these would prove to be the 'cup that cheers') and drove straight over to her place after my facial, hoping I wouldn't look so fabulous she'd feel even more depressed. I didn't want to push her any closer to the edge of the cliff, after all.

I must say, it gave me a bit of a shock to see how badly she's letting herself go – her hair was a shocking mess, and she was wearing, I'm absolutely certain, chain-store jeans and an old shirt of Huw's. She's lost weight too, but not in a good way. I mean, she was almost a size zero before, now she must be a minus two. A leggy little stick with huge red eyes and blotchy skin.

'Oh My God!' I said when she opened the door. Well, I mean, one always intends to spare one's friends feelings but sometimes the shock is just too great to hold back.

'Cress, I don't…' she began, on seeing me there.

'Nonsense,' I said and swept past her and into the sitting room.

I found a couple of glasses and opened up the old champers and poured her out about half a pint.

'Drink that up, Poppet, and you'll feel fab in no time. I don't suppose you're eating properly?'

She curled up on the sofa opposite me, her fingers gripped the glass the way I used to cling on to the satin edging of my pink blanky when I was three. I watched her, worried. She had huge dark circles under her eyes. What a bastard Huw is, to do this to her. She sipped some Bolly. Then a bit more, and in no time at all I was topping her up.

'Do you think he'll come back?' She asked me later, her voice plaintive.

I blustered a bit, after all what could one say to that without adding to the pain? I finally settled on answering her with a question of my own.

'Would you want him to come back, after what he's done to you?'

'Yes!' For a moment she sat up, all bright and perky, then all the energy went out of her again, and she sagged back. She made a helpless gesture. 'No. I don't know. If he did come back, would he stay? Would it be because he loved me or because it was more convenient to live at home? How would I know he wouldn't do exactly the same thing in a few months or years? I'd never be able to trust him again.'

She took a sip from her glass. I was about to murmur some kind of agreeing noise when she added,

'Not that he will ever come back. He's with her now. He loves her. I don't mean anything to him anymore. He's gone forever!'

It seemed a bit pointless to contradict her – who knew what was going on in Huw's mind? And besides, what if he really loves this Manddi with two Ds? I desperately wanted to comfort Monica, but I just couldn't think of anything to say apart from how sorry I was and that it was all such a horrid mess.

'Oh God, Cressida, what am I going to do? I can't bear to live without him! I wish I was dead!' She began to cry, not softly but with huge racking sobs, her thin chest heaving as she gulped for air and tried to talk, and her eyes and nose streaming, tears and saliva and stuff running down her face, onto her shirt, onto her hands, all dripping into her hair, and I could no longer understand the words she was gasping and spluttering through her fingers.

I found some tissues in my bag and pushed them into her hand, scooching onto the sofa next to her and putting an arm around her shoulders. She collapsed against me and wept and wept. My own eyes prickled with tears, all I wanted was to make everything better for her, but however much I wanted to, I knew I just couldn't take away her pain. I may have said this once or twice before, but men are such bastards!

It was dark when she finally sat up, drank the last of the champagne and then went out to the cloakroom to wash her face. When she came back, it was with the embarrassment of the controlled person who has experienced a bout of abandonment. She apologised to me about twenty times and begged me not to tell anyone I had seen her so distraught, so messed up. Not to mention without her lash extensions.

'I won't, I wouldn't.' I assured her. 'Are you sure you won't come back with me for dinner? You need to eat, you know. And Mrs H is bound to have made something yummy for dinner.'

'No, no, I'd rather not. Thank you, Darling, but I couldn't face anyone, not even dear old Thomas. I've got a few easy things in the freezer, I'll just nuke something and sit in front of the television and watch **Britain's Got A Top Talent Idol**.'

'Well, if you're sure,' I said, still a bit doubtful I should leave her. But actually she really did look much better now.

'I'll be fine.' She said, and she smiled. 'Go home, Cress! You've done your bit to bring me back from the brink. I'm fine now, really, I'm much better. Thank you for everything. Go home, Darling and I'll call you tomorrow!'

So I left. She waved off me from the door, and I felt sure she was calm and relaxed after her cathartic emotional storm.

Of course I had to explain to Thomas why I was so late – it was quarter to nine by the time I got home. But anyway, when I promised not to tell anyone about Monica, obviously he wasn't included, she would know that I was going to tell him. Mrs H had left us her excellent pheasant and claret ratatouille in the kitchen, so I popped that in the microwave, and whilst Thomas was choosing some wine I told him about poor Monica.

He let out a long whistle as he wiped the bottle and carefully drew the cork.

'Wow,' he said, 'I can hardly believe she would give way to that extent. Not that I blame the poor kid, but, well, I mean, it's only old Huw, isn't it, I mean he's not the sort of chap you'd think girls would get all hot and bothered about.'

'Darling, he's her husband! And he's done something truly terrible! The poor woman is completely crushed. Anyone would be, under the circumstances.'

'I suppose.' He said, a bit uncertain. He swilled the wine around in a large glass jug.

'Thomas, Darling, what are you doing?'

'Letting it breath a bit. Meant to open this earlier, but I forgot. Would you be like that?'

'What? Distraught like Monica? Yes, Darling, I would, of course I would! You know how I adore you.'

He smiled. And dropped a quick, distracted kiss on the tip of my nose.

'Hmm. Most gratifying to hear, I shall make sure I never abandon you for my secretary. Of course, my secretary is about 90 and male but even so...'

The microwaved pinged, and dinner was served.

Wed 1 August - 11.45pm
This morning I drove into town and dropped by Huw's office. It was an unpardonable breech of etiquette of course, but I didn't think he'd make too much of a fuss, and at least he could rely on me to behave in a civilised manner. In any case he'd already shown that he himself had no sense of propriety whatsoever by turning up at a dinner with his mistress within two days of separating from his wife.

    I had hoped to be able to speak to Huw privately and to make him see reason and make him ditch his tart and go home to Monica and beg her forgiveness, but all that changed as soon as I reached the lobby. I was forced to put Plan B into operation.

    Manddi was there. I could see her through an open doorway, sitting in the outer office that protected Huw's from visitors. So, a friendly smile firmly in place, I waved at her and I went in.

    Her mouth dropped open when she looked up from her game of computer solitaire and saw me. Her wad of gum fell out of her lipsticked mouth with a soft thump onto the desk leaving some tiny, tiny splash marks on the surface of the wood veneer.

    She was not exactly the image of a classically trained secretary. Three inches of black roots showed through her over-bleached hair, her low-cut blouse just barely remaining buttoned over the strain of her bust (at least that explained the double D!), a massive muffin-top hung over the top of her tight black trousers. My first reaction was God, she's so common. My second reaction was, God she's so common. I think I managed not to let her see how much I despised her. She smiled, so it must have been okay. Although she would probably have said 'must of been'.

'Hi. Dun I know you? Din I see you at that fing the uvver night?'

'You did indeed. And I thought I'd pop in as I was in Town, and say how sorry I was not to have more chance to chat with you.'

'Really?' Probably she was remembering the Barbie incident as she sounded a little more surprised than was strictly polite, but never mind. I turned up the wattage on my smile.

'Yes, really. Thomas and I are Huw's oldest friends and so obviously we don't want to lose touch just because he's with someone else now.'

'Oh.' She said, still surprised, but this time more accepting. She grinned, and nodded. 'Cool.'

'Perhaps we could have lunch together?'

'What, now?'

'Well, whenever you have your lunch.' I suggested. She looked a bit puzzled.

'I can have it whenever.' Said Manddi with two Ds. 'But it's only eleven o'clock.'

'So shall I come back at about half past twelve?' I said. She thought for a second.

'Cool.' She said, which I took to mean 'that would be lovely, thank you, I'm looking forward to it.' Choking back my irritation I gave her another huge smile and said,

'Later, girlfriend.'

'For sure.' She said eagerly.

She didn't seem to realise I was being ironic.

Well, I don't mind admitting it was not only the lunch from hell, but the expensive lunch from hell. If I had somehow assumed she was an independent adult, she had clearly assumed I was her elderly Aunt come to buy her stuff.

I paid. Though in hindsight, I suppose that didn't matter, no one was likely to check. There was no difficulty getting her to talk – and talk – about herself and Huw. About what he said about her new tattoo, what he said about her new Facebook picture, in fact what he said about – well, almost everything she did or said or even thought of doing or saying. She talked about her time at secretarial college where she had only got through her course by the skin of her teeth, largely because her main priority had been to party as much as possible. She told me how she loved to meet up with her old pals, how she would often stay out late drinking, and get up late in the mornings, hungover.

'But it don' matter if I come in to work late, right, cos I'm bangin' the boss so it's cool.' She explained. I nodded and smiled.

'Cool.'

She told me everything I wanted to know, didn't seem to find any of my questions odd or too invasive, and when she went to the ladies', I had no trouble acquiring her driving licence, even though I wouldn't have been surprised if she hadn't had one. Judging by the number of points on it, she wouldn't have it for much longer.

And when I walked her back to the office I had no difficulty getting her to give me one of the company's business cards 'so I could phone her for a chat'.

Cool.

I had made up my mind.

I went straight home and ordered a rental car, using Manddi's name and arranged to collect it later in the afternoon.

I spent half an hour practising Manddi's signature, and a further half an hour messing up my hair and face so that I looked reasonably similar to her licence photo (if you imagine someone viewing it through another person's reading glasses in very poor light). I pulled on a top that was too small and a pair of Thomas's track-suit bottoms.

I had obviously done something right as the spotty young chap behind the counter at the car rental office didn't do more than glance at either the photo or my signature. I walked out twirling the car keys on my forefinger with a sense of elation.

He talked me through all the little dents and dings and drew my attention to how much petrol was in the tank, asking me to bring it back with approximately the same amount. Cool, I told him with a dazzling smile. He left me, and I put on my driving gloves.

I was ready.

At five minutes to five I was waiting in the rental car. I'd parked it a little way up the road from Huw's office building. The road sloped quite steeply down towards the office block, and I had stopped near the top of the hill, with an excellent view of both the road and the entrance to the building's lobby.

I'd already rung up Manddi and pretended to be an old girlfriend from secretarial college keen to meet up for drinks. That had got her out of the way. I didn't even need to disguise my voice. She had sounded a bit puzzled, as if she couldn't quite remember who I was (or rather, who I was pretending to be) but that hadn't stopped her agreeing to get together at five o'clock at a pub five minutes' walk from the office. I'd promised to drop her at her home afterwards. I couldn't believe it worked. It's no wonder people are always getting killed when they're always so gullible and do stupid things like agreeing to meet up with complete strangers in bars.

She left the building almost as soon as I arrived in position, teetering along on impossible heels and texting someone with both thumbs as she went. She looked happy.

I settled down to wait. Worried that he might simply stay at the office until late enough to take Manddi home, or that she would come back almost immediately having found no one at the pub waiting for her, I was already half convinced I was going to have to come back another day and try something else. So imagine my relief when only a few minutes after Manddi had departed, Huw emerged from the building, briefcase in hand.

I saw him stepping off the kerb, heading for the underground car park where he'd presumably left his top-of-the-range current-model BMW.

I was actually going quite fast by the time I hit him. He, with the usual arrogance of the pedestrian these days, had assumed I would simply stop when I got to him, and he just stepped into the road and began to cross without actually bothering to check if it was safe. As I reached him, he was still ambling across the road and clearly wasn't about to hurry himself. I think he may have even seen me, as he glanced around at the very last nanosecond with suddenly frightened awareness, and there was something – some little look on his face – no, not even on his face, it was just the strangest suggestion of a shade in his eyes, the little lines between his brows contracting. It was a look that said, 'I always knew she hated me,' followed by a sudden realisation of what was about to happen and a strong impression that he suddenly thought, 'oh shit!'

But then he bumped up in the air and over the top of the car (I was doing quite a speed and of course, it's downhill and on a slight bend at that point – not at all a good place to cross really), and I saw him in my mirror, almost in slow-motion, as his head whacked down on the boot and then he hit the tarmac behind me with a strange flomping sound I could hear even though the window was up and Michael Bublé was blaring out of the speakers.

Huw bounced once more and lay still on his face on the road. There was a smeared streak of blood and tissue a foot long where he fell to earth. For a busy street in the evening rush-hour of the City it was amazing that there didn't seem to be another soul around. Not too worried about being seen as I was in my Manddi disguise, I got out of the car and teetered back to him, stepping carefully round the blood that was beginning to seep and to thread its way through the minute grooves in the temporary road surface – I didn't want to ruin my Jimmy Choos.

There was a nasty second when I thought that he was still alive, but if he was, that moment passed quite quickly as I bent over him and saw that his half-open eyes already looked glassy. He was quite neat and tidy really, apart from that little stream of blood, and as he was lying on the scraped side of his face, he really didn't look too bad, all things considered, but it was the angle of his head that revealed the truth of the matter.

I hesitated for a second, wondering whether to try to find a pulse so I could be sure, but already a couple of elderly busybodies were coming out of a charity shop further down the street, so I just had to leap back into the car and drive off as fast as I could, zooming round the old dears on the zebra crossing. Glancing in the mirror, I could see a walking stick being waved furiously, and I heard a shout of outrage. Old people, I ask you! Surely anyone could see I was being a Gangsta? Why did it surprise them that a cold-blooded murderer should also lack principles?

From there it was only a twenty minute drive to my next destination. I pulled the car off the road onto the drive of the semi-detached love-nest Huw had been sharing with Manddi. She wasn't home yet from the pub. So I stood by the door and waited. After about another half an hour, she arrived, looking furious.

She didn't seem surprised to see me, didn't bother with pleasantries, just started immediately shouting about how fucking useless people were, how she'd wasted so much fucking time waiting for people who didn't show up and had to pay for her own fucking drinks and then even Huw hadn't bothered to answer her texts and he wasn't at the fucking office, though there had been a couple of cops further down the road, not that she had any truck with cops after the way they banged up her dad when all he did was drive the poxy car, and then there I was in the tiny sitting room on the leatherette sofa before she even drew breath.

Now there was a certain amount of time pressure, because I was expecting the police to turn up at any moment to announce the terrible news. And of course, at the back of my mind, I couldn't be one hundred per cent sure that he was actually dead. Emergency medical treatment has come on in leaps and bounds in recent years, and the local hospital enjoys an excellent reputation. What if they'd managed to pull him back from the brink? What if, even now, he was sitting in bed in hospital, giving a full statement to the police whilst gorgeous young nurses plied him with sweet tea and painkillers?

I must have started to breath a bit heavily and look flustered, because suddenly taking a break from all the interesting things that she had said and thought and said again, Manddi put out a hand on my arm and in a really sweet voice, she said,

'Hey, Crezz, are you cool, man, or what? You look like shit, innit?'

Desperately reaching for something to tell her, I told her I thought Thomas was having it off with Mrs Hopkins, (it was the only thing I could think of – fortunately she hadn't met Mrs H so that was okay) and said I thought I was having a panic attack, and that I wasn't able to sleep because of the worry and what on earth was I going to do? She jumped up and clomped upstairs in her massive 70s style heels. A moment later and she was back with a little brown medicine bottle with a foreign label, she shook out a few little capsules and shoved some under my nose.

'Take a couple of these. They're well good, Crezz.'

'What are they?' I asked, hoping I sounded more curious than cautious. One must retain one's cool at all times.

'Just sleeping pills, innit. Nuffing dodgy. But they're strong. Really strong. One of these and you'll feel all relaxed and cool and that. But don't take it till you get home, they work really quickly. I take 'em all the time, just one to help me sleep, they're brill, knock you out like a light in literally five minutes.'

'So have you got anything to give me a little buzz now? Not pills, I don't mean. Some nice vodka or something? I just need a bit of a pick-me-up. You know.' I asked, beaming at her. She beamed back. She thought I was pleased, and I was. She thought I was pleased because she'd literally handed me the answer to my problems, and of course she had, but then I had lied about what my problem really was.

She went to get the booze. And I dug a pair of nail scissors out of my handbag. We drank a few glasses, got a bit tipsy, she called in at the loo on her way to the kitchen to get a bag of mini poppadums from the kitchen, and I cut open about two dozen capsules and let the powder fall into her drink, giving it a little swish to dissolve it properly. And when she came back from the little girls' room, we toasted each other's health and I sat back and waited.

I had my gloves on all this time. Fifteen minutes later, I was grateful to the huge thatch of pampas and untamed hedging that concealed me as I half-carried, half-dragged Manddi out into the rental car, stuffed her in behind the wheel, and ran the garden hose from the exhaust. She smiled drunkenly as I waved goodbye then I helped her lean forward to rest her weary head on the centre of the steering wheel. The car was filling up quickly and I doubted this was going to take very long. And she looked so happy.

I dashed inside to wash up my glass and put it away, careful not to leave any prints, obviously. The remaining capsules, the poppadums, some chocolates and the empty bottles I left on the coffee table in the sitting room. The whole time I was tidying up, I was worried about the police arriving in the middle of things. In fact to be really frank, I was almost wetting myself with nerves about it. Yet on the other hand, I couldn't believe how long it was taking them to get round to informing Manddi of Huw's tragic demise. But nothing and no one seemed to notice anything amiss as I slipped out the back door and down an alleyway, emerging in the street behind the one where the love-nest was. I left my gloves in the top of a rubbish bin drawn up to the kerb for the following morning's collection. A small sacrifice, but I felt it was important to get rid of them.

I felt remarkably chipper when I got home. I'd done all that and it was still only twenty to seven when I got in.

Mrs H was still there, in the kitchen giving Tetley her dinner.

'I've left you both summat in the fridge,' she said, and I couldn't help wondering if it was the same stuff that she was giving to the cat. I giggled a bit. She looked at me oddly.

'Oh I'm so sorry, Mrs Hopkins,' I said, 'I'm afraid I'm a little bit tipsy. They gave me rather a large glass of wine at the beauty salon this afternoon, and I'm afraid it went straight to my head. On an empty stomach, you know.'

'Oh dear, Mrs Powell, p'r'aps you ought to 'ave a little lie down?' She suggested. It seemed like an excellent idea, and ten minutes later I was snug as a bug. I heard the front door bang as she went out, and the house was quiet until Darling Thomas arrived home at about half past seven or so.

He came straight upstairs and sat next to me on the bed. I woke from a short but deep sleep, and my head was pounding. I felt sick.

'Darling,' he said, 'something terrible's happened.'

I sat up a bit too quickly, and clutched my head groaning. He was all concern.

'What is it?'

'Just a headache. That's why I was having a lie-down. What's this terrible news?'

'You'd better brace yourself.' He said and I saw he looked pale, upset. I grabbed his arm.

'Darling? What? What is it?' I managed to inject quite a lot of unrehearsed alarm into those few words, as I had half-forgotten what had actually happened and the sudden memory of it rushing back was a bit of a shock.

'Well, it's – it's Huw. He's dead. He's been killed in a road accident.'

I gaped at him. Unable to believe the wonderful news.

'He's – he's dead?'

'Yes, Darling.'

'Huw? Huw's dead? Monica-and-Huw Huw is dead?'

'Well technically, Manddi-with-two-Ds-and-Huw Huw, but yes, I'm afraid so, the poor chap. Monica rang me at work.'

I continued to look at him like an idiot, my brain a whirl of excitement.

'But...' I said. Because it's one of those things people always say and it sounds suitably inane for this kind of situation.

'Yes, apparently the police called her as his next of kin. She told them about him leaving her for Manddi, so I dare say they will be going round to break it to her next.'

'Poor Manddi.' I said, 'I mean, I didn't much like her, and I was still far too angry with Huw, but for him to just be snuffed out like that, here one minute, hit by a car the next.'

'I know.' Thomas nodded sadly.

'Poor Monica!' I said suddenly, leaping up, 'we should probably go to her. She'll be in a terrible state.'

'I believe the police got her sister or someone to go round. She sounded quite flat and well, numb, I suppose, when she rang me. She was worried about how you and I would take the news.'

'God, what a nightmare.' I said, and slumped down on the bed, my head on Thomas' shoulder. We sat like that for almost five minutes, then went down to get our dinner out of the fridge.

Thurs 2 August - 4.30am
Oh my God! This is the most incredible mess, and it's all my fault!

A couple of hours ago, or rather a bit more than that, it was at about two o'clock this morning, there was this terrific, apocalyptic pounding on the front door, and looking out the bedroom window, we saw Monica down there on the drive, screaming and shouting and sobbing curses. When she saw me looking down, she staggered back from the door the better to see me and with one hand was waving what looked like a gun at me and with the other, what appeared to be a bottle of vodka. And she was screaming.

'Come down here you bitch! It was you! You did this! I know it! I'll kill you. How could you do this to me? I trusted you! You were my best friend! It wasn't supposed to be like this! I'm going to kill you!'

Thomas put on his dressing-gown, preparing to go downstairs – I begged him not to - she looked terrifyingly unstable, was obviously pissed out of her head, and very definitely beside herself with grief. And she was armed – God alone knew if the gun was loaded or if she had the faintest idea how to use it. This didn't seem to be the best time to find out.

'Nonsense,' he said in his astonishingly naive way, 'we're her friends, she needs us.'

I ran down the hall after him, desperately afraid something would happen to him, imagining her aiming at his heart in her blind unreasoning fury.

We reached the end of the landing where the stairs from the attic floor come down to our floor, to meet Mr and Mrs Hopkins there, both in less than truly adequate night attire. We looked at them, they looked at us somewhat sheepishly. I was confused. Thomas merely shook his head.

'I knew it.' He said. 'We'll talk about this in the morning.'

He continued down the stairs and I gaped after him, looking back at Sid and Mrs H.

'What the hell?' I began, but remembered Monica and raced off down the stairs after Thomas. He was drawing back the bottom bolt on the front door and I could still hear her screaming outside on the drive. I panicked.

'Thomas, wait!' I yelled. But he had pulled back the top bolt and was turning the knob to open the door. At the same time I was vaguely aware of Mrs H lifting the telephone receiver and pressing a few buttons. She asked for the police and ambulance and in a remarkably calm way gave our address and embarked on a brief recent history. Sid pushed his vast bulk past me and filled the frame of the door. I could see through a gap by his bent elbow.

Monica stepped up to the door, peering through the gap between the men's bodies to find me.

'Cressida!' Overwhelming emotion turning her mellow voice to a harsh grating roar. 'Get out here now! I'm going to blow your fucking head off! You killed him! You bitch, I hate you! I hate you! I want you dead – now!'

Sid and Thomas stepped up to her and as Sid held her arm, with one simple tweak Thomas had the gun out of her hand. I didn't have time to gasp with horror or to be afraid for him, he had done it before I had even realised his intention. When she saw she had no weapon, Monica fell on her knees and crumpled to the ground sobbing and helpless.

Neighbours' lights were going on all around our little cul-de-sac, so Thomas and Mrs H pulled Monica to her feet and walked her into the house, Sid waiting outside for the police, and I went into the kitchen to make tea for everyone, but mainly to hide from Monica and her accusations and the terrifying rawness of her pain. I felt a bit stunned. I felt full of self-loathing. It was as if I had stepped back from the canvas, too late, and could finally see what I had done.

Thomas came into the kitchen to see if I was all right, and found me half-fainting, my head down on my knees, weeping. It was perfect actually. Again! He took the tea through into the drawing room, though I doubted that anyone would want it. The police had arrived, and apart from a very brief conversation, Thomas wouldn't let them speak to me.

After about forty minutes, an ambulance took Monica, now quiet, away. Subdued and all too obviously exhausted by the ordeal of her outburst.

After taking statements the police finally left too, and then it was just us and Mr and Mrs H, and the pale ghost of dawn coming across the hedges through the trees and onto the lawn.

Thomas and I sat in the drawing room with the fresh hot cocoa Mrs H had made. The two of them hovered uncertainly in the doorway, Sid adjusting the fraying string of his aged pyjama trousers.

'Perhaps you'd be good enough to wait until the morning for my resignation, Madam.' Mrs H said softly. Never had her enunciation been so careful. Never could I recall her calling me Madam. Or at least, not meaning it. I shook my head.

'What is going on?' I asked her, baffled.

'Don't you know? Haven't you worked it out?' Thomas said. I shook my head, confused.

'They're living here.' Said Thomas. 'In our attic. Like Borrowers.'

'What?' I still didn't understand. He pointed towards the ceiling.

'It's true.' Said Sid.

'Living here? In our attic?' I said, too spent to take it all in properly.

'He lost his job, got made redundant when the factory closed down.' Said Mrs H. 'That's why I'm always 'ere. I don't know 'ow I fort we'd get away wiv it, but I just 'oped… I mean, you've got a lot of room up in the attic, and not much up there. So when the bank repossessed our 'ouse a month ago, we jus' fort, I mean, we know it's wrong, 'course we do, but we were desperate. It was that or go and live with my married daughter in Milton Keynes, which would mean giving up my job 'ere. And it's not just that it was our only means of support, I love my job and it was only supposed to be for a short while, till Sid got another job and we got back on our feet. I sort of 'oped you'd never notice, being as you're both often out all day.'

She looked at us both for a moment, biting her lip, and I felt the prickle of tears at the back of my eyes.

Mrs Hopkins half turned to go out of the room.

'We'll leave first thing in the morning.' She said softly.

'But...' I said. I turned to Thomas. 'I don't want them to go, Darling. We can't manage without them.'

'No, of course we can't.' Said Thomas, suddenly all brisk and in-charge, just how I love him the most. 'Don't be silly, Mrs H, I won't hear of anyone leaving, of course not. You must both stay on as long as you need to. Obviously it's a lot easier to get back on one's feet if one has a – well - a base so to speak – from which to – er - well, you know what I mean. And really, you know, you could have said something before. I'm not an ogre, you know.' But his eyes twinkled a little at the thought that for the first time in his life, someone, however desperate, had thought he was an ogre, even if for only a few minutes. Poor darling, he's so soft-hearted!

Mrs H dabbed her eyes with her nightie and I snuffled into my lacy hankie, whilst Sid pumped Thomas' arm like real ale would come out at the wrist and told him quite gruffly that he was a top bloke.

A trifle awkwardly we all broke up and went to our respective rooms. It felt strange knowing that they, not rats, were up there in the attic. But in a way, it was nice to know that someone else was in the house.

When we were in bed, I half expected Thomas to ask me what Monica had meant by her accusations, but he didn't. Instead he said,

'By the way, Darling, apparently Huw was deliberately run down. He was murdered, that policeman told me. By Manddi.'

I hadn't expected this. I sat bolt upright.
'What?'

'I know,' he sat up again and put an arm round me. 'Shocking, isn't it? Apparently the police went to the house where he'd been living with her, and it seems that she'd got herself all boozed and drugged up and then gassed herself in the same car she'd run him down in. The people at the rental company remembered her. The police found the pills and everything. They reckon he must have told her he was going back to Monica and she couldn't handle it and did him in, then herself. Shocking tragedy.'

'Yes, shocking,' I murmured. I slipped out of bed. He looked at me, querying.

'I need to get a drink and sit quietly for a little while. It's all been a bit much.'

'Of course, Poppet. Do you want me to come down with you?'

I shook my head.

'No need. Get off to sleep, you've got work in the morning.' I dropped a kiss on his hair and took myself off downstairs.

I'm moving like I'm in shock.

I can't believe it.

It's as if I thought it was just some game. I'm so lucky things worked out so well. I just can't believe how smoothly it all went, and how everything has just fallen so neatly into place. But it's as if I've only just realised what I've done and the immensity of the achievement.

I mean, I'm thrilled, naturally. But the sheer audacity of it takes my breath away – so many things could have gone wrong (could yet go wrong, I quickly remind myself – the fat lady ain't singing yet!) But…

Wow, I did it!

And some day, Monica will thank me for it. Though that may not be for quite some day if this evening's palaver is anything to go by.

I popped out to the fridge and grabbed myself little glass of bubbly, even though I know I've already had more than is good for me these last two or three days.

I stood in the little den at the back of the house, looking out into the garden, to where the fairy lights are still twinkling around the terrace, where someone had forgotten to turn them off when we went to bed. The garden was softly gleaming in the dawn glow, so pretty. I lifted the glass and whispered a toast before drinking the glassful down in one.

'To absent friends.'

Same day – 6.30 am
I didn't sleep well, once I did finally get to bed. Probably the champagne and all the excitement, but I just kept seeing them in my dreams, reproaching me.

I saw his face as he looked at me as his body was hurled past the windscreen, the look in his eyes, the knowingness.

I saw her face, heard her soft giggly voice with its irritating lisp, saw her dopey smile as she drifted away into unconsciousness, saw her eyes watching me through the car window as I plugged the gap around the hose with loo paper, saw the eyelids drooping closed and the smile on her face as she lay with her heavy head on the steering wheel and watched me as I turned and walked away.

And now Monica. Monica wanting to kill me, Monica's life ripped up by the roots because of me and now she wants me dead. She knows what I did. It was what she wanted me to do, what she was saying, showing me when we went to The Cube that night.

Why doesn't she get that I did it for her? For my best pal? Criss Cross, Monica.

Same day – 11am
Oh my head, it just won't stop aching! I feel that if I make any sudden moves it's just going to tumble down off my shoulders and roll under a chair or table and I'll have to fish it out with a broom or something.

I still can't believe I pulled it off. When I think of all the things that could have gone wrong, it's a little bit terrifying.

The police were here again earlier, and that in itself gave me a few nasty moments, but they were just here to settle a few details, nothing much. I answered all their questions in a sad, sombre little voice, and told them of Monica's terrible depression of the last few days following Huw's departure. As far as I can tell, it's all done and dusted, there wasn't (I'm glad, even relieved, to say) the least hint of suspicion in their manner. So I live to fight another day, as it were.

But of course the main fly-in-the-ointment, Monica, has been calling me seemingly every five minutes, leaving increasingly obscene and vicious messages. So much for her being in some kind of secure detention centre for mad people. I mean, I know she's upset and everything, but for goodness sake, what about me? No one thinks about how I feel in all of this. Well, of course, no one thinks about me because no one knows I'm involved, but you know what I mean. I'm the one who's had all the trauma to deal with, and whose time and money and effort went into this project.

Well, if she didn't want me to kill her philandering, cheating, lying bastard of a husband she shouldn't have kept going on about it. Stupid cow, how was I supposed to know she only wanted the girlfriend whacked? Why didn't she make her meaning a bit clearer? What am I, a mind-reader? He'd only have gone off with someone else sooner or later, anyway - she should be thanking me! How is it a proper Criss Cross if I only get rid of someone who doesn't matter? Personally I think I did a brilliant job, setting it all up so it looked like Manddi killed Huw and then herself – it took me ages to think of that. And there was always the possibility of getting caught. She's not thinking about what it's cost me to do this.

    Think I'll do a spot of shopping, that will cheer me up. After all, only a week or so until we go to Jessica's, and obviously I need to look my best in the wilds of Scotland.

    Well, it's not really that wild, I mean, it's a twelve bedroom shooting lodge with its own sauna and hot-tub and indoor heated pool etc, but one still needs to maintain appearances. Also, Thomas will need a nice new jacket, it might be a bit nippy up there, even if it is August. Scotland is so dreadfully unpredictable.

    Thought I'd better let Mrs H know I was going out, so I popped into the kitchen and got a bit of a shock when I saw Sid there too. I'd completely forgotten about that weird turn of events. He appeared to have a lawn mower in pieces on the kitchen table, all spread out over sheets of newspaper. Not sure if the mower was ours or not. Maybe he's taking in repairs like some people take in washing, who knows? Anyway, he said goodbye cheerfully enough, and Mrs H seems a lot more relaxed. She wanted to talk about 'that dreadful business last night', by which I assumed she meant Monica and Huw and everything, but I told her it was dreadful, but that I'd have to dash, but that we'd be sure and have a chat later.

Fri 3 August - 11.35am

I did spend rather a lot yesterday, but I must admit I feel heaps better. I got the most divine little evening gown, perhaps a wee bit too low in front, but I was feeling a bit daring, and I know Thomas will love it, though it's not really the thing for the country unless we have some very refined company.

And then obviously I had to have a teeny little evening bag to go with it, and the shoes. And a wrap.

Must try to remember to do something about Thomas' jacket. Might just get away with having the old one cleaned and possibly patched up a bit. After all, it doesn't matter too much if it's not perfect, it's only for hanging about in whilst waiting to shoot some poor innocent creature. And he's bound to stuff half a stoat or something in the pockets, or fish bait or something. As it is it practically stands up on its own, it's that rank. I don't know why he loves it so much, he such a mild sort of chap most of the time. Men are such funny creatures.

Monica is out of the hospital now – already! Some mutual friends called me and told me the good news, and said they'd visited, and said she'd been asking for me. I told them I don't think she really wants to see me except to scream at me again and subject me to all her vile accusations. Which was a bit of a daft thing to say, as due to their stalk-eyes, I could tell they were dying to know why she would say such things.

But in the end they just smiled sweetly and said no, she's calmer now, more sensible, she knows she was wrong and just wants to see me, to apologise, to weep on my shoulder, that sort of thing. So I said I would go and see her, which will have to be tomorrow, as I've got my waxing appointment this afternoon, and it's always such a bother if I have to cancel then try and re-book, they're always so busy. Oh and tomorrow evening we've also got drinks at Nadina and Jeremy's new apartment, which I take to mean they've moved into a flat in town to save money, but anyway, we'd already said we'd love to go, so of course we shall have to.

Sat 4 August – 5.25 pm
Well I popped in to see Monica just after lunch– a bit reluctantly, actually, but I suppose that's hardly surprising – I wasn't expecting her to greet me with open arms, more like a 12-bore. But in the end I thought it was best to get it over with. So although it was a bit of a squash time-wise, at least it gave me an excuse not to stay too long if things were a bit…you know.

And if I'm honest, I'm still not too sure how things went.

I found her sitting in the garden by quite a pretty little lily pond that I had no idea they even had – it's in a part of the garden I hadn't seen before. I must ask her – at a more appropriate time obviously – who they had in to do it, as whoever it was, they made a lovely job. We could do with something like that, I would love to have somewhere like that to sit, right next to a pretty little pond with a nice cup of tea in the afternoons and just let the world drift by.

Apart from the fact that she was wearing black silk trousers and a gorgeous little black top, she looked pretty much as normal. Paler, possibly even thinner, although after only three days or so – well, perhaps it was just an illusion, but she looked like someone recovering really slowly from an illness.

She didn't look up as I approached, didn't speak. For a couple of seconds I hovered, a bit unsure what to do but when she didn't make any sudden moves I thought to myself, what the hell, and I pulled up a chair and sat down next to her.

'Hello.' I said. Genius, I know. I don't know how I do it.

She looked at me now.

'Hello,' she said. There was a pause and I tried to think what kind of thing would be best as a conversational opener, but then she spoke again, looking away from me and down at her restless hands.

'I'm sorry about the huge scene the other evening. Sorry for calling you a bitch and all that sort of thing. I didn't mean it. I was just so upset.'

I felt awful then.

'Darling! You don't need to apologise! Please…'

'I'm not saying I've changed my mind, or anything. I know you killed him. But I also know it was a mistake, you just did what you thought I wanted you to do, I do realise that. It's just – the pain, Cress, I can't seem to get past it. I feel as though half of my body has been wrenched away. I feel like I'll never be warm again, and I feel bruised and broken. To think that I'll never see his face again.'

She began to cry, softly. Somehow that was even worse that the ranting and screaming. I wanted to say something, anything that would help, that would change what had happened, but there was nothing. Apologies would be pointless, so I sat on the edge of my seat in voyeuristic silence.

Eventually she scrubbed her face dry with a handkerchief, and she looked at me properly now for the first time. Not accusingly, just sad. It hurt me to see it.

'It wasn't a game, Cress. Not the way you thought it was. We're not in some strange kind of Hitchcock-land where I do your murder and you do mine. True, I tried to manipulate you and I failed. You see, I wanted you to kill Manddi for me. You got that bit right. That night in your garden, with the bird. I knew you'd have the guts to go through with it, whereas I never would. You see, we were the opposite way round. You said, how could you kill your mother-in-law if you couldn't kill a bird. I was thinking, if this was that bitch Manddi it would be easy, but it's not, it's an innocent little bird. And suddenly it all seemed such a clever idea – no one would ever suspect.

    'So I let you think that I had killed your mother-in-law. I knew what you were planning – like I said before, you weren't exactly a genius when it came to covering your tracks. And I could see you were up to something that evening, you were so excited, so on edge, and you kept stealing glances at your watch. So I left you waiting in the lobby, went straight out the back way and was soon on my way to Clarice's. I knew I wouldn't have to wait long, although in the end, it was a bit longer than I expected.

    'I stood in the shrubbery near the house. Sure enough you came sneaking along, all stealthy and ready for action. But you quickly discovered what I already knew – someone else was already there. I watched you go in, but you didn't come out again. The other person came out - I saw them – but not you. In the end I decided to leave you to it and go back to the Health Spa. Afterwards, I was sorry I hadn't gone into the house to make sure you were all right. I still feel really bad about that, though at the time of course, I didn't realise anything was wrong, I thought you were just tidying up the loose ends your beloved Thomas had left behind.'

Yes, that's what she said.

She looked at me with a kind of air of triumph, as though she'd been dying to tell me this for ages – which she probably had – and now she was going to have her big moment. I think she knew she would be able to hurt me more this way.

But I couldn't take in what she was saying.

'What?' I asked. I shook my head. As if that would make things clearer. She leaned forward, a huge grin on her hollowed face.

'Thomas.' She almost laughed as she said it, part glee, part disbelief that I could be so dense. 'It was Thomas who killed Clarice, you moron. I know you always thought it was me, and for a while it was handy to make use of that, but in fact it was your precious Thomas who smashed his mother's head in, and obviously, Thomas who tried to smash your head in too. Thomas tried to kill you.' She smirked at me, watching me carefully with hungry eyes. 'They say the truth hurts. Does it, Cress, does it **really** hurt? I certainly hope so. You may be my best friend but you killed my husband and I want you to at least suffer a teeny little bit.'

But the icy venom in her voice, the carefully modulated rage in her face, the polite, tea-party smile as she said it, none of these things meant anything to me beside the enormity of what she had told me. I felt as though I had been poleaxed.

I remember groping my way to my feet, stunned, not caring that she was laughing a little tinkly party-laugh, or watching me with triumph, I didn't care about any of that. All I could do was to think of Thomas. I had to go, to find him, to ask him.

I don't remember anything of the drive home – I did it all on automatic pilot, I suppose, as I am here now in one piece, and the car is fine.

Mrs Hopkins opened the door to me, I remember she seemed surprised to see me as I hadn't used my key to get in, but had rung the bell and waited to be admitted to my own home. She asked if I was all right, if I needed anything. I remember saying no and just wandering away from her up the stairs. I turned when I got to the top and in a voice that seemed to barely stir the air, I said,

'Is Thomas still out?'

'Yes, Mrs Powell.' She said. She moved forward, put her hand on the stair rail as if to climb the stairs to me. I remember she was looking at me as if she couldn't understand me. As if we weren't speaking the same language. 'Are you sure you're all right, only…'

'Yes, Mrs H,' I said. 'I'm fine. I just need to lie down. Could you please ring Nadina Cooper for me and apologise that we won't be able to make it this evening. Perhaps you would tell her we will have to cancel due to ill health? Her new number is on the invitation, it's on Thomas' desk.'

And I've been lying down ever since, shivering under the bedspread. I must ask him. I wish he would come home. But I dread seeing him. Did he try to kill me? How will he react when I tell him what I know. Suppose he says yes, he wanted me dead. Or perhaps he'll simply try to laugh it off. I know Monica didn't give me any proof, and I know she was deliberately trying to hurt me. But in spite of that, I know. In my heart I'm certain of the truth of it.

I can't seem to get warm.

She was telling the truth.

Sun 5 August - 2pm
He came home much later than expected last night, and Mrs H must have been looking out for him, because as soon as I heard him come in the door, I heard the sound of voices and immediately he came bounding up the stairs to see me. He came into the room carefully. With the slightest pressure on the springs, he moved onto the bed slowly and gently, gently and slowly pulled the eiderdown back a bit to lay a kiss on my cheek.

'Poppet? What's the matter? Not feeling well?'

I kept my eyes closed. I felt exhausted. A weak tear or two squeezed under my eyelids and ran down onto the pillow and damped my cheek. I was too exhausted to do this now. But, because I had to say something, I gathered what strength I could and spoke, though in a strange, flat voice.

'Monica told me.' I said. And I knew that whatever I was going to say next would change everything. 'She saw you that night coming out of the house. You killed Clarice.'

I felt the jolt as he moved, shocked. I opened my eyes. If he hated me, if he wanted me dead, to hide all traces of his guilt, I had to know it now. I had to see it for myself, in his eyes, in his face.

'You hit me.' I said, and my voice broke.

His face crumpled, he lay down on the bed next to me and gathered me into his arms, and weeping, begged me to forgive him.

'I panicked, my Darling, I didn't mean to hurt you, I didn't even know it was you until it was too late. And I – I simply - panicked. When the police contacted me later that night... Until then I thought there had just been some random burglar in the wrong place at the wrong time and my only thought had been to get out of the house before I got caught.

'But later I was just so afraid of losing you, I couldn't find the courage to tell you what I'd done. I mean I specifically chose the weekend you were away so you wouldn't have any idea what was going on. In case the police found out, or had any suspicions of me, I didn't want you to be involved. And - I didn't want you to know what I'd done. This whole time I've been so terrified you would find out what I had done and I would lose you!

'I never meant to hurt you, Darling, I swear it. And the whole time you were in hospital I was terrified I was going to lose you. Eventually the doctors told me your injuries weren't serious, but before that there was a short delay before they found out, and – and I hated myself for what I did to you, for the terrible risk – that I had almost - yet I didn't know how to tell you. I hated having secrets from you. And you're always so strong, so organised, so good. Oh God, Cressida, I'm begging you, please forgive me, I don't know what I'd do without you. I never meant to hurt you, Darling. I'm sorry, so, so sorry.'

And he sobbed in my arms whilst I stroked his hair and promised him everything would be all right, the weight lifting off my shoulders and floating away and taking my tears with it. As far as I was concerned everything was all right now. My heart sang.

An hour later, in the darkness, he spoke to me.

'Why were you there? At my mother's? That night?'

It seemed he was curious for the first time. Hardly surprising. After all, he knew I hated her as much as he did. And now I felt a wave of relief. I was going to tell him the truth at last. No more secrets. I could tell him all that I've thought and done these last few weeks. I reached out to put on the bedside lamp.

'I was going to kill her,' I said, 'I was so sick of her interfering in our lives, of her bullying and meanness. That's why I booked those few days away. I just couldn't stand it anymore. But I wanted to protect you, to keep you out of it. And then when I got there and Clarice was already dead, well, I was convinced Monica had done it. In fact, she deliberately encouraged me to do just that.'

'Why would she do a thing like that?'

I was a bit surprised he wasn't more upset over my confession that I had killed his mother. It gave me the courage to continue.

'She wanted me to do a kind of **Strangers on a Train** thing, where we did each other's murders. You know, cross over our murders. So no one would suspect us.'

'And she wanted you to kill…' he was looking at me expectantly. I took a breath. This was it.

'Manddi. But I cocked it up, as Mrs H would say. Because I thought she wanted Huw dead – to pay him back for leaving her. She had been so angry and hurt by him. So - I killed him, and I killed Manddi too, and made it look like she killed Huw then herself. And now Monica hates me and wants revenge, blood even. That's why she told me about you killing Clarice. She wanted to hurt me by telling me it was you who attacked me. She thought I would think you were trying to kill me that night. She thought it would destroy us.'

He gaped at me, hardly able to take in what I was saying, the enormity of what I'd just confessed to. I was vaguely surprised at how calm I felt, how matter-of-fact about it all. But in reality, I was just too depleted to care very much about anything. I just let myself drift away on a tide of thoughts and images. I knew he'd be shocked to begin with, but after what he'd already confessed to me, I hoped eventually he would come to see things just as I did.

I slept late this morning and awoke feeling drained and listless. Thomas too seemed subdued. We made hardly any reference to our conversation of last night, apart from a moment when Thomas, clearing his throat a little nervously, as if he was about to broach something that he had been putting off, said,

'Do you think she intends to tell the police? Or will she blackmail us? Monica, I'm talking about.'

I shook my head.

'To be honest, Sweetheart, I don't really know what she's planning anymore. But I do believe her capable of anything.'

After that we spoke very little, and even during breakfast we were almost silent, just clasping one another's hands across the table and poking our food around the plate without really consuming any of it. It was all very strange. I felt like there was something enormous hanging over us. I felt like we were marking time.

Tues 7 August - 5.45pm

We haven't seen or heard anything from Monica for three days now. At first I was relieved and felt that I could relax for the first time in I don't know how long. I felt that finally she was coming round to my point of view, that at last she must be seeing sense.

But now I've realised that in fact she hasn't given up, she is just waiting, out there somewhere, until the most opportune moment. I feel a growing tension and I'm on edge all the time, every little sound making me jump out of my skin. She's toying with us. Waiting.

By contrast, Thomas and both the Hopkins' seem unusually calm and relaxed. With the Hopkins', I suppose it's because their secret is finally out and they have no need to worry about the future and it's quite clear they are completely happy and at ease now, judging by the number of times I've seen Sid wandering round in his vest and Mrs H humming and practically dancing around the kitchen as she prepares some delectable dish. And she is spoiling us. Every meal seems to be her own personal attempt to outdo herself in showing her care and gratitude. Nothing is too much trouble.

With Thomas, it's a similar thing – now that his long-harboured guilty secret is out, now he's told me what he did and I have forgiven him, he has nothing more to worry about. His conscience feels cleansed by the confession he made to me, he has nothing left to fear or feel anxiety about. But I feel more and more weighed down by the fear of what might happen next. I feel as though I've absorbed not only my own fears, but theirs as well, and I am bowing under the weight of it all.

Bizarrely he dismisses what I have revealed to him as unimportant, it doesn't trouble him at all – I don't understand that man sometimes. Why isn't he upset that I murdered his friend and his friend's mistress? He just shrugs his shoulders and says Huw was a worm, and Monica is better off without him. And besides, it was just a misunderstanding.

Huw's funeral is tomorrow. The official decision remains unchanged – murder by Manddi Morgan who then took her own life in an act of remorse slash grief. The whole thing has been reported in the tabloids at length – I've read Sid H's 'newspapers' – and there has not been so much as a breath of suspicion attached to myself or to anyone else. And even all accounts of the bereaved widow's feelings, all her recorded comments and so on have been in keeping with the official line of both police and coroner - even Monica has kept my secret.

And yet none of this comforts me. It only makes me even more certain that Monica is planning to exact some terrible revenge, and whenever I think of it, which is every minute of every hour of my every waking day and a considerable part of my dreaming too, I feel numb and unable to function.

She is planning something. I know she is. I feel her eyes on me. Even though I haven't seen her or heard from her in all this time. I feel as though she is here, watching me, judging me and planning, planning, planning. It isn't over.

We need to get away. It's not long now until our trip to Scotland. But even that still seems too far off, like a life-raft on heavy seas. I suggested to Thomas that we should go a week earlier than planned, but he can't get away from the office. He was keen for me to go on ahead without him, but I can't bear to be apart from him. So I sit here at home, waiting, staring out at the garden. I've cancelled all my appointments, I'm afraid to go out. Even with both the Hopkins' here most of the time I feel so naked, so vulnerable.

And the funeral is tomorrow. Thomas suggested we ought to go, and I have to admit, I thought it was the stupidest suggestion I'd ever heard. Poor Thomas! But, all I could think was, how could we, of all people, go to this funeral? And how would Monica feel upon seeing us there. Nevertheless, Thomas is, unusually, quite stubborn about it. He says it's up to me if I go or not, but he is going to go. No matter what has happened recently, Huw was once his friend. It's his duty to attend, he says. So I suppose I will have to go too.

There is an upside, of course. I've got a simply gorgeous black frock and coat in my dressing room, and of course there's a big black hat with the sweetest little veil, and my usual black high heels.

Wed 8 August - 8.30pm

Well that was tedious! Funerals should always be miserable affairs, conducted if at all possible in persistent rain, or at the very least overcast conditions with occasional drizzle. But today at Huw's funeral the weather was contrary to convention – warm and sunny, it was practically rude with birdsong and flowers. We might just as well have been there for a picnic.

Monica looked stunning, of course, and although it was a little awkward to start with, to my surprise she actually came over to us, and kissed us both and thanked us for coming!

All understated stricken glamour, she apologised quietly and discreetly for her 'foolishness' of several days ago. Of course, she said, she knew now Huw's death was the result of the terrible tragedy of his misguided infatuation with the Swansea Siren Manddi Morgan, and Monica said how much she regretted her outburst and hoped we could put it all behind us? We were still friends? Of course we were, I smiled, and kissed the air by her cheek again.

Then as she turned away to welcome some business acquaintance of Huw's, Thomas and I were able to exchange a look of complete bewilderment. Surely she hadn't forgotten that I had actually told her I had killed Huw and Manddi? How could she now say it was Manddi's fault? How could she have forgotten everything she had screamed at me?

An air of unreality persisted all through the funeral and then the 'do' at Monica's house whence we all gathered for refreshments. Monica hardly left my side, and so I was there to hear all the little things that the mourners said as they came and went and condoled with the widow. Occasionally Monica seemed almost overcome by grief, and she would cling to my arm, and accept a hankie or a tissue from me, and I found myself patting her arm and offering comfort in a way that a little part of me felt was a wee bit hypocritical. But what else could I do?

As the numbers began to dwindle, Monica invited us into Huw's study, and asked Thomas to look at a few things on Huw's computer.

'I want to sell everything, make a fresh start, but some of the information on his computer may be confidential – could you take off anything that needs to be kept private? I might not understand what I'm looking at. But you know, one hears so much these days about identity theft. I just want to err on the side of caution.'

So Thomas spent almost an hour going through the computer files and deleting confidential items and generally wiping everything off the hard drive whilst I helped Monica to decide which of Huw's office knick-knacks could be kept, and which given to charity ahead of the house sale.

When we had finished, she thanked us profusely and asked if we would come for dinner tomorrow evening. We carefully avoided catching each other's eye, and smiled our false friendly smiles. It would have been too awkward to decline, so although I was sure we both hated the idea, we thanked her and said we'd be there at seven-thirty.

But in the car, on the way home, we debated the topic. And by the time we reached our front door, we were still none the wiser. What was she up to? Why did she want us to go to dinner?

Surely, after everything, she didn't really want to still be friends?

Thurs 9 August - 6.20pm
A dull day. And all I've been able to think about is the approaching dinner party at Monica's. If there are only going to be the three of us, I can't see how it could be anything other than really uncomfortable. How could it be otherwise? Thomas says he's planning to get roaring drunk, and I've told him that isn't fair, because I want to do the same. It seemed like stalemate until Mrs H offered us Sid as a chauffeur.

' 'E can wait in the car for you. Don't worry about 'ow long you're out for – 'e won't mind, after all you've been very good to us. 'E can take 'is soodookoo book and 'is iPod, 'e'll be 'appy for hours.'

It was a tempting idea. We tentatively accepted, and she hurried back to the kitchen looking pleased.

Other good news today – we've finally had an offer on Clarice's house, Highgates. At first the offer was a bit on the low side, but then the agent came back to us with a better one and we accepted. Hurrah! At last, that old albatross is off our necks! (So long as there are no hitches, of course, and let's face it, there usually are with house sales) Do albatrosses hang round necks? Or is it backs? And albatrosses doesn't sound right either, it sounds like one of those words that should end in an 'i'. Albatrossi? Anyway, the old ruin is as good as gone.

Once we were ready to leave for Monica's, Mrs H pottered into the hall where we were getting ready and said, ' 'Opkins is bringing the car to the front door, Madam.'

I swear she's got a new housekeeping outfit – a sort of smart navy skirt and white blouse with a little cardigan over the top – not as conspicuous as a jacket, but setting the whole ensemble off nicely. I've noticed she's started wearing it in the afternoons, when the actual cleaning is out of the way, and when she has to go to answer the door etc. Next thing I know, I shall find we've got a parlour-maid.

I was a little thrown by her sudden formality but I thanked her. I've noticed she always seems to launch into what I call her Downton Abbey manner any time she is called upon to do anything in her 'official' capacity. As we were going out the door, Thomas whispered to me,

'I think we've acquired a staff without realising it.'

'No,' I replied, 'I think it's more that the staff have acquired us. I think we're being transformed into gentry. Next thing we know, there'll be hampers arriving from Fortnum and Mason's.'

'Opkins' got out of the driver's seat of the Audi and came to open the door for me. He looked truly magnificent in a chauffeur's uniform and peaked cap, his chin neatly shaved for the first time in our short acquaintance. I thanked him as I got in. He gave me a shy half-smile.

'You're most welcome, Madam,' he said.

I felt a thrill of elation. As the car pulled away I turned to Thomas and said,

'You know, I feel suddenly so much more important!'

'I know, it's all very glamorous!' He thought for a moment then said, 'I suppose I shall have to pay him.'

'Hmm. I suppose you shall.'

And I supposed we had already, without even knowing it, paid for that chauffeur's uniform.

'I think the cap is a bit much, though.' I said to Thomas. He nodded.

'Yes, I don't think he needs the cap. The uniform is pretty cool though.'

And we had a quiet little debate about salaries and other such things. Before we knew it we were at Monica's and I hadn't even had time to worry about it.

Hopkins opened the car door for me, and I went up the steps to the door, feeling a little anxious, but Monica was all smiles and welcomes, hugging and air-kissing, and complimenting me on my dress.

We went in, and after a few cocktails to break the ice, settled down to dinner.

The whole evening was very pleasant – as if nothing had happened, as if I had never killed Monica's husband just a matter of days ago, as if there had been no glitch in our friendship. It was the oddest evening. The only tricky moment was when Thomas accidentally alluded to Huw, and there was a slight pause in the conversation, but then Monica just smiled and said, yes, he was right, it was just like Huw to say that, and the moment was over.

When we were leaving I was pleased to see that the car was back, as I had noticed that Hopkins had gone off after we had gone into the house. I suppose in all fairness, we couldn't expect the man to sit outside for four or five hours, even with his 'soodookoo'. But it was a relief to see that he had remembered to come back for us. In fact he seemed quite good at the chauffeuring thing and I began to think that perhaps the sum Thomas had decided on was not so exorbitant after all.

On the way back from Monica's, tipsy but not totally sozzled, we both remarked with some surprise that it had been a nice evening.

As he got ready for bed, Thomas said,

'I think everything's going to be okay. Maybe she's forgiven you and realised it was all just a misunderstanding, and there's no point in making a massive fuss. I mean,' said my sensitive husband, 'it's not like hurting us would bring Huw back, and even though he was my friend, I'd have to say he was a bit of a bastard. I don't think he'd have gone back to her. Or at least, not for long.'

'Yes, Darling,' I said, and put out the light. I could only hope he was right. But it seemed too good to be true. Somehow that didn't seem to me to fit with Monica's nature. Somehow, somehow I was sure something was brewing, because I knew that despite appearances, Monica was not the type to forgive a mistake of that magnitude.

Fri 10 August - 11.50am

Tomorrow we're going to Scotland! I'm so excited, not to mention relieved! It will be lovely to get away for a week or so. (And doubly nice now that we know we won't have Clarice with us to spoil everything and make us all tense and crabby with each other.) And I think it will do us good to get away from all the recent events and give us a chance to relax and forget about horrid old reality for a while. And I can't wait to see dear Jessica and Murdo.

So I've already done most of the packing, and Mrs H even asked if we wanted Mr H to drive us. Reluctantly I had to say no, though it would have been really quite wonderful to be chauffeur-driven all the way to Scotland! But no, I've decided to give them both the time off.

I went into the kitchen first thing, as per Thomas's request last night, and sure enough, there was Sid sitting at the kitchen table in an old shirt and jog bottoms, looking every bit the out of work navvy or something, reading the paper over his elevenses. Tetley was asleep on the windowsill. Mrs H was doing something at the sink. They both looked up. And I cleared my throat, suddenly a bit nervous, I mean, one never knows quite how they will take things.

'I hope you won't mind my saying, Mr Hopkins, Mr Powell and myself were delighted with how well things worked out last night when you drove us to our dinner engagement.'

I had their full attention. Mrs H turned round and Mr H dropped his paper several inches. He nodded sagely, as if I had hit upon some hidden superpower he had been cunningly disguising.

'I don't know how the job-hunting is going on, or quite what branch you're hoping to – er – branch into…' I continued. 'But, my husband and I (oh dear, I thought, poor choice of words, a bit too much like the Queen or Maggie Thatcher or someone, a bit too power-mad slash uber-regal) - er – we were wondering whether you – er - would consider taking up the position of chauffeur slash handyman with us on a formal, and indeed er, permanent basis. The position would attract the salary of – er' and I named the figure Thomas and I had agreed on the previous evening in the car, and then at the last minute added on another £2,000. What the hell.

Mr Hopkins' eyebrows rose almost up to his slightly receding hairline, and he glanced across at his wife. Mrs H was staring at me, her mouth open, her eyes wide.

I wasn't quite sure if I should say anything else. It was difficult to gauge how they felt about the offer. Was it too low? Were they offended? Was this the despised 'charity' of the loveable porter in **The Railway Children**?

No one said anything.

Feeling uncomfortable, I began to step back out of the kitchen.

'Well, perhaps you'd just like to think about it…' I said, and I was beginning to feel a little disappointed by their lack of response, when suddenly Mrs H launched herself at me and enveloped me in the tightest hug I'd ever received. Mr H got to his feet and with a surprisingly nimble tread, came over to me and was crushing my hand in a vice-like grip and telling me how pleased he was, and how we'd never regret it, and that it was bloody good of us. Mrs H released me and stepped back to grab a bit of kitchen paper-towel to wipe the tears away.

'Well,' I said, feeling even more awkward than before, 'well, that's nice. Very nice indeed. I must say. I'm glad you're pleased. Er – and of course, we're very pleased to have you – er – on board. As it were.' I finished a bit lamely, not quite sure of the most appropriate thing to say and even more unsure of how best to extricate myself from the situation, I made a desperate dash for the door once again and heaved a sigh of relief on reaching the privacy of my bedroom, shutting the door a bit more firmly than I meant to and busying myself with refolding all the clothes I had packed.

I feel peculiarly drained.

It's very odd, the way this world we live in works. Some people have more money than they know what to do with, and even people like Thomas and I look impoverished against them, and yet the world is full of them, people for whom our little fortune was barely more than pocket money, people who could buy a whole country and not noticeably miss the cash. And yet there are around the world millions upon millions upon millions of people with next to nothing, people who could be immeasurably helped by people like us giving them a hand when they most needed it. And, equally strangely, the ones with the least wealth always seem to have to work so much harder to earn their pittance than those who have so much money it can't be counted by mere human beings.

And although (obviously) when one thinks about this, one realises it's completely wrong, obviously (obviously!) one doesn't want things to change too much, because one doesn't want to lose the masses one has and become one of those who has to work like a dog for next to nothing. One feels ashamed, yet afraid to change. I could never clean someone's bath or cook their food or wash their underwear. I mean, how horrid! And yet apparently, that's considered quite a good job. Strange!

Anyway, altogether too introspective!

So I refolded my designer sweaters and my silk and hand-made lace underwear, and felt glad we had been able to do our little bit towards making the world a better place, at least for Sid and – what is Mrs H's first name? I believe I've never heard it. Don't think it was even on her original application form. Hmm.

Sat 11 August - 7.40pm
We sat in the cafeteria at the service station ignoring all the noisy hordes of football fans and the holidaymakers with excited children scampering about the tiled floor of the food court and, sitting in a dim corner, we gazed across our lukewarm cappuccini into each others' eyes.

I don't know what other people thought. I didn't care then and I don't care now. I never want to forget how I felt, how I think Thomas felt in those few moments. I was oblivious to everything and everyone around me. All my attention was riveted by what he had just said to me, out of the blue, stopping everything.

'Let's try again.'

We were well into our journey after an early start, and were probably almost halfway to Jessica's by then, so we decided to risk a bit of lunch and a hottish drink at the motorway services. We found the only table not either occupied or covered in the debris of half a dozen earlier forgotten lunches and almost as soon as we sat down, I knew this was going to be one of those life-changing conversations one has on a few precious occasions throughout one's life with the man one loves.

I couldn't think what to say – I had so wanted to hear those words over the last three years and I had thought I never would.

Our previous attempts at IVF had left us broken, bereaved and hopeless. Did he really want us to go through all that again?

He continued to look at me. He reached out and took my unresisting hand in his two huge paws. His hands were warm and I hadn't even realised I was cold. A little tuft of hair had been raked out of place by his fingers a moment earlier and stood out on end endearingly, and I put out a finger to smooth it back into place, so full, so full of love and happiness just to be with him.

'But…' I said. I couldn't think of any more words than that. He smiled, lifted our entwined fingers and dropped a light kiss on the back of my hand.

'I know it was traumatic,' he said, 'I know it didn't work. But I'm ready to try again.'

I closed my eyes, not wanting to relive the pain of previous failures, the despair of the miscarriages I'd – we'd both – endured. I shook my head but he got my attention with a tighter clasp pulling me closer across the table-top towards him. But even as I thought to myself, I can't go through all that again, his eagerness urged me on.

'It'll be different this time,' he said, smiling, confident, 'somehow I just feel it. This time it's going to work. And I won't be in Dubai or Hong Kong this time, I'll be here with you the whole time, we'll be together for every step. And with the Hopkins' as well to look after you – Darling, I really feel it might work this time. You know what Mrs H was like when she thought we'd got her a cat – just think how she'd dote on us if we gave her baby to coo over! Let's go for it, Cress. Let's have a baby!'

I looked at him now, but had to look away again, afraid to let myself be drawn in by his enthusiasm. Yes, what he said was true, but that didn't mean it would work…

'I don't know…' I pulled my hand free, pulled on my jacket, cold. I looked out of the window to where some children were flinging McDonald's buns to ducks on a dingy pond.

'Thomas,' I began again. He leaned forward.

'Please, Darling. I know how much it would mean to you. And this time, it means so much to me – I may have been – well – I know I failed you.' His voice wobbled slightly and I began to protest but he continued. 'No, it's true - I wasn't sufficiently involved emotionally, I know that now. I don't know why – I just think I wasn't fully behind the whole thing last time, but this time…' He looked down at the table, stirred his coffee, then glanced back up to me, his gorgeous eyes on mine. 'I really would like to be a Dad. We've now got the time, the money, the home. We're older, wiser, healthier, less stressed, more ready. Please Darling. Let's go for it. Tell me it's not too late.'

I brushed some tears from my cheeks and glanced quickly over my shoulder, hoping no one had noticed. I tried to smile at him but my lips couldn't quite do it, and my vision blurred and my voice wobbled and in the end I just nodded and took a big gulp of my cold coffee whilst a huge teardrop rolled down my nose and sploshed onto my jacket. I swallowed.

'Okay.' I said, nodding so that he couldn't miss my meaning. And then, finally, I could smile. He gave me a hankie to blow my nose and wipe my eyes and we sat and held hands and gazed at each other like newlyweds.

It was the best journey we've ever taken together. We talked, we listened to music on the radio, we were silent. When we saw the sign telling us it was two miles to Jessica's village, I was sorry the travelling was almost over. I wanted to drive on and on and on, just Thomas and me, together.

Same day – 11.45pm
Jessica spoils us, she really does. She's put us in the most gorgeous room usually reserved for visiting dignitaries – her parents or his, or a decrepit old aunt or someone, but this time, seeing as they've almost all died since this time last year (how strange!), it's ours.

You'd expect it to be a bit dark and overpowering in here with all the heavy old panelling and floorboards and beams but because it's so big and well-lit, it's not dark at all, it's just warm and charming.

And of course there's the odd bit of tartan here and there – well, you've practically got to haven't you? The whole place is done out in the 19th century's idea of what it would have been like in the 17th century – so there's lots of plaid and dirks and shields all over the walls – pure Jacobean-era kitsch. But at least there's no bagpipes playing folk tunes on the sound system.

The place was built by Jess and Thomas' great-grandfather, a Lancashire – or was it some other shire – but no, I think it was Lancashire, he was a cotton or wool or something baron, and he wanted a 'little place in the Heelands' so that he and his nouveau riche buddies could do a spot of shooting and fishing and wenching to unwind from the strains of 1870s industrial life well away from the prying eyes of their virtuous charity-founding wives. The fact that it's only forty minutes from the border was neither here nor there and he seems to have decked the whole place out mainly from his imagination.

It's a bit embarrassing if any actual Scottish people come here, Jess says, or any of those overly-earnest American family history researchers, because they always want everything ABSOLUTELY authentic and are always saying things like 'but of course that style of tam o'shanter only came into popular use between 1727 and 1734', as if one cared, but otherwise I doubt anyone realises it's basically a pastiche of what Victorians thought of as Gaelicnicity.

Jess's late father put in the central heating, God bless the man! Jess's hubby Murdo put in the discreet, well-crafted double glazing, another man upon whose head blessings should be showered! So the result is that it's actually very cosy in spite of the size of the place, with none of the nasty draughts one would normally expect of an old country place elaborately decorated in generic Gaelic. Thomas and I love it, and if anything (which I hope it won't) ever happens to either Jess and Murdo, or their four sons or their offspring, it will come to us.

The bed – naturally – is a four-poster – huge and comfortable – an unusual combination. Obviously we had to try it out – and we were almost late going down to dinner!

When we did walk in, hand in hand, Jess arched an eyebrow at us and said to Murdo,

'God, they make me sick, anyone would think they were newlyweds.'

Her husband agreed, adding,

'Good thing we haven't got other guests here this evening. Surely by this time it should be separate beds eh? And sensible winceyette nighties? Especially for Thomas? Down to the ankle and up to the neck, just like Grannie used to wear.' He guffawed far too loudly and moved towards the alcohol.

We drank rather a lot of wine over the marvellous dinner. What Jess has lost over time in the svelteness of her figure, (after all she's had four sons!) she has gained in the generosity and quality of her hospitality and dinner was a relaxed, indulgent affair and we lingered over it for hours. We talked, joked, teased gently and affectionately. The men told tall stories from their fishing and shooting exploits while we girls talked about the social faux pas we'd had the privilege of witnessing lately, and of the torture of school reunions. It was a wonderful evening.

As we wandered out of the dining-room at last, Murdo slapped Thomas on the shoulder.

'I might as well let you go up, I know you'll not be any good to me in the gun room just now. You've clearly got other things on your mind. Just keep in mind we've got an early start in the morning, and I'll need you to help me get a few things ready.'

We laughed. I kissed Jess goodnight and we made our way upstairs under their indulgently fond gaze.

Sun 12 August – 11.45pm
Today has been the most wonderfully relaxing, romantic day. I'd forgotten that the 'Glorious 12th' fell on a Sunday this year, and so the season will begin properly tomorrow as there's no shooting on the Sabbath, of course! All our worries are behind us and I feel more relaxed than I've felt all year.

Mon 13 August - 6.00am
We lit the candles last night, turned off the electric light and slipped naked under the covers, laying there drowsy and warm and together. It was like a new beginning. I felt as if we were married all over again. It was bliss.

Now, after what we talked about Saturday morning in the cafeteria, I feel as though we are at the start of something new and wonderful. Hope fills me, even now as I write this whilst Thomas is showering before we go down to breakfast. It's as if the future is there for us to grab hold of more than it has ever been before. I feel so strongly that nothing is beyond us now, our lives lie at our feet like a newly unrolled Persian carpet, ready for us to take the next step.

Same day - 10.45 am
It's mid-morning now and Thomas went off ages ago, all excited like a puppy going out for a run in the park, after a hearty breakfast with Jess and Murdo and a couple of early arrivals.

I've never gone shooting or hunting myself, and so I know I don't really understand the appeal. Probably the closest I've come was sitting in that rental car waiting for Huw to show his face before I ran him down – now that really was blood-sport! But even I can appreciate the almost overwhelming sense of anticipation that this morning brought.

Murdo and Thomas were up hideously early, checking the guns and whatnot with Murdo's man before showering and breakfast etc. Then the chaps all gathered together in the big main hall for a quick dram before heading out, and I just gave him a quick wave and called out that I'd see him later. I went back upstairs for a quick nap then a nice long soak in the bath – returning to society at a far more suitable time!

Jess and I are going to try a spot of Christmas cooking today. Yes, I know it's only August, but she wants to trial a few new recipes, and as she's renowned for her cooking skills and expecting a houseful, she obviously isn't going to wait until December 24th to make sure everything is perfect with her catering plans. She likes to do quite a bit of the 'special' food herself at Christmas, so she's having a crack at a few different things today, which is good news for me as chief taster. It was a relief to find she'd got rid of all the staff for the day, I hadn't relished trying to squeeze into her kitchen with her cook and maid and butler etc there, and one could hardly have a lovely cosy chat with them all there ear-wigging.

So we will spend the main part of the day in her amazing, state-of-the-art kitchen. Mrs H would be so jealous if she saw it, she'd be pestering me for renovations. Although knowing Mrs H, I've probably already signed my approval of them and just don't realise it and I'll get home to find everything is completely different! And Jess and I will accompany our baking (well, her baking) with gossiping and drinking wine and while she is mixing, and rolling and baking, I will be in charge of the tasting of all kinds of delicious things. I think I can manage that.

Same day – 4.15pm
We have had a whale of a time this morning and afternoon, I have made an absolute pig of myself 'testing' Jess's recipes for her, whilst poor old Thomas is outside traipsing about the grounds above the house in search of some poor scruffy little bird or another in the surprisingly unseasonal weather. It's been a bit blowy and changeable, Jessica tells me, this last few days and now - can you believe it's actually quite dark and very heavy skies – surely they'll have to come in soon, they'll all be drenched and cold. In August! He could have taken me to the Caribbean, but I knew he had to have his shooting in Scotland. Well, I know where I'd rather be – the sun will always lure me. No, second thoughts, actually I wouldn't, I'm having a fabulous time.

    Between fruit tarts, I told Jess what Thomas said about another go at the IVF and she gave me a big hug and said she thought it was a wonderful idea. Then we both had to dab our eyes and blow our noses, so soppy, but I'm so happy today. Everything is coming together so beautifully, and who knows, perhaps Thomas is right and this time it'll work out. Not that I want to be one of those sextuplet mothers. Twins at the absolute most, one of each, obviously, and preferably the boy will grow up tall and broad and dark like Thomas and the girl smaller and blonde and blue-eyed like me, though I don't suppose it'll work out like that.

    I wonder how Thomas will feel about calling the girl Natasha? I love that name. And I've been thinking of David Thomas for a boy – I know it's not very exciting, but with today's penchant for the strange and ridiculous, the so-called 'individual' names for children – I think it's solid and reliable, a name that won't furrow brows or make people puzzle over the spelling. And it's too stupid to call a child after a celebrity or other public figure – what if they turn out to be murderers or paedophiles?

I just heard my phone do its funny little message-received beep, so thinking it might be Thomas out in the wilds, bored or just missing me, I fished it out of my bag to check it, nearly knocking my wine over into the bargain. It wasn't Thomas. It was Monica. Considering I haven't heard from her since you-know-when, I think it's a bit bloody pointless just sending a short little text like that.

'Criss Cross.'

That's all it said.

Stupid cow. What the hell is that supposed to mean? Is that supposed to mean something to me? 'Criss Cross'? Why can't she send a normal text like anyone else? Why these stupid, childish guessing games? I'll delete it in a minute. I'm not replying, that's what she wants, but I'm not playing her stupid games any more. It's about time she learned some respect for peoples' lives. I suppose she means, remember when we went to the cinema together.

Jess is calling me, the next batch is out of the oven, so must top up our mulled wine and start knocking back mini-stollen, mince pies, tiny little panettone, cheese straws etc, etc. Heaven! Shame to have a baby belly before being pregnant though! Thomas doesn't know what he's missing!

Fri 24 August - 3am
Thomas is dead and gone and I am alone. My Thomas. All our plans, our dreams, those last few days two weeks ago, it's as if it never happened. No baby now. No old age holding hands together. Nothing. I'm empty, and so is the world. I don't want to write anything.

Later - 4.10am
And I wanted him to be buried, laid in the ground in a beautiful polished box, so I could remember him for ever and ever, sitting on the grass beside him, as if he were still there, talking, telling him things, telling him about my life. But they cremated him, burned him to dust and now the dust has blown him away between the rose bushes and there's nothing left. I can't find him anywhere. He's gone. I have to keep fighting the urge to go out and look for him. Because he's not just out there somewhere, he's not lost, he's just – not.

Sat 25 August - 11.05am

I feel like my heart's been ripped out. Is that a cliché? I don't care. I don't care what anyone thinks. They look at me, at the broken wretch with the unwashed hair and raw eyes, my nose running as I howl into my jumper-sleeves, curled up like some animal in a ridiculous, over-stuffed, over-designed, over-priced Elegance of a Chair, and I can see there is something that is almost fear in their disgust, their thin veil of sympathy drawn tight across their faces.

Comforters. Visitors. Sympathisers of the Bereaved. Why can't they all just go and fuck themselves? Leave me alone. And then my rage dies and I hear the words my mind has been screaming at the walls. Alone. And the pain washes over me again. He's gone and I will never, never again see his dear face, his smile, hear his voice, see his lovely, solemn eyes looking at me.

There's no more of him, his whole being is at an end and I am so lonely, so afraid, and so fearful of forgetting him.

Same day, later - 2.40pm
I look back over the entries I wrote just over two weeks ago, when my whole world was sunny and happy and I had the man I love by my side. It seems impossible to process the fact that so much can change in such a short space of time. And there I am wittering on about Jessica's bloody baking whilst out on the moor the only man in the universe that I love was not, as I supposed, having tons of fun shooting innocent animals – but he was the one being shot. He was being culled, put down like vermin. And I didn't even know. I didn't sense it. I was laughing and eating and drinking in Jess's kitchen. Why didn't I know?

My first period after Thomas's death came today and it's a day or two late. I had half convinced myself I was – miraculously – pregnant, but there will be no baby to remember him by, no one to share Thomas with, and now I am feeling so wretchedly dashed and miserable. Another lost day curled up on the sofa staring at nothing.

My whole body aches with the enormity of what I've lost. And I just can't help it, I just keep saying it again and again. Thomas is dead. I hear my voice saying it out loud and every time, it surprises me. I sound normal. I sound just like my normal self, I can even say it in a happy voice. I look in the mirror and see myself, ruined, wrecked, hollow-eyed, grey-skinned. But outside the trees are leaved, the flowers bloom, the birds even sing. Everything is perfectly normal.

Mrs Hopkins brings me food and drink every so often, and I eat a little of it, or drink some of it, because I know it helps her. At least she's stopped crying.

Later still - 9.50pm
Mr and Mrs Hopkins drove up to Jessica and Murdo's to meet me on the 14th. In fact they set off as soon as they heard. And every little thing that needed doing, they did it for me or helped me to do it. They have really been wonderful. But even they keep looking at me with That Look – sympathy and fear together.

Thank God we came home last week right after the memorial service, as soon as the ashes were out of the urn. What with the hysterics everyone was having, and obviously the rest of the shoot was off, there was nothing for anyone to stay for. And we'd had the police and the sheriff and various people upsetting everyone and traipsing in and out of the house and examining the grounds at all hours. Eventually it was ruled as an accident and no one was really blamed, except the procurator fiscal did make the comment that the shooting should have finished much earlier due to the unusually poor weather conditions and the bad light etc.

They're working on the assumption that it was just an accident, though I know differently. Officially, Thomas was walking along with his gun not broken, tripped over a root or rock or something and shot himself in the neck and up through the face. As if he would do such a moronic thing. No one let me see him, I just saw him in the hall, and as they loaded his body into the ambulance, just a long mound on a stretcher under a long dark cloth. I think I can assume that his lovely face was just a bloody mess. Whatever. There's not the least suspicion there was any malice involved. Just stupidity. My poor Thomas, and he always took such great care.

Then since we came home, it's been endless. People I haven't seen for years, people who didn't even come to my wedding have been endlessly descending on the house these last few days.

And my sister – I know very well the bitch hated Thomas (because she tried it on with him and he wasn't interested. He told me all about it.) - yet she's going around in a black frock dabbing at her eyes and saying in a delighted hushed little voice how terrible it all is. If she says it once more I will find something heavy and hit her with it, anything to shut her stupid mouth.

Mon 27 August - 8.30pm
Thank God my family only stayed for a few hours. But there have been plenty of friends, colleagues, acquaintances, an endless happy stream of them.

It's that look in their eyes. I know I've said it already, but it's making me insane, I hate it, that look, all coy and anxious and piteous and empathetic. And I know inside they're enjoying the whole exciting misery of it. Those slanting eyebrows, the heads on one side, the little understanding nods and little noises of sympathy and the little pecks on the cheek and pats on the back. I'm going to punch someone sooner or later. Probably sooner. And once I start, I probably won't be able to stop, and I'll just keep punching and punching and punching and punching and punching until their faces are a bloody mess just like his was.

That day. To me now, 13 August is the only date on the calendar, everything else has disappeared. Unlucky for some. It's a good thing there is a calendar on the wall here in Thomas's study where I sit to write my journal otherwise I'd have lost track of the date ages ago.

That morning when everything was so, so wonderful, and all the time, lurking in the wings, that doom, that sideways-knocking disaster. I was a fool. I feel so stupid, so humiliated, there I was, fannying around in the kitchen with Jess and her cooking and dreaming about getting pregnant, and he – he was lying in his own blood gazing up at the sky. It's like a terrible joke has been played upon me.

And it was too soon. I couldn't say goodbye, I couldn't hold him, kiss him, make love to him one last time, I couldn't look back at him as I walked away, couldn't refresh my memories, which already seem so faded, so dull, so unreal. I feel like the only one not let in on the joke. I feel so - unprepared.

    I came back to this house by car, retracing the steps – or rather, the wheels of our journey just days before, but everything, absolutely everything about that same trip was different. It's like he never existed, like I dreamed him up. My Darling. How can it all be gone so quickly?

    We didn't kiss properly when he went out with Murdo that morning – Jess and I were going to be busy later so after we had our breakfast, I went back to bed for a lay-in before I had my bath and so I barely paid any attention to him going – just a quick wave to him and Murdo and everyone, then I raced myself to get upstairs and under the covers. He called something back to me and it made me laugh, I can't remember now what it was he said – I was already halfway up the stairs, it didn't seem like it would matter. I didn't know that would be my last chance to kiss him or to hear his voice.

    I hate wearing black now. I hate flowers. I hate the heady scent of them, drowning all the fresh, freeing air out of the house. I hate finger-foods and soft, muted music.

    I hate the way people just stand there looking at me, waiting to see what I'm going to do. I hate the way they all keep trying to hug me and keep telling me, never mind, Darling, it's shock, that's all, the tears will subside and you'll start to feel better.

    I heard someone telling some other moron that I needed to move on with my life. It's only been 14 days. Is that all we get now, to mourn our soulmates? 14 Days? Then it's time to pick yourself up, dust yourself down, stop standing around like a wraith and have some fun. Let your hair down. Get back on the horse. Plenty more fish in the sea. Time heals all wounds.

    I don't know why she was so surprised when I went over and slapped her.

    Move on with my life? Move on with that, bitch!

    My life ended with that gunshot that blew my husband's face off. Tell me how you think I can move on from that.

Thurs 30 August - 12.15pm

The day before yesterday, we had another little memorial service down here, for all Thomas's colleagues and those of our friends and acquaintances who couldn't get to the main one in Scotland. It went as well as these things possibly can – very much a case of gritting my teeth and getting on with it, and once it was over, going up to my room – once our room – and shutting the door against it and sinking onto the bed to sob my heart out. I suppose the service was rather beautiful. But the words of the minister did nothing to comfort my aching heart – I just don't want to be comforted – as soon as it stops hurting, I'll know I've forgotten my lover. I don't want that to happen. So I just listened politely and tried to remember to say all the right things to the right people at the right time.

Just before the service began, I got a text from Monica. It said the same as the last one. Just two words, Criss Cross, but this time followed by several little Xs as kisses. At first I thought she'd accidentally sent the old text again, then I saw the kisses and realised it was a new one, and I cursed myself for not blocking her number.

But now, now I've finally realised what it meant. What she meant. What she was saying last time.

She was telling me she did it. Making her proud announcement. Monica killed Thomas.

Same day - 10.10pm
I'm going to kill her. I'm going to rip her fucking head off her shoulders. She's boasting and sending me kisses to say she has killed my husband. She's destroyed the most important person in my life and what's she concerned with? Her little in-jokes and making sure I know her clever, clever secret?

He was my whole life. How could she? How dared she? Just joking about it like that with her bloody little 'Criss Cross xxxx'. Like she's just throwing it into the conversation, oh, by the way, I've just killed your husband, aren't I a clever little sausage?

I'm going to kill her.

Sat 1 September - 9.35am
The first day of September and already it seems so autumnal. I don't know if it's just me, my 'low mood', as the doctor terms it, getting the better of me. It seems cooler, and there's the slightest hint of decay on the sharper breeze that seems to suggest that winter is about to arrive a little sooner than expected. I feel like wrapping myself in shapeless old cardigans and jumpers and hiding in Thomas's office. I don't want to see anyone, but thankfully very few people call, they've finally taken the hint. Either that or they're all suffering from compassion-fatigue. Suits me, whichever it is.

    I just don't know what to do. I can't get interested in anything, can't rouse myself to anything. Every time I get some tiny spark of enthusiasm, it dies away almost immediately and I'm left on the old leather sofa in his office, wrapped in scruffy woollens and staring out of the window at nothing, utterly absorbed by my misery.

    This time a month ago he was still here with me. I wish I could go back and tell myself to run away with him and hide. Or to kill Monica, it wouldn't matter if I went to prison, at least then I'd still see Thomas once a fortnight and know that he was alive and safe.

    And each day seems the same, no alteration, nothing to distinguish it from its fellows. And my life stretches out in front of me the same, an endless trickle of grey days of nothingness. I feel a slight relief that it's not August any more, but that's about all I seem capable of feeling. I'm dead, I think. Or sleeping, like a daffodil bulb. Sleeping under the earth like Thomas should be if only they hadn't burned him away to dust.

Mon 3 September - 10.35pm
I started to sort out Thomas' things today. I've been putting it off – obviously. Actually it wasn't quite as bad as I'd expected. I mean, once I got over the initial bit of opening the doors and starting to take everything out. At first I felt a bit – guilty, I think it was, very odd – a bit faithless, throwing out all his clothes and things as if he was never coming back, which well, clearly I realise that is the truth but it still felt somehow like a betrayal, a denial of him.

Mrs H helped me, and I was very grateful to her. We did it in little batches, and every now and then, she made a comment like, do you remember when he wore that shirt to that Do and came home with Cabernet all down the front,' (though she said it more like cabinet), but it was such a help, we ended up having a lovely little chat about him, all rosy and blind to his practically non-existent imperfections.

Towards the end, when I was getting a bit tired, I got a bit teary, and she knew, didn't tell me to try and pull myself together or to move on, she just patted my arm and said, 'time for a pot of tea, Duckie.' And she went downstairs and left me to weep a bit then she and Sid brought up a big tray with strong tea and plates of sandwiches and little cakes.

I kept a couple of his shirts, a jumper, his bathrobe, and his watch, and the pair of cufflinks I bought him last Christmas. Sometimes I just snuggle up in his giant bathrobe, it swamps me of course, but is unbelievably comforting to curl up in it on the sofa.

Miranda Kettle, one of Thomas' colleagues, (beaky nose, no chin, cheap coffin handles, remember?) came round this evening and was very generous with her time – she was a bit nervous, I could tell when she first arrived, but when she saw that I wasn't hysterical and she could mention his name, she relaxed, and again, it was quite a nice time in an odd way.

    She looked through all his business stuff for me, which reminded me of how Thomas looked through Huw's stuff, only a few short weeks ago. She gave me a generous amount for his laptop, on behalf of the firm – it's easier for her to take it away to divvy up the clients etc, so once again, that's another nagging little thing out of the way. Although I can't help feeling a bit worried that she is going to make a vast profit out of Thomas' death – she seemed to be going to huge lengths to keep her obvious glee under control and remain suitably sombre. Oh well, again, I suppose it's only money – and it's not as though I'm short of a bob or two. I suppose I'm very lucky…

    I'm exhausted though, I feel absolutely wrung out. And teary again. And just full of how much I have lost and how empty and alone I feel and so, so lonely without him.

    I can't face the thought of going to the hair salon, or anywhere else. I don't think I've been out of the house apart from that memorial that went so well.

    And although Thomas' personal things and work things have all been sorted out, there are still so many little annoying things to deal with. I don't feel like answering any of the letters and notes of condolence that I've received. They are on the sideboard in the drawing room, and there's already a little film of dust on them, so obviously even Mrs H hasn't felt like doing anything with them either.

I eat with them in the kitchen now. It's pointless setting the dining table for one, and anyway, I'm not really interested in eating, so it gives Mr and Mrs H the chance to nag some food into me, and I get some human contact – my doctor says that's important - and they are the only people I can bear to be around. Usually they just carry on with their lives around me and I let my mind drift off to the moors and that strange and terrible day.

Last night, I went into the kitchen for a glass of water, and they were sitting there at the table, talking. I don't know what I said, just some casual remark, and then the next moment I was sobbing uncontrollably again. And Mrs H got up and came over and put her arms around me and she hugged me while I cried, then gave me some kitchen paper-towel to blow my nose on when the emotion subsided. She made me some cocoa and toast and while all this was going on, never once told me it would all be all right, let it out, get on with your life, etc etc,. It's as if she knows those are all lies. She and Sid are the only people I can bear to be with. They are the only ones I can trust.

But I don't know what is going to happen. With my future, I mean. I'm rich, or will be once all the legal rigmarole is sorted out. The sale of Highgates is almost complete, so that will be a couple of million in the bank, not to mention Thomas' estate including his pensions and insurances, and of course, this house is all paid for. I'll never need to worry about money. I suppose I'm lucky. Women lose their husbands every day and have to worry about bringing up their children single-handedly and pay bills and mortgages and how to manage everything on top of their grief. But I'm lucky.

I'll never have Thomas' baby. That bright morning in the motorway cafeteria those few weeks ago, when we talked about it again for the first time in ages and we were both so happy…God, it hurts so much just to think of it.

It's so grey outside today, so dull and overcast. A thin rain is falling but barely enough to wet the ground, it's almost like a mist. Twinkle has just emerged from under a bush and I can see something feathery hanging from his mouth, and I don't know whether to laugh or cry at the irony. I'm going to put my journal away and go and see if there's anything on television. Little bastard, he can kill it or leave it, I'm too tired to care anymore.

Mon 24 Sep - 2.25pm
Well they've finally gone, duty done, Cess and Parker I mean, Thomas' sister and her useless husband, and not a moment too soon. I actually hate them now, even if they are the last members of Thomas' family (apart from Jess and Murdo – I could never not love them!) I mean, I hated them before Thomas died, and now, having had them here trying to muscle in on Thomas' fortune and the proceeds of the sale of Clarice's house, all the while pretending a concern for my well-being and happiness, well I loathe them so much the very thought of them makes me feel sick.

And they never gave me a moment's peace to collect my thoughts and they made such a fuss if I cried, like I shouldn't be doing it, or like I should consider getting counselling or something. Like my grief is somehow excessive. But now, thank God, they've gone home for a day or two, though coming back about Thursday, so I'm sitting here enjoying the quiet and just watching the garden.

I never thought it was possible to hate anyone this much. Apart from Monica, of course, but that's kind of a special situation.

And their veiled threats. The insinuation that I have a moral obligation to give them some of the money. That although 'obviously Thomas did technically leave everything to me', obviously with Cess being his only relation – and with Clarice being her mother too, it seems only fair, 'obviously, in the current climate, that I should reconsider my financial needs just a little bit, as I am only one person with modest requirements' and they have a larger household, and there are two of them, and 'of course in life, both Dear Mummy and Tommy were so generous and understanding…' And of course they wanted to 'assure me that they wouldn't even dream of taking any kind of legal action, no of course they wouldn't, because after all, we are family, and that, after all, obviously, is what really matters because of course if one didn't have one's family where would one be?'

Bastards. I want them gone. For good.

So I had an idea. I did a spot of research on the internet.

As I said, they've just popped home, ostensibly to get some more clothes and make arrangements for their housekeeper to get in and out – apparently she doesn't live in, 'one wouldn't want Servants in the old-fashioned sense, no a Daily is much more modern and cost effective, no meals and board to pay for. No, one's staff these days are effectively contractors, so one has none of the old overheads associated with keeping live-in servants.' Stupid bitch. I hate her.

Anyway, as far as they're concerned they will be back on Thursday afternoon with a fresh set of undies and revitalised for making my life a misery. As far as **they're concerned**…

However, I now have several small but key components from their car's engine in a jar in the garage, and at any moment I am expecting a visit from the police bearing the most terrible news. Tee hee!

Tues 25 Sept - 10.45am

Dear Mr H informed me, immediately the police had reluctantly left me huddled at the kitchen table sobbing into a hankie on Mrs H's shoulder, that he had taken the liberty of removing the engine parts I had left in the jar in the garage and had then buried them deep in the middle of our rather messy compost heap 'just in case anyone got ideas'. What a sweet man! I can't believe he's aiding and abetting.

    Threw out Thomas's aftershave, his moisturiser, shower gel, all his shaving stuff and even his toothbrush. Seems almost petty to dispose of someone's toothbrush.

    My own toothbrush, sitting all alone in the little Wedgwood jug, looks a bit pathetic.

    I feel terrible throwing away all his bathroom things – so guilty, so wasteful. And it's just so final.

Thurs 27 Sep - 3.15pm
I don't think we need have worried, the police have now been back a couple of times with more information. They are now satisfied that Cess and Parker's deaths were due to the excessive levels of alcohol in Parker's blood – who knew he was a drunk-driver? So they are not looking for any further cause of the accident. Shocking! I mean, it's truly disgraceful, really, when one thinks of the innocent lives he could have wiped out by his blatant irresponsibility. Thank God he is dead, I say, and her of course. Never liked either of them, as I may have mentioned once or twice. The nice policeman commiserated with me over the tragedy, coming so closely on the heels of the loss of my husband only 6 weeks ago. I didn't say anything about the terrible losses of Huw or Manddi or Clarice only a few weeks before that. Didn't want to point him towards a pattern.

    I told them all about Cess and Parker being on the point of moving in with me, to help me recover from the loss of Thomas, and that he and Cess had been close, and that she and her husband had come up to stay when Clarice died, and how they had only popped home for a few clothes and to make a few essential domestic arrangements, and now they were gone forever, snuffed out due to a moment's human weakness. It was all very affecting, and the poor policeman was so upset, I began to think he was never going to leave. I hope I haven't made him think he's on the wrong career path! He may very well require some counselling.

    I went out of my way to assure him I had the Hopkins' to take very good care of me, and he finally left. So, another episode closes satisfactorily!

Tues 9 October - 2.40pm
And now I've got their house and savings too, as they had left everything they had to Thomas, and so obviously that all passes to me under his will. Croesus had nothing on what my bank balance will be in a few months' time!

But I'm glad they didn't leave any children – it would have been awful to orphan some poor little children. And I probably would have felt responsible for their future care and upbringing, so really it was a good thing all round that they hadn't any children. Especially if he was a drunk.

I've got a cold. Don't know from whom; some selfish bastard – probably Cess or Parker - gave me their germs. Am wrapped up in Thomas's old gardening jumper. It was a baby-blue golf jumper in a former life but has a snag on the hem from him leaning over a gorse bush to 'play it' where it lay. It still smells of Davidoff. Wish my nose was as stuffy as my head slash throat, as the scent of it has made me weepy and ridiculous. But don't want to take it off as it is cosy and reassuring. Who knew even old clothes have ghosts?

Mon 31 Dec - 11.50pm

I'm so thankful this awful year is almost over. I've made my New Year Resolution. Only one. It's not really going to come as much of a surprise.

I'm going to kill Monica.

That's all I care about, all that means anything to me. She must pay for what she did to Thomas. And this coming year, I'm going to see to it that she does.

Christmas was dire. All I did was sit in front of the television in the small drawing-room, with Mrs H and Sid. My skin is disgustingly spotty and patchy from eating too much, and I've been drinking too much and trying not to feel sorry for myself, and trying not to think too much about Thomas and how happy we were this time last year and all the places we went and all the things we did and waking up lying next to him and realising with a rush of joy it was Christmas morning.

Tonight I'm going to sit up with a large glass of champagne and a big bowl of fresh strawberries and cherries. I'm going to welcome in the New Year with my vow, my oath to fulfil my promise to myself, or God, or Thomas or the Universe, or who or whatever the hell we pray to these days – probably the TV – the little God-in-the-corner – and I am going to exact my revenge. And the fruit is to perk up my skin a bit, as I'm looking so scraggy at the moment.

Slowly and deliberately I will kill Monica, and as I do so, she will know what is happening to her and she will know why, and when she begs for mercy, or pleads with me, I shall just remember back to that morning the day before he died when we sat in the motorway services and decided to try again for a baby – that is what she has robbed me of, that is what she took from me – the future Thomas and I planned together.

And the New Year is a real psychological hurdle for me. It really feels as if, once I get past tonight and into the start of the year, things will get better, get easier. I feel such a sense of relief that it's almost January.

And I do want the pain to lessen but at the same time I feel guilty letting go of it so quickly. I know I owe it to him and the memory of our love to keep my grief alive and to keep on missing him, but the thing is, it's not easy, and I am so tired of misery.

Every now and then, something happens, something small and insignificant, and I find myself smiling, or I look out at the garden and I find myself planning a new border, or I start thinking about decorating and I realise all of a sudden that I am beginning to pick up the threads of my life again in some small way, and although I know Thomas wouldn't want it any other way, wouldn't want me to mourn him for an extended period, any more than I would want him to mourn for me if the situation were reversed, nevertheless I feel so wicked. I mean, he is dead and nothing can bring him back, but I don't seem to be able to hold on to my sense of loss as I did in those first few weeks. I feel I'm denying the truth and depth of our love by moving on, by coming to life again. I know that's ridiculous, and as I say, I know he wouldn't want me to give up on life and freeze inside but I just feel so awful for being alive.

I'm going to sell this house. And with the money from that, and from the sale of Highgates, and the money from Cess and her waster of a husband, well, I can pretty much afford to go anywhere and do whatever I want to do.

Which obviously brings me back to Monica. My last act of love for my husband will be to kill the one who killed him.

Ooh, it's midnight! Thank God for that. What a relief 2012 is over. Must have a quick swig then run and say Happy New Year to the Hopkins'.

Thurs 3 January - 6.15pm
Okay, well, January. At last. I feel such a sense of relief, a sense of casting off the old burdens.

The Hopkins' have been amazing. They have been there for me – and still are – whenever I need someone to talk to, but they never presume. They have become my family. When I move, I shall make sure it's to somewhere they like, that's now as important to me as my own happiness, as I want them to come with me. I'll ask them tomorrow where they think they would like to live. And I'm going to send them on a nice cruise or something as a big thank you for all their care and support over the last few months, I just wouldn't have survived without them, my friends.

Fri 4 January - 11.00am
Did I mention that I had to employ a firm to clear out Cess and Parker's house in Weybridge? Well, I got the bill today – almost £5000! Bloody cheek! Still it's only money, I suppose, and I didn't want to have to go down there myself, although Mr and Mrs H did offer to help out if I changed my mind.

Am thinking of having a few days away – probably at Chapley's again, I could do with the pampering and I know the place. I mean, there are a few unpleasant associations, seeing that last time I stayed there, Monica gate-crashed my private little party. But I don't see why I should let her spoil things for me, and it's not all bad memories, after all Clarice was killed last time I was there, so that cheered things up a bit.

Mind you, that was when I thought Monica had done it, but now of course, I know it was Thomas and I still find that a bit too weird to take in. But obviously Monica encouraged me to think it was her because of that stupid criss cross idea and the film and everything. I can't bear to watch Hitchcock films anymore. The Birds was on the other evening, but I only watched a little bit and had to put it off.

And that reminds me of the texts Monica sent me with just those two words, 'criss cross', and it was those two words that made me realise what had happened. I haven't heard from her in a couple of months, and obviously I'm happy about that, as I hate the very sight of her, but I must say this silence makes me wonder what she's doing with herself these days. It makes me think about what might be the best way to kill her, as it won't be so easy if I never see her.

I don't know if it's just winter blues, or what, but I just can't seem to get down to doing any serious planning, I just haven't got any interest in doing anything except sitting around in front of the television or pottering around the house or garden. So a few days away for some R and R should be just what I need to pick myself up and then when I come back I can really take myself in hand and crack on with this new project. After all, I can't just drift through life, I must achieve something. God knows what, or why, but I just feel I must.

Have sent for some house details. I must say, it's awfully difficult to find a really nice home in the Cotswolds (Mr and Mrs H's favoured spot, he has family in that neck of the woods apparently) for a max of £4,000,000. (But don't want to spend my entire wodge of cash!)

Oh and wonderful news! Jess and Murdo are coming down for a few days next week. I think they really just wanted to check up on me, make sure I'm eating and coping okay. It will be lovely to see them – a bit emotional too, I imagine, but that's only natural and I'm not too worried about that, really I'm just looking forward to it.

Sat 12 January - 10.30 am

The house is so quiet again, now Jess and Murdo have gone back to Scotland – they tried to make me go back with them, I think it was something along the lines of getting back on the horse etc – they're afraid I won't ever go back there as it's where Thomas died – but any way, I told them I was planning a trip to Chapleys again next week, and didn't want to cancel it as it's so hard to get a booking, they're almost always full.

We had a lovely few days, didn't do much, just pottered about and ate and drank and went out in the car to look at the local scenery.

One of the things Jess commented on, apart from the fact that I looked shockingly in need of my upcoming visit to Chapleys (bless her!), (and I know she didn't mean it in a horrible way), she said she'd noticed how familiar, even intimate, I had become with the Hopkins'.

I told her they weren't just my employees any longer, but that I really cared for them, almost as if they were my own family, like surrogate parents or something – and that they had been wonderful to me after Thomas died. I told her all the little and even quite big things they'd done, how they'd looked after me and hugged me and held me and listened to me in those early days when it was all so fresh and unbearable. I told Jess that if it hadn't been for them I wouldn't have got through it.

But wonderful though she is, I could tell she just didn't quite 'get it' – and why should she? Her family is still intact and even if she lost Murdo, God forbid that should happen, she would still have her four sons, her mother and her younger brother and his family in Toronto. She wouldn't be as alone as I am.

Not that she was telling me to distance myself from them or anything of that sort, no. But she did laugh and say something about how Bayliss, her butler, would never permit such familiarity. But then she's got a different set-up to me. They are in a huge, feudal manor arrangement, literally The Lairds of the area, we're just well to do and with a small staff. I mean, I – not we – I am just well to do etc. It's just not the same kind of set-up at all.

 Mind you, I've met Bayliss and he's a miserable old git. He is the epitome of the Golden Age type of butler – one instinctively knows he refers to Jess and her family as 'My Family', and no doubt he serves them dinner in 'our dining-room', and he is utterly rigid and formal. And he's in command of at least a dozen troops, and with us it's just Mr and Mrs Hopkins – and in my house, there isn't that formal 'upstairs' and 'below stairs' distinction – anyway, they live in the attic, so technically, they're even 'upper' than I am!

 So it was lovely to see them, but after a few days, I wanted them to go – I just found it so hard having other people in the house, and besides Murdo was bored with no men to speak to (he would rather have died than chat with Sid H!) and Jess was missing her home and everything. Now, although the house is very quiet, it's all back to normal, which I find a huge relief.

 But much as I love normal, I'm really looking forward to my trip to Chapley's the day after tomorrow – three days of mindless relaxation and beauty treatments, and then next weekend, Mr and Mrs H and I are off to the Cotswolds to look at a few houses that could be half-decent, just four from the dozens of properties the details of which various agents have sent us. There's one in particular near Stow-in-the-Wold that looks as though it has distinct possibilities but I'm not going to get my hopes up too soon, just in case! But fingers crossed, it could be just what we need!

Mon 14 January - 5pm
Feel a bit deflated. I suppose I should have realised it wouldn't be the same, coming here on my own. And in January! I mean, last time I came to Chapley's, I had Monica with me (okay so that was a bit unexpected, I admit, and it took me a couple of hours to get used to the idea, but after that it was great) and it was all so exciting, I was full of plans about Clarice and of course once I reached the end of my stay here, I had Thomas to go home to.

As it is, however primped and pampered I've been today, and shall be again tomorrow, all I'm doing is going home to my housekeeper and my chauffeur – however much I've come to love them – and a second-hand tabby cat with sardine-breath.

And it's not as much fun doing all the treatments on your own. However pleasant and friendly the staff are, however kind they are when they come back to sort you out after your seaweed wrap, and find you've suddenly started crying because you're thinking about your dead husband, it's just not the same as having an actual friend to spend time with.

Dare I say it, it's even been a bit dull. And pointless. I've not enjoyed all the fuss and the treatments this time. I'm just lying there all the time with no one to talk to and no one to, you know, share the experience with.

If only I hadn't killed my best friend's husband. It would have been lovely to have Monica here with me – and I'm sure she and I would have had as much fun as we did the first time we came together. After what she went through with Huw last summer, she could probably have done with getting away from it all for a day or two.

Anyway. So I'm glad I'm going home the day after tomorrow. I'm driving myself – one of the few occasions these days when I get to drive my own car. And it's quite nice just to sit there in my own car with the music I like on the radio, and not have to keep answering queries about my comfort and my preferred route etc.

By the way, I should probably do something a bit more definite about selling Thomas' BMW – it's too big for me. I like my little 2-seater Mercedes. And obviously when Sid drives me anywhere, we go in the Audi so it seems a bit silly to keep hold of Thomas' car as well. Sid might know the best way to sell it. I'll ask him about it next time I see him.

Same day – 10.15pm
There's something particularly pathetic about eating a sumptuous four-course dinner in a restaurant at a place like this, and eating it all alone, in one's nicest dress and most expensive perfume.

On the first night they asked if I'd like to be seated with another woman who was here on her own, and I wasn't completely against the idea. Then I took a look at her shoes and declined apologetically. The waitress seemed a bit surprised, I think, but there's no point in being nice just for the sake of it. We wouldn't have had anything in common and the last thing I wanted was to have to sit and look at photos of someone else's grandchildren or dog.

But all the same, I did feel a bit ridiculous sat at the huge table, elaborately dressed, all on my own. Felt a bit like Miss Haversham when all the guests had gone off and left her to it in her wedding dress. (Before the fire, obviously).

Wed 16 January - 9.30pm
It's so nice to be home. I've already had Mrs H's tea and cake shoved into me and heard about a dozen different anecdotes that could be filed under the heading 'Tetley's Tales'. Honestly she's completely besotted with that cat. I'm sure she loves it like a child.

One new thing. I don't know if I've done the right thing or not. Probably not. Oh dear, I'm having second thoughts, but I've already said yes…

Mr and Mrs H told me something about their son. Didn't even know they had any offspring apart from the daughter in Milton Keynes, but apparently she's merely one of a batch of three. Matthew, one of their sons, is just about to come out of prison – yes, prison! - and he will need somewhere 'decent' to stay 'just until he gets on his feet a bit'.

I must have gaped at them like some kind of lunatic because they hastened to assure me 1) he wasn't dangerous which means he probably is – I mean, regardless of the original reason for his incarceration, who knows what nasty tips he's picked up in prison? His own parents would be bound to say he wasn't dangerous, wouldn't they? Then 2) he'll keep out of my way - now he's starting to sound like a stray puppy – 'he won't eat much and we'll feed him out of our pocket money' so that, 3) I'd not even know he was there - surely that's not a good thing with Criminals? I would have said it's much better knowing exactly where they are at any given time and 4) it's only for a few weeks until, yes, you've guessed it, he gets back on his feet a bit. They must think I came down with the last shower. How do I let myself get talked into these things? It's that cat all over again.

Oh God! What have I agreed to? Mrs H hugged me and blotted tears with the hem of her apron and Mr H just puffed up with happiness and kept on saying I'd not regret it which I already am, and they'd never forget my kindness.

Oh My God!

And now I've got to drink more tea and eat more bloody cake, provided by Mrs H's overactive gratitude. I've ballooned to a size two, I just know it. I know it's too late to tell them I've changed my mind, even if I claimed mental exhaustion following the drive home. I have made my bed, and now I'm going to have to lump it.

Have been on the phone finalising arrangements to view some houses. Wish I could just stay in bed for a week and sulk with my head under the covers, instead of yet another trip looming on the horizon.

Thurs 17 January - 3.20pm
It's so hard to cram everything in – we're driving down to Gloucester tomorrow to base ourselves there, and starting out exploring a variety of properties the following morning.

We've now got three houses to see on Saturday and one on Sunday. We couldn't do two and two, for some reason to do with someone going to a wedding, so Saturday will be quite busy, and I hope I don't mix up all the kitchen and bathrooms until I can't remember any of them clearly and the whole experience is a complete waste of time.

And then it's a quick nip back home for a day or two, and I believe the Hopkins' will be flung headfirst into preparing for the arrival of their Bundle of Joy. I'm not very clear about the precise arrangements either for his accommodation or for his conveyance to the house, but Mr and Mrs H tell me not to fret, it's all under control.

Which is exactly what worries me.

I know I'm being a bit silly about it, but what if they brainwash me into leaving all my money and everything to them? What if the three of them gang up on me and make me into their slave and I end up waiting on them and doing all the housework and everything? Or. What if they wait until I'm asleep and they creep in and murder me in my sleep and, again, take all my money and everything? What if he moves in and then starts bringing in all his prison buddies? What if he turns my home into a half-way house for murderers and rapists?

And then after that there's a quick dash up to Scotland for a long weekend next weekend for Murdo's birthday. I'm a bit anxious about that. I mean, I haven't been there since…and I'm a little bit scared of how it's all going to feel, how I'm going to feel, how I'll cope…but it's just for a couple of days so I'd be silly not to go, and anyway, I can't let what happened stop me from going there – we had so many lovely visits, and there are good memories too, it's just that they are mostly submerged by the loss and all I can think of is the dark panelled hall, and the shape of Thomas's body on the stretcher, of how I felt seeing the stretcher and the big sheet over the top of him, and the way the sheet curved up and down with his body and I was thinking, that's my husband under there, that's his body and his blood soaking through the cloth and he's dead.

And then only two weeks after that, it's our tenth anniversary, and I can't bear to think about that because Thomas had promised to take me to Tahiti to celebrate and we had said (although half as a joke) that we would have one of those recommitment ceremonies on the beach, a sort of cheesy re-marriage, but I had it all planned out in my mind – though I never told him, I wanted it to be a surprise – and I could visualise the flowers and the clothes and it would be sunny and all perfect and beautiful and the sea would be gently lapping the sand and we would be there, gazing into each other's eyes.

But now that will never happen.

Fri 18 January - 7.15am
I've been feeling so down since yesterday when I wrote that bit about Tahiti. I had to stop to go off to find a hankie because I was crying. Then I went to lie down and when I got up, I didn't feel like doing anything except sitting in front of the television. All night I had a terrible headache, and I've woken up still with it this morning, and I just feel like sobbing or smashing things. I wonder how long I'm going to feel this way. I wish I could lose my memory or something. It must be wonderful not to be haunted by your own history.

    Mrs H has been very sweet both last night and this morning. Last night she fussed over me with cups of tea and bowls of soup, and this morning she's spoiled me with French toast. I know she's trying to cheer me up, and I'm touched that she wants to, or even that she knows me well enough to gauge my mood, but really, I sometimes wish I could just be alone.

    She's done my packing for the trip. Mr H is getting the car ready and then we'll be off. I feel like the whole day is yawning in front of me and I don't know how I'm going to get to the end of it – bedtime seems so far off.

Same day - 10.35am

We are on our way down to Gloucestershire, and we've made good time, should be in Gloucester itself in around half an hour or so. Mr and Mrs H are sitting in the front together, so I've got plenty of room, sprawling here in the back playing Angry Birds on my phone and listening to my fave tunes.

We stopped for a coffee, and I earned about a million brownie points by making them go and find a nice place to sit whilst I went to buy the refreshments for us all. I get a bit embarrassed though – when we go anywhere they're always far too grateful and far too ready to accommodate my wishes – I wish I could get them to relax and be themselves a bit more and not behave like grateful orphans on a daytrip.

Anyway.

Had a call about an hour ago, bit of a nuisance, from the estate agent, saying that the owners of the first house we had planned to see today have called to cancel due to the kitchen ceiling coming down after a flood in the bathroom above it. If he'd only let us know sooner, we wouldn't have had to leave quite so early this morning. But I suppose it can't be helped. But that's one scratched off the list. Fortunately it wasn't 'The' house.

So, on arrival at the estate agent's office, and after meeting the man I've been speaking to almost continually over the last week or so, we will go straight to house number two, which I'm pleased about – well, not just me – as it's the one we all like the most so far, in spite of the rather rubbish description the little agent chappie has furnished us with. And all the photos are too dark or blurry to be of much use, so fingers crossed! In spite of all the lack of information, it seems to have that certain something.

It's quite exciting, having all these potential new homes to inspect. I'm looking forward to walking round with the Hs and hearing what they've got to say. They certainly seem to have very firm opinions about how they want me to spend my money!

At home, our current home, Mr and Mrs H have been clearing out one of the smaller guest rooms for the arrival of their son. (Next week!!! Eek!!! How did that come round so quickly?)

Everything has been cleaned and the bed aired, the curtains washed and rehung, the linen is neatly folded in the airing cupboard and the eager parents are full of excitement. I keep finding them chatting together in hushed voices around the place. This means so much to them. I do hope he's not a scumbag, for their sake, they are so happy and excited. They obviously love him heaps more than my parents love me, or Clarice loved Thomas.

I don't know if I mentioned it before, but at Christmastime, I persuaded Sid & Lill (yes, that is her name – I began to wonder if she even had a first name at all, then out of the blue, one day a couple of weeks ago, call me Lill, she says!) to move out of their cosy little attic hideaway where they'd secretly stashed themselves last year following their financial difficulties.

I've let them convert the guest suite into their own little spot – they've got their own little sitting room and a private bathroom, so it's quite nice and cosy for them, and it's nice for me too, knowing there is someone there within calling distance and not miles away up under the eaves with the tea-chests. When one no longer has a lovely husband to snuggle up with, one suddenly feels very – well, I don't know, but vulnerable doesn't even begin to cover it – naked is more like it. Like one of those little baby birds in a nest, unable to feed itself and unfeathered and liable to get chucked out of the nest to its doom at the slightest whim of a light breeze. So they are such a comfort to me. I'm not quite so all alone with them just a few yards down the hall.

 Probably by now they could have moved out and back into their own place again, even if it was only a rental, but they haven't suggested it, and I've been so thankful for their company, I'm happy for them to stay forever. They're no trouble whatsoever and of course, they pamper me to within an inch of my life. I don't know what I'd do without them.

 I've asked the agent in Gloucester to put the sale of my present house in the hands of his counterpart in my area. I'm a little concerned now, because apparently the property market is very depressed at the moment, but he assures me there is still plenty of money around and that it shouldn't be too difficult to find a buyer for a superior property such as mine.

 At least I don't have to wait to sell that house before I can buy the new one. In fact I suppose it's pretty obvious that the reason I'm getting such a good personal service is due to the fat commission the house sale is likely to generate for the agent if I decide to buy – what is 1.5% of £3.8 million? I never was very good at sums at school, in spite of the private tutor who (God alone knows how!) managed partly to coach and partly to bully me through my exams. But however much commission that is, even I know it's not to be sniffed at, and it'll only be that low if I decide to plump for the cheapest one on the list – the one we really like is actually a fair bit more than that.

But whatever happens, I'm going to choose one of them. I mean, how bad could a house worth £4 million be? I've got to move, I've made up my mind. I can't bear the thought of staying in my house a moment longer than I have to – 2, 3 months at the most I can manage, I'm resigned to it taking that long. But longer, no, I can't even begin to think about facing that length of time. I get this feeling of dread in the pit of my stomach just at the thought of not being able to escape. It's too big, too cold, I'm beginning to have dreams about it, I feel like I'm being chased, well not chased, just - vaguely menaced, pursued, I can't explain it, it's just as if someone is after me. I'm afraid to go outside, yet I'm scared to be indoors, and I feel like I have to keep away from the windows, I'm afraid to be seen. I want to just find somewhere safe and small and cosy so that I can hide away where no one will ever find me.

So even though Sid and Lill have advised me to 'wait and see' and 'keep an open mind' and keep telling me not pin my hopes on finding the right house immediately, privately I've decided that I'll take the best one available out of the bunch we're viewing this weekend. I can't wait any longer, it's got to be now. If I don't move now, I'm beginning to fear I may not be able to move at all.

I only hope the Hopkins' do keep their promise to come with me, I'd be lost without them, and…

Oh good, Sid says we have arrived.

Same day – 11.05pm
Amazing! We've seen the loveliest house. It was the second of the day, or technically would have been the third if the first one hadn't been cancelled. (That first one we saw, the one we were all so keen on, was absolutely ghastly, by the way. Really dark and weird. Definitely haunted!)

I wanted to cancel the other viewing. We all loved the house that much. Of course, the agent was all doubts and caution. Was I really so sure I liked it that much, after all I might see something even better if I looked at others. I shouldn't go rushing after only the second I'd seen. Like I was a kid in a sweet shop pointing and screaming.

But I was adamant. Mrs H agreed with me - she had fallen in love with the kitchen, with its perfect little breakfast nook, preparation island, and Belfast sinks (yes two!). And the almost silent extractor fan above the smooth, cool expanse of the double ceramic hob with superfast temperature control and plate warmer. There was a double wall oven and more cupboards than even she could fill, and a lovely aspect over the kitchen garden with bird table. No, nothing is going tear that room from her heart now that she has seen it. I believe even if I didn't want the house, she'd try to talk me into it.

But I do want it.

Anyway, eventually we managed to talk Mr Lavish into cancelling our viewing appointment for tomorrow and he has arranged a further viewing at The Beeches instead.

There are six bedrooms, so it's only a little place, but so cosy, so homely. And anyway, I don't need anywhere bigger, I only have the occasional visitor.

The master bedroom is done out in a really lovely pale peach jacquard design paper, clean and fresh, elegant but also warm, with a really good carpet, brand new, only a few shades darker, then there's a simply huge dressing room, leading to the ensuite bathroom. The whole suite looks out over the rear garden, so that's lovely.

The other bedrooms are neat and clean, good light and plenty of storage space. Two of them have ensuites, and of course there's a decent-sized family bathroom, which is admittedly a little tatty, if we're honest, but renovating a bathroom is not the end of the world.

I think the Hs have selected their room already, a biggish one at the opposite end of the house to 'mine' and up its own little flight of stairs, almost in the attics, and the set-up is a little like the one they have now, with their own bathroom, and a little sitting room and stairs down to the back part of the house – very Upstairs Downstairs.

There are doors into the garden from the drawing room and the study, leading first onto the wide paved area of the terrace (not sure if they said they were leaving all those little pyramid-shaped box trees? Must check tomorrow, they were just perfect), and from there you go down a few steps into the garden itself, first to a wide lawn surrounded by borders and the fence separating the property from the neighbours on one side and from the kitchen garden on the other; and from there you go to a rather nicely kept shrubbery beyond which is a little summerhouse by a lily-pond (a bit like Monica's but nicer), and then on again to another shrubbery, and then to a lovely shady spot, all cottage garden flowers and overgrown roses, a delightful little retreat. In all about 250 feet long and a good 150 feet wide, so quite a bit smaller than my current home, but then as I keep reminding myself, I am down-sizing. I don't need so much room now I am alone.

The entrance hall is a little smaller than I would have liked, but it is a bright, regular square, with some storage and of course the downstairs cloakroom, and the stairs come down with a little bit of a sweep and some nice cornice-work, it's all very pretty.

The sitting room, or 'Family slash Drawing room' as the agent kept calling it, putting imaginary quotes in the air every time he said it, is a large rectangle, and I can just see how I want to arrange everything – a nice seating area around the old-fashioned fire place – actually it's not that old – it's really a modern thing made to look old – the best sort, in my book. A nice surround and a mantelpiece and those lovely doors out to the garden at the far end.

I can't really remember the dining room, apart from the fact that it was almost as big as the sitting room. Then there was the study, currently used as a home office, which I suppose is the same thing, smallish, but neat, clean and cosy, with more doors to the garden. Shame Thomas won't be there to use it – I could just picture him wandering out those doors to potter around the garden, coffee cup in hand, mulling over some contract or deal or something and deep in thought, with that little frown line between his eyebrows as he concentrates. Such a shame he won't ever see it, I think he'd approve.

And there was a small sitting room, very, very sweet, and then the games slash hobbies slash fitness room, which I probably wouldn't use but my guests might like to.

Off the kitchen there is also the utility room and a small boot room with a nice big area for outdoor coats and shelves for all one's stuff. Outside, a double garage with a workshop, Sid's little empire, the usual shed and greenhouse, a nice little walled kitchen garden area, it's all a bit like a grand country house in miniature.

The house is off a quietish road just on the outskirts of Stow-on-the-Wold, in a tiny little village – or really, it's a hamlet, it's all terribly picturesque, like something off a chocolate box, and everyone seems very, very nice. There's a pub and a shop and a sweet little church. I think I'm in love!

Finally! The agent has just got back to me to confirm tomorrow's appointment has now been cancelled and a further appointment has been made to view The Beeches, after which, I'm almost certain, I will be ready to make my offer. If I don't, Mrs H will probably give notice, and I'm not about to go back home on the train, let me tell you! I'm getting used to being driven everywhere.

I'm spending the evening in my room. I had dinner sent up, and have been sitting in bed all evening doing crosswords, watching a bit of television and writing in this journal.

Mr and Mrs H have gone out for dinner and to the pictures, they were so excited to be away, anyone would think they've never had any time off before! Before they went out, Mrs H insisted on ringing her friend at home who is cat-sitting for us, to check on Tetley. I'm only surprised her pal Maureen didn't insist on putting the cat on the phone so Lill could talk to it.

We've arranged a late breakfast and then we're going back to The Beeches for around 11.30.

It's a lovely house. And I have to live somewhere. The Beeches is a great find, and is not the kind of house to come on to the market very often, so I'm lucky to have the chance of it now.

The way I'm feeling, any place is better than where I live now, with all those things he said, he did, all those looks, embraces, I can't bear the empty intimacy of the house anymore. I believe sometimes people say that the memories keep them going, that they are healing and consoling – but that's not been my own experience. I'm haunted, not by a spirit or a ghost, just by the happiness we once had. I have to get away from there and try to fix myself.

Of course, I could live in a hotel all my life. There's something to be said for that – blank impersonal rooms, no emotional investment required, very little space so no chance to accumulate all the 'stuff' we humans acquire these days – no personal belongings, nothing that ties you to a place, no baggage, no demands. It's wonderful just for a few days to be simply me, in the here and now, no past, no future, no pain or memories, just to relax and be at peace for this short while.

But it can't last, of course. The real world drags you back and insists you keep company with all those memories and experiences and ghosts that hurt and haunt you and leave you feeling broken. But at least that way you know you're alive. If that's a good thing. And I'm not too sure any more that it is.

Wed 23 January - 10.30pm
I met Matt today. I don't know quite what I was expecting. I came back from shopping (bought some ab-so-bally-lute-ley amazing shoes!!!) to find Mr and Mrs Hopkins in the kitchen, Mrs H making yet another of her endless pots of tea, and there he was sitting at my kitchen table, perfectly relaxed, as if he'd lived here all his life, chatting away to his parents and just giving me a wave and a wink as I came in, and saying something along the lines of 'Alright Darlin'?'

Congratulations, I thought to myself, it's a boy!

Their son and heir. As I say, I'm not too sure what I was expecting, and I know I said he could stay with us for a short while, but even so I was still a little surprised. I mean, he's exactly like his father must have been thirty years ago – big but not fat, good-looking if you like that sort of thing, and a bit of a bad 'un, I'm absolutely certain.

Well, I was definitely expecting prison pallor, not the tanned, healthy look of him, and he's obviously been allowed to keep himself fit whilst detained at Her Majesty's pleasure. His hair, although not cut according to any truly gentlemanly style, was at least in keeping with the type one sees on the high street (usually outside pubs and betting shops), and moreover, I have to grudgingly admit, it was recognisably a style, not just an all too obvious snip around a pudding basin with a pair of nail scissors.

His clothes were modern, not really terribly tasteful, but clearly from the higher end of the high street chain-store range, and worn with an undeniably cocky flair. But at least he doesn't wear his jeans halfway down his thighs, causing him to waddle like a duck as in so many men today and revealing far too much boxer-short.

Mrs H made me some tea, introductions were made and as I made my hasty exit, massaging my crunched fingers, I distinctly heard him say something about me being 'not bad, not bad at all'. Charmed, I'm sure.

Well I only hope he makes himself useful whilst he's here, perhaps he could do some of the things that a man of Mr H's advancing years oughtn't to do. That might at least help to rebuild some of the self-respect he's probably missing behind that ill-constructed mask of arrogance. I know he's their son, and they've been terribly good to me, but I don't think I'm going to like him – in fact I already don't like him – so I'm desperately hoping he won't stay long. Unfortunately, I don't think I actually gave a specific time frame for his rehabilitation and moving out into the wider world. Blast!

I'm actually a little bit nervous about having him here in my house. Matt, I mean, obviously. I mean, I suppose it's normal to have concerns as I don't know him yet, and what little I've seen and heard of him hasn't exactly inspired my confidence – he has just come out of prison, for God's sake!

I wish I knew what he'd been in for.

Saw Monica yesterday afternoon. It was a bit of a surprise, I hadn't heard from her in absolutely ages which I was glad about, but Mrs H had already told her I was 'in' so I wasn't really able to get out of it.

She apologised for coming round without phoning first, but said she wouldn't stay long, she'd only wanted to stop by to say how sorry she was, she's been getting some therapy or something, and she had come to realise the shocking reality of her actions, that she had been told by her therapist that she'd had a breakdown and couldn't be held accountable for her what she'd done but had to accept it and make amends if possible. As I was about to protest, because I just couldn't hold back when she said that, she said yes, she knew that it was wrong to make excuses.

'I know now that nothing could ever excuse the misery and the torment I put you through,' she said, adding, 'I know you can never forgive me or view me as your friend again, but it's important to my own healing to face you as my victim with an admission of guilt and regret. And so, Cressida, I just want to say I'm sorry.'

What can you say to something like that? And it did make me feel just a teeny bit bad about killing Huw and his girlfriend – what's her name? – Molli? Sanddi? But I decided it was pointless to make a fuss - I mean, I can't bring them back. And even if I could, he would still be with his new girlfriend and not with Monica, so that wouldn't be any better, would it? Monica would just be miserable again and at least she's apparently now got the money from the sale of the house, so she's not exactly strapped. In fact she should be quite comfy for the rest of her life, as long as she doesn't spend it all on daft therapies, of course.

I didn't exactly appreciate her coming round or the nice things she said about Thomas, but I suppose it was nice to see her looking better. She said it would be lovely to have me round to her new place for coffee like in the old days, and I murmured something along the lines of, yes, I've missed it too, then she gave me a quick hard hug and left. Really lovely flowers though. But I must say, it's all left me a bit on edge and upset. I didn't think I'd ever see her again. If anything it sounds like she's living even closer to me than before. And now it seems she wants to be friends again. It's completely insane.

As if I haven't got enough to deal with at the moment with Junior.

Would anyone notice if I locked my bedroom door at night, do you think?

What if he was in for breaking and entering?

Or rape?

Thurs 24 January - 11.00am
Just heard from Mr Lavish the agent that the Beeches (as in Mr and Mrs Beech – très bizarre, I'd thought the house was named after the trees – surely it should be Beechs?) have accepted my offer. In fact he indicated in his rather polite and hinting manner that they pretty much took his hand off for it. I've been onto my solicitor and told him to sort things out asap, I don't want to hang about, I can't stand the thought of being here any longer than I have to. I've just got to get away.

    So I went into the kitchen to hand over the good news to the many Hopkins in the place, and Mrs H was ecstatic and came and hugged me before jumping back almost immediately and apologising, and 'Her Sid' came over and shook my hand a little shyly for him and said he was 'right pleased' for me, and 'Our Matt' just nodded and smiled and said nothing, just looked at me in that way he does that makes me feel prickly, like I need to take an anti-histamine. I left Mrs H to sort out the details about removal firms and so on, and came up here to lock myself in my ensuite bathroom. I notice she can't take her eyes off her precious son. Neither of them can. I wish he'd leave.

Same day - 10.15pm

I feel sick. I want to cry and never stop. Don't know what's the matter with me. I just want to hide away and not see anyone or speak to them.

Mrs Hopkins just came up and knocked on my door. She asked if I was all right. I managed to pull myself together enough to tell her with a little laugh that of course I was all right, never better, just a little tired, and that I fancied a soak in the bath to relax.

I turned the taps on and heard a tiny movement which meant she had gone away. The steam filled the room till I could hardly see, and under the cover of the sound of the water, I sat on the carpet and sobbed into a towel, then I felt exhausted and cold and dragged myself into the bath to try to get warm.

What's wrong with me? Have I got whatever syndrome or disorder Monica has got? I feel so angry, but I don't want to shout or punch anyone, I just want to cry, curled up in a little ball in a dark quiet corner.

I just need this move to take place as soon as possible so I can get away from all these ghosts that whisper about me constantly. But at the same time, the thought of leaving here scares me. Going somewhere new. People asking me if I'm married or 'with' someone. Having to keep explaining, seeing that look in their eyes, pity and at the same time a sense of delight that they've found something salacious to tell their friends and family when they get back home – 'you'll never guess what!'

I want to hide. I don't want to be on show, there for everyone to comment on, speculate on, saying 'isn't it awful?' with that look of greedy pleasure on their faces as they try to consume my grief, my loneliness. But I've got to pull myself together, I can't stay in here like this, or the Hopkins' will be banging the door down and that son of theirs will be looking at me with his cheeky-lad look and saying 'alright Darlin'?'

On impulse I rang to invite myself round to Monica for a coffee some time. As soon as I began to dial her number, I regretted the impulse, but luckily for me she wasn't home.

Had dinner in my room this evening, listening to sad old blues songs on my ipod and staring out at the rain running down the black windows.

Fri 25 January - 9.45am
Oh God. I knew it was a mistake to call Monica last night. Now I've got to go for coffee one evening next week. She saw my number on her 'while you were out' bit on her phone, and of course she simply had to call me back, the bitch. Why can't she just erase her messages unanswered like normal people? I was just about to get into the car, Sid was taking me to the station to get the 11.30 train up to Jess and Murdo's for the weekend, and I was already feeling horribly overwhelmed and stressed about that.

Same day - 1.15pm
Why do people always chew so loudly on the train? There's a quiet carriage in the middle of the train for people who don't want to listen to other people's phone conversations or music. But are there are any rules about chewing? No! I can hear that woman with her bloody bag of toffees six seats down the carriage.

Had quite a nice cup of railway coffee to go with Mrs Sid's sandwiches. I've listened to all my music and now I'm starting a new book. Feeling a bit more relaxed now that the chewing person has got off. But I'm trying to pretend to myself that nothing awful is going to happen at Jess's, that it will be a nice, relaxing and happy time, though secretly I'm dreading it. At least it's only for a few days.

Wed 30 January – 3.15pm
Monica's tonight – and I'm desperately nervous.

    Just got back from Jess and Murdo's last night after a gruelling and not quite great long weekend. It was better than I'd expected so I suppose that's a good thing, but I felt awkward, it just wasn't quite the same as being there with Thomas.

    They made me so welcome, and Jess fussed over me like a mother hen, but I just couldn't seem to assert myself, plus the journey itself really knocked me for six – next time I must take Sid up on his offer to drive me all the way. Anyway, I did it, so that might lay ghosts to rest a bit – maybe my next trip up there will be more relaxed and less like gazing into the past.

    But I was so exhausted I just fell into bed last night. Then I slept late this morning – and I'd half-forgotten about Junior until I bumped into him when I was having a little potter in the garden. He smirked at me and said 'wotcha', I believe it was. I'm probably being a bit mean, I suppose he can't help being common and a jailbird. He then said 'I expect you're glad to be 'ome?' I said yes, but then I know I was a bit rude, I turned away and went back indoors and shut the door on him.

    Then I've spent an hour going through papers from the solicitor about the house purchase, and other post. And only then did I remember, when Mrs Sid brought me some lunch and asked what time I'd like dinner, that I was due to go to Monica's this evening for coffee, and since then I've been alternately planning on cancelling and telling myself it'll be nice. But I'm so nervous.

    Oh it'll be all right. Won't it? I mean I've got to face her sometime, and this will return her call to me in a relatively painless way and then no one can say it's my fault we're not still friends.

It's just coffee, for God's sake, it's not like I'm going to Chapley's with her.

Later same day - 8.20pm
Fortunately I haven't seen as much of Junior as I'd feared. I think he went out just after I saw him in the garden. Perhaps he's found a nice flat or bedsit or something. Or a job. Then he could move out, have his freedom, be independent, his own boss, and I could stop worrying about what to tell the Hs when they find out I've started locking my bedroom door.

Had a nice dinner in the little sitting room upstairs on a tray in front of a re-run of Inspector Morse. V pleasant. Now I'm just going to fling on a nice top and some decent jeans and pop round to Monica's. My stomach churns at the thought of it, but I suppose it'll be okay. At least the Hopkins' know where I am so if I don't come home this evening, they'll know where to tell the police to find my corpse.

Same day - 1.10am
I'm so glad I went.
I've been round there four hours – a long coffee! But it didn't feel long at all, the time just flew by, and when I left, I saw she had tears in her eyes as she thanked me for coming, and I said that it was my pleasure and was a bit surprised to find that I really meant it. I said, we must do things together more often, go out perhaps, being single isn't easy for anyone these days.

She'd bought some gorgeous mini Florentines and little buttery melt-in-the-mouth biscuits, got fresh flowers on the little side tables, chilled some wine 'just in case', and the whole place was full of the delicious scent of filtering coffee when I got there.

It was a little bit awkward at first, which was only to be expected, but then things warmed up and we talked and laughed and she told me about her therapy, and had a little weep, and of course there was the coffee and the accompaniments, and it was all very civilised. I was able to thoroughly relax and enjoy myself, and I think – I hope – she enjoyed the evening too.

And I really learned something about myself this evening. Something which surprised me a little, and pleased me too.

I learned that after everything I've been through, everything she's been through, after all that's passed between us, I discovered that I could sit there and smile and chat and laugh and eat her Florentines and drink her lovely crisp wine and her deep and rich coffee, that I could sit and enjoy her hospitality and sparkle. And all the time be thinking - how much I hate her and - of the best way to kill her!

It was wonderful, actually, because as I say, I was there for four hours, more or less, and I really had a great time – planning how to do it. That laughing bitch, chatting oh so candidly about her therapy, about her regrets - she killed my Thomas. I will never, never, ever forgive her for taking him from me. I hope she burns in hell. Sooner rather than later if I have anything to do with it.

Hmm, burning. That's an idea. Must start some serious planning. It will have to be soon, because of course, once I move, it will be so much further to come, and so much less convenient.

But no, not burning. I hate the smell of anything charring, and burning flesh would be simply too much. I've already done a spot of research – this is my chosen medium – Ethylene Glycol.

Ethylene glycol is a good one, because it's basically the active ingredient in anti-freeze, screen wash and numerous other household chemicals, cheap, easy to use and readily obtainable. Perfect!

According to the Crime Channel on the TV, it's sweet to the taste, and although it's usually coloured light blue or a greeny blue when in its 'official' form, it can be insinuated into soups, beverages, jellies, or other desserts and is very difficult to detect as the initial symptoms resemble the onset of a flu or a nasty tummy bug (very nasty!). It's also the kind of thing that can be found in almost anyone's shed or garage without arousing suspicion; it's a perfectly normal thing to have sitting around forgotten on a shelf. Usually administered by a loving spouse in some specially prepared dish, I can't think of a single reason why I shouldn't use it on Monica. I've been thinking about this for quite a while.

But I need to think a bit longer about this, work out the details. Obviously I want it to look like either an accident or suicide. I don't want to fall under the least amount of suspicion. Obviously!

Hmm.

I wonder what he was in prison for? Do you think I could ask? Would it be a bit rude? Or just in really bad taste?

But what if he knows some interesting ways of disposing of bodies or obtaining weapons? What if he knows someone who knows someone who would 'get rid' of a person, any person, no one in particular, for a pre-agreed sum of money, no questions asked?

Tempting. It would be so easy for me, so convenient. But then I wouldn't have the satisfaction of watching the light die in her eyes as she drew her last breath, and it is very important to me to have some kind of closure, so reluctantly, I think I'm going to have to do the job myself rather than outsourcing.

Right then. Give me twenty-four hours to rack my brain and come up with a cunning plan.

Oh goody, another little project!

Wed 13 Feb - 3.15pm

Oh dear! Mrs H in tears due to Tetley-versus-Twinkle shrubbery-based conflict. Thank God Sid was here with the garden hose to break things up. Not quite sure who was winning – there seem to be similar quantities of clumps of fur in each of the shades and it's all over the lower part of the lawn. Sparrows are stealing bits of it to snuggle in around their first clutch of babies. Mrs H has given me fair warning that the peach soufflé will not be up to her usual standard and, in her words, 'we might as well get a Mackers in and 'ave done wiv it.'

The vet came personally to supervise the recovery of the patient (and how much is that going to cost me? I shudder to even guess.) He declared her to be out of danger but in need of rest and recuperation.

Aren't we all?

Thursday 14 Feb - 9.35am

This morning, before I did anything else, I nipped into the kitchen and enquired about our little convalescent. Then I had to endure ten whole minutes of Mrs H's descriptions of all the real and imagined symptoms of our battle-scarred feline. I made all the right concerned-sounding noises, and was 'relieved' by the vet's report. Well, not so much the report as the fact that his fee turned out to be mercifully lower than I had feared. Finally, as I turned away to go, feeling quite proud of my ability to feign interest in our beastly little memento of Clarice, I caught Sid's eye and he gave me a broad wink above his tabloid and nearly caused me to laugh and spoil everything! I managed to turn it into a cough at the last moment and then had to fob-off Mrs H's concerned attempts to call me a vet, I mean doctor, too. He's a cheeky one, that Sid Hopkins.

Tues 2 April - 5.10pm
I've sold the house and we're getting ready to move!
I'm surrounded by boxes. If Mrs H is excited, and Mr H is stressed (don't know why, it's my Royal Doulton on the line here), then Son Matt is as relaxed as the April days are long.

Yes he's still here. It's been two and a half months now. For some reason I fondly imagined he would have moved out by now – the idea, as I recall, was for him to come here for a short while until he made other, permanent, away-from-here arrangements and got on his feet a bit, found a job, that sort of thing.

Not only that, but I suspect he's coming with us to the new house! As I was going into the kitchen this morning, I'm sure I overheard him, (now known to me, secretly of course, as Hopkins' Darling) saying something to his parents about how he hopes he's got a bit more space in his new room at The Beeches as his room here is, and I quote, 'ardly any bigger than me bleedin cell at Wansworf.' Bloody cheek!

So, he was in Wandsworth, was he? Isn't that a high-security prison?

What the hell am I going to do? I mean, all this time I've been assuming that when I move house, it will be just myself and my two members of staff – I hadn't expected to be opening a half-way house for ex-cons down on their luck. It really is too bad! How can I get rid of him? I still don't even know what he was imprisoned for, it could have been absolutely anything! And whenever I see him, which is mercifully rarely, I find myself shaking and horribly intimidated. I'm scared silly and I hate myself for it. Surely this can't go on much longer?

I know I should talk to the Hopkins', but…I just can't face it at the moment. I just keep hoping and praying that somehow they'll just kind of know that it's time for him to leave. Surely they at least remember this was just supposed to be a temporary arrangement? He must have some friends to turn to? Some old lag? Or some ex-girlfriend? Why doesn't he go out more? I mean, surely it's not healthy for a young man of his age - whatever that is – to stay in so much with his aged parents? Why doesn't he – I don't know – go to the pub or bingo or something? I feel like a prisoner in my own home. Even though I hardly see him, I feel as though he's always there, watching me. I'm convinced they tell him about me, what I'm up to, things I've said, things about my past, about Thomas. I mean, perhaps they don't, but somehow I'm convinced they do.

Same day, a bit later
Oh My God!!!!
Now I can't even walk around what used to be my own home without literally bumping into half-naked ex-prisoners in what used to be my own hallway!

I just came out of my bedroom to run downstairs for something, and there he was, practically dripping on the carpet, a very inadequate towel wrapped around his waist, and that daft self-satisfied look on his face as I gave a little frightened gasp and a squeak of surprise and then got all flustered and ridiculous because of all that chest on display. I was so embarrassed and he just laughed! And he didn't even apologise! And what on earth was he doing using one of the upstairs bathrooms anyway? There's a perfectly – oh yes, the shower isn't very good in the little bathroom in the Attic, and yes, actually, now I think about it, it is very small, and a bit dark, if he wanted to have a shave. Wouldn't want him to cut his throat, would we?

But even so, he could have still either forewarned me or taken a bathrobe or a bigger towel or better yet a full set of clothes, or – or something! Why did he have to let me bump into him? Why did he have to emerge at that precise moment? And there are plenty of much larger towels in the house!

Could he have possibly engineered it? Surely he wouldn't, would he? What could he possibly have to gain from it? Apart from exposing himself to me, that is? Or undermining my confidence? Shall have to ask Monica about it.

Another dinner out this evening with Monica. As I haven't felt like writing any journal entries for a couple of months, I should just say she and I have seen each other at least twice a week since that first time, plus we often go to parties and events together. 'The Two Merry Widows', as Nadina called us a few weeks ago at her bash, though she didn't know I'd heard her, but even so…I wanted to rip her face off!

I haven't actually done anything about getting rid of Monica other than to day-dream happily about it. Still don't even know if we've got any Ethylene Glycol, let alone managed to figure out how to deploy it.

But Monica's getting so clingy of late. She doesn't want me to move, and all the time it's 'let's do such and such – before you move'. That phrase is constantly on her tongue – before you move. Before you bloody move. We've got to do everything before I move. I mean, it's not like I'm going to Australia (I'm beginning to wish I were) – it's only bloody Stow-on-the-Wold. It's as if she thinks she'll never see me again. I wish! She's getting on my nerves! But I'm desperately hoping I'm not letting her see that. I want everyone, including Monica herself, to feel that the two of us are on the very best of terms – for future necessity.

Oh, must stop, Mrs H needs me.

Same day - 00.45am

Anyway, all through dinner, I was thinking how easy it would be to slip a little drop of the 'good' stuff into her drink, into her sauce, into her dessert coulis. Especially as she'd already had a skinful. I can't believe how much that woman drinks. Like the proverbial carp. Or a salmon, drinking her way upstream only to flap about and gasp and die in the shallows. And we were in a quiet part of the restaurant (I really did wonder if the waiter thought Monica and I were a couple, he put us in such a lovely dim, romantic spot, the old softie). When she went to the loo (twice) I could have easily enhanced her food slash drink with a little drop of something from a special little bottle in my bag.

    She wouldn't have noticed, I'm absolutely certain. I mean, the waiter brought a second bottle of wine to the table at Monica's own request as we were about to tuck into our entrées, and she was already slurring then, and trying to be funny, saying 'an exchellent vintage, my good man, thish ish the best sherry I've ever tashted.' And he pointed out it was exactly the same wine as the bottle of white she'd already drunk, to which she replied 'thash worr I mean' and she hooted like the Queen Mary at that. She'd had at least four G & Ts (with almost no T) waiting for me, then three glasses of white wine to my one, all on an empty stomach. The woman's a total lush.

    And of course, if 'after the fact', the police asked me about our meal, I could say that she'd had a lot to drink, that we were very close friends, that she'd wanted to be more than just friends (hence romantic table in a dark corner at her request), and that she was depressed and upset about my moving out of the area and my unfortunate but unequivocal rejection of her romantic advances. I could then say that, 'to tell you the truth, officer, my main reason for moving away is to avoid the difficult situation, to whit, the strain her increased desire for intimacy is placing on our long-standing friendship, added to her possessiveness. She's making me feel uncomfortable.

'Not only that but I've noticed how much alcohol she has been consuming, which can't be good for someone on so many antidepressants slash antipsychotics. And when I took her home after our dinner, as she had to leave her car behind at the restaurant due to being under the influence of a considerable amount of alcohol, she became…' (and here I would delicately avoid becoming unladylike and graphic) 'upset and – a teeny bit difficult when I refused to stay the night. She started to cry and beg and to say how much she loved me, and it was all very uncomfortable. I assured her we would always be friends and when I tried to leave, she started to cry and cling again. Of course, I felt uncomfortable leaving her, but, well, one didn't for one moment think she was so desperate as to take her own life, one simply thought she'd wake up in the morning feeling embarrassed and with a frightful hangover. Poor, sad Monica, how tragic! Do you think she did it with her sleeping pills, or the medication she takes for her mental disorder?'

Feel so much better now! I wonder how much antifreeze you need to kill someone? Must Google it. I could probably put it into an old perfume bottle and put it in my bag without any real difficulty (unless of course you do need a pint or so of the stuff in which case, I'd probably need a rucksack, which might look a tad out of place with high heels and an up-do). Then if anyone should see me with the bottle in my hand, I could just say I was having a little spritz of scent whilst Monica trotted off to the ladies' because – how embarrassing! – I'd just realised I'd forgotten to put some perfume on, and I didn't want her to think I was depressed and un-self-caring following the recent death of my husband, as I knew she'd worry. And I could say I waited until she went to the loo so that she wouldn't see it as a sign I was ready to move on…oh dear…and then at this point I could become upset again and incoherent with emotion.

Well, if I were a police-person, I'd be convinced!

Same day - 1.30am
Wow, I've just been looking on the internet and it looks like quite a small amount of this stuff is a fatal dose. I'm quite impressed actually – the stuff has really gone up in my estimation, it's absolutely lethal! So long as you don't use the more modern, kinder-to-the-environment-and-you organic stuff. I need to find some grotty old back street place with low moral fibre as well as cheap deals on car stuff.

I'm so excited! I haven't felt this good in months! I can't wait to start on my new project. And I will have to really crack on with it as we are moving in just 11 days! I'd better invite Monica along to a couple more 'before I move' events – I know, I'll tell her there's a late frost due and I want to protect my car engine, something like that. I might even be able to get her to handle the bottle or something, make it look more convincing than leaving a bottle wiped completely clean of prints in her garage. That always arouses suspicions.

Right. First thing tomorrow (or today, really I suppose it will be) I'll have a little nose around in our garage. I'll pretend I'm chucking out old stuff we don't need to take with us when we move, or I'm concerned about chemical spillage in the removal lorry, something like that. Then, if we've got any, especially if the bottle's old and a bit grotty, it's all local colour as far as the police will be concerned. And that will save me the bother of having to do any actual procuring of the poison.

Though of course, there's something to be said for the idea that, feeling depressed, Monica went out specifically to buy a product to help her make away with herself. But how likely is it she'd choose anti-freeze? I mean, surely she'd be more likely to choose sleeping pills rather than a product with really messy side-effects?

And also, how would she know in advance that she was going to be depressed after I'd turned her down and gone home, leaving her to her misery? I have to say, this killing people lark leaves a lot of I's to dot and T's to cross. There is just so much to take into consideration.

Hmm. Spur of the moment or planned suicide? A tough choice.

Will sleep on it. Feel like I will have a really lovely refreshing sleep now that I've got something interesting and fun to muse on.

Thurs 4 April - 2.40pm
Feel ridiculously fluttery and pathetic. And quite cross, though I'm not sure if I'm cross with him or with myself for being embarrassed etc. Bloody hell!

I bumped into Junior coming out of the garage with no shirt on (it's only the first week of April for God's sake! Why can't he wrap up warm like the rest of the world?) and of course I was rendered totally stupid by all that bare male flesh (again!) and he knew it too – the Bastard – he just grinned at me in that stupid God's-gift kind of way he has and I felt myself blushing like a school-girl and couldn't remember what I'd gone out there for – and then, when I did remember, I was completely flustered because obviously when I remembered, I couldn't just say, oh yes, I came out to see if we've enough anti-freeze on hand, as I want to kill my friend with it, so then I just had to turn on my heel and go back into the house, and I'm absolutely certain I heard him laughing to himself. Hateful man. Why the hell is he still here? And why haven't I got the balls to tell him to get out? Well. To be honest I mainly haven't got the balls because his mother is such a divine cook and an excellent housekeeper. And his father will drive me anywhere I want to go at any time I choose to go there. But that's all beside the point.

Same day - 5.15pm
Anyway, I've now managed to sort out my hormones sufficiently to get past Junior and into my own garage, and I can't believe my luck, I've found exactly what I wanted - a bashed about grotty can that looks about fifty years old and is only half full or so; it's even got a little skull and crossbones design on it with a warning about the dangers of misuse. How thoughtful!

I've arranged to see Monica for the pictures and supper at her place this evening – gave her a lot of guff about not wanting to inconvenience Mrs H as she's up to her ears in packing up my Royal Doulton and fussing over the cat, and Monica said all sweetly, well would I like to pop back to hers afterwards for a night-cap slash snackette and so of course I said, all surprised and pleased, well yes, that would be really lovely if she was sure she didn't mind and she was absolutely not to go to any trouble...

Tee Hee. I'm on a high, I can't believe how nicely it's all falling into place.

Pity we couldn't just skip straight to the anti-freeze soup but I suppose one must build up to these things. So another bloody film to endure with Her Hitchcockness. I suppose it's the least I could do for my best pal! And it is her big send-off, after all.

I've got a Gucci perfume bottle that is almost empty, and as I'm ready to sacrifice the last precious drops (and as I've already got about another three bottles of the same one) to the cause so I'm going to swill it out and half-fill it with you-know-what and add a drop of pink food colouring just to make it look a bit more like something other than what it is, if you see what I mean, after all a can of anti-freeze in my shoulder bag would look a tad odd even in our enlightened times.

    Bottoms up!

Same day - 11.55pm
What a bloody disaster! I can't believe that selfish cow is still alive and kicking, it's so fucking unfair!!!

Well, I sat through the worst film I have ever seen (Lost in Translation x The English Patient = This Evening's Tedious Offering!!!) – it was about absolutely nothing, nothing happened and it took almost two and a half hours for it to not happen. Critically acclaimed my arse.

So I wasn't in the best of moods, and I'd be the first to admit I may have been a bit snippy with her – moaned about how she'd said she was taking me to see something good, etc, and then we went back to hers as planned, but both a bit snotty with each other by this time, and I was half-inclined to bin the whole idea and reschedule, but then I thought of all the fun I'd had planning it and all the trouble I'd gone to, so I thought I might as well go ahead with it, and tried to be extra-nice to Monica to make up for it.

So we got ourselves comfy in the den and she left me to sort out drinks and she pootled off to the kitchen to drum up a bit of food. Only when she came back it was all dim-sum and that sort of dry finger food, nothing you could slosh a bit of anti-freeze into without anyone noticing.

But I didn't despair, because I thought I would simply stick it in the drink once she'd had a few of her usuals. Only she wandered off with her drink and chucked it down the sink and came back with a nice lemon tea, said she fancied a change and was trying to lose a few pounds, and would I like to try some?

It was all a bit frustrating.

Like she needs to lose any weight, if anything she could do with gaining about 10 pounds, the bony cow.

So anyway, I went to the loo, came back and she'd got me a fresh voddie, but this time she'd put it in a bright blue glass, said she'd dropped the old one and smashed it, and wasn't she an idiot. All a bit odd, I thought, but nothing to trigger any alarm bells.

And then I went to take a sip.

I think I'd read that anti-freeze doesn't have any particular smell, though I'm not sure. But there was just something odd about the drink. I'd had a few drinks by then myself, so although I was not exactly sober I was hardly three sheets to the wind, but even so, it was as if the whole world slowed down as I lifted the glass to my lips, and over the rim, I could see her eyes, bright and shining and eager, watching me greedily, her lips a little too moist at the corners as if she was almost salivating, as the liquid tilted towards my mouth, and I just suddenly became convinced – as I say there was a very slight odd sweet smell, and this bluish tinge which could just have been from the glass, and then there was the way she was avidly watching me, her eyes shining, her lips disgustingly wet.

So I just slammed it down on the table and leapt up and gabbled something about forgetting to tell Mrs H something about the china, and I grabbed my bag and raced for the door, Monica following me slowly and calmly with this strange, half-amused smile on her face as if she knew I knew and thought it was really funny, not put out at all, but it was as if it didn't really matter, there was no rush. As if she knew she could just get me next time.

So I just did a quick air-kiss and fled. And it was only once I actually got back home and was putting my jacket on the stairs that it occurred to me that Monica had not said one syllable from the moment she handed me the glass, nothing except that weird smile and her excited eyes and her wet lips glistening.

That woman's a total whack-job.

Fri 5 April - 10.25am
I think it must have been the drink talking. This morning I can't see why I was so freaked out last night. My imagination must have been working overtime. That or my guilty conscience. It's because I know what I'm planning to do to her and deep down I'm afraid of her retaliating, probably in exactly the same way – after all she's on the internet, she can do research, like anyone else. And after Thomas, there no doubt in my mind she's got over her squeamish couldn't-kill-a-crow-ness. I could believe her capable of anything now.

    Or else the tension must just be getting to me. Moving is a very stressful experience – one of the worst stress-inducing events one experiences, apparently. That and changing jobs and losing a partner.

    Must think of another way of getting this dratted anti-freeze into that cow.

Sat 6 April - 10.05am

Slept late this morning and was woken up by a terrific pounding on the front door, and I was halfway down the stairs screaming 'don't let them in!' before I realised that 1) Junior was gawping up at me with great interest because 2) I was only wearing my baby-doll pyjamas and 3) Mrs H was already there, sliding back the chain and opening the front door

I needn't have panicked – it wasn't the police, just some wretched Hot-tub salesman Mrs H sent away with a flea in his ear. But it meshed so perfectly with what I had been dreaming only a few seconds earlier – the dream in which Monica had sent the police after me for trying to poison her – and so quite reasonably, and subconsciously, when I heard the pounding on the door, I absolutely shot out of bed in sheer terror thinking the game was up.

Then I didn't want to turn round and go back upstairs because of my little tiny baby-doll knicker-short thingies but I could hardly walk up the stairs backwards, so in the end I had to brazen it out and turn and go back up the stairs to my room, but I'm positive he stared at my bum – it felt as if hot little holes were being drilled into it by a lecherous ex-lag.

I heard Mrs H say to him,

'She really don't like them door to door salesmen, does she?'

'But how did she know who was there?' He asked her a little too shrewdly for my liking. I could visualise her usual shrug as she said,

'Well she must of, ay?'

Fortunately, you can't argue with logic like that.

But as I rounded the top of the stairs I glanced down to see him still standing down below in the hall, looking up at me. Our eyes met briefly before I turned away with the distinct feeling that I'd been rumbled. As I reached my room, I heard the kitchen door softly thump closed behind him but I could still picture his eyes, missing nothing, and I knew that sharp ex-con brain of his was puzzling over the small incident.

Got showered and dressed really, really quickly and then dashed to the shops to buy bigger pyjamas to ensure no more awkward incidents like this morning. Chose six pairs, all pink flannelette, with collars, sleeves and long trousers that I'll have to turn up if I don't want to trip over them and break my neck. No part of me will be visible apart from my head, fingertips and big toes. I just know I'm going to look like a five-year-old in her big sister's pyjamas, but I don't care, it will be worth it. That'll teach him to ogle my bum!

Same day - 8.20pm
But what am I going to do about Monica? I keep thinking about what happened the night before last, and I can't quite make up my mind. Did she really try to turn the tables on me or was it all my imagination? Did I just panic and lose my nerve? I can't help remembering how cleverly she has manipulated me before – first making me think she had killed Clarice, and then, making me think she wanted me to kill Huw and that girlfriend of his, making me feel we had a kind of unspoken pact to help each other out with our little problems. She's smart enough to know how to use my own brain against me, how to twist my thoughts, my emotions, how to push me into a course of action I would normally think twice about taking. Is she still messing with my head?

I just don't know. I thought I smelled something weird in my drink last night, and now in the sane light of daytime shopping, I feel like I over-reacted and could she really have been staring at me the way I thought she had? And now I can't even remember if anti-freeze has an odour? I remember reading it had a sweetish taste, but nothing about smell. And I don't want to go out to the garage and find it and have a bit of a sniff, because ten to one a certain Someone would come in at that exact moment.

Well, I mean. She was drunk, wasn't she? Wasn't she? I mean, we'd both been pretty much piling it away as usual, until she hauled out the herbal tea and outmanoeuvred me once again. So she probably was sort of staring at everything with a kind of glazed, happy look, or else she was so drunk she couldn't focus properly and was staring at me oddly because she was having trouble getting a fix on me? I bet that's it.

I can't believe it! I completely panicked and let my over-active imagination freak me out so that I didn't go through with my plan. For God's sake, Monica could have been dead by now! Why am I such a spineless moron? I could have got back from shopping just in time to receive the terrible news about the sudden and tragic death of my best friend!

I'm such an idiot!

Another lost opportunity!

Now I've got to think of another time and place and scenario and everything. Shit! Shit! And thrice shit!

Same day - 10.45pm
What about a leaving party? I could invite all my friends. That will provide me with lots of witnesses! If we pack all the furniture and carpets and everything, hire plastic catering-ware and have a lovely buffet and some music, and, obviously, lots and lots of bubbly, and of course, colourful antifreeze-laced cocktails, it should be fun. Surely at a party in my own home there should be sufficient opportunities to a) provide an excruciating scene in which Monica comes off looking like a psycho and b) nip a spot of the good stuff into her Buck's Fizz or – I know – her Pimms, because Pimms always tastes weird and then there's the colour and all the old tat you stick in it will mask any amount of anti-freeze or screenwash or whatever.

    Oh goody! Game on again.

Sun 7 April - 3.30pm
Mrs H is not in a good mood now I've broken to her the news that I want to host a party in this house next week. You'd think I'd suggested burning babies at the stake judging by the horrified expression on her face. She's banging about like anything in the kitchen – I'm upstairs in my bedroom with the door closed and I can still hear her ranting above Beyoncé! Even Tetley is giving her a wide berth.

'A party, Mrs Powell? Here? Not before we move, Mrs Powell? Surely not?'

I could hardly have it after we move, could I? Not that I said that to her of course, I'm not completely mental. I was a bit tart with her, which I'm sure I will live to regret slash pay for one way or another over the next few days. I simply said quite snottily,

'Yes, Mrs Hopkins, in this house. It should be possible to arrange to hold a party here as we don't move until next week, and I don't need anything truly elaborate. I'm going to go and ring round my friends now to get an idea of numbers.'

But I wish I hadn't called her 'Mrs Hopkins' like that, she and Sid have been so good to me.

Anyway, I told her how I wanted it to be done, gave her a rough guesstimate re number of guests and food and drink and so on, and went back to the sitting room to sort out my guest list and now, I'm happy to say, I've rung all sorts of people and although some can't make it at such short notice, most of them can and said how delighted they'd be to come to my 'leaving do'. I'm quite excited! It's been ages since I had a party! Not since before Thomas…

I've let Monica know, of course, and soothed the troubled waters with much oil not to mention soft soap, and she sounded pretty keen too, but whether that's because she thinks she'll get another stab at poisoning me before I can poison her, I'm not too sure. Anyway she went out of her way to be excited and happy and accommodating. She made too many suggestions of course, so that already the affair is going to be far more lavish than I'd originally intended, which won't please Our Lill. But it doesn't matter, Monica's happiness will be short-lived. And I've roped her in to kind of co-host it with me, told her I want it to be a party to remember.

'Oh Cressida,' she said, 'it will certainly be that!' I could definitely hear the malice in her chuckle as she said it. She sounded exactly like an arch-villain. I could practically picture her rubbing her hands together in glee at the prospect, could imagine her going 'mwah ha har!'

Thurs 11 April - 7.10pm
The house is looking absolutely stunning – I can't believe how much effort the Hopkins clan have put into making my party go with a swing! And even Junior has been fetching and carrying and getting up and down ladders hanging fairy lights everywhere and flirting outrageously with Monica whilst she swagged the place out with exotic flower-and-twig creations.

I didn't really make much in the way of introductions but of course she already knew who he was, and curiously, he seemed to know a good bit about her too – yet more proof that Mrs H has been keeping 'everyone' informed about my life, as if I had any doubts!

So – an hour to go until the earliest of my guests arrive - there are always one or two who arrive inconsiderately early to any party, some people just don't know how to behave! And at the other end of the scale there are those who don't leave until well after the rest of one's guests – that's even more of a faux pas than being too early in my book. But of course, if one cut out all those sort of people from one's guest list, well, the list would be a bit on the short side, wouldn't it?

I'm almost ready myself, so just thought I'd make a quick note of my thoughts etc.

There's lots of gorgeous-looking food, and plenty of drink, obviously, couldn't manage without that! Junior is the self-appointed DJ for the evening, though in reality he'll just be changing the CDs. Mrs H is going to ferry the food around and Sid is going to stay out of sight in the kitchen as he looks like a bouncer at a borstal, and that will be apt to spoil the mood. Don't think we'll need his special 'talents' this evening. At least, I hope it won't be that kind of party!

We've still got the sofas but apart from those and a couple of tables for the booze, the downstairs part of the house is completely empty. Eerily so, in fact. It reminds me of a corpse – all life extinct and of course it's the life that makes a house into a home, layering it with warmth and familiarity and individuality, and the lack of it makes an empty, soulless house. But of course, that's just perfect for a party!

It's a good thing there are oodles of people coming, because to be honest I'm finding it rather unsettling here now that almost everything has been packed. Still, it's only for another 2 days, then I'll be off to sunny Gloucestershire. The Hs go the day after tomorrow, to give them a day to start getting things straightened out a little bit before I join them at the new house on Sunday – their suggestion.

I was going to remain here up to the last moment, because my bed will be one of the last things to go, but now I don't know. If the house isn't populated with other people, I'm not sure I can bear to be here. I still have vague concerns about Clarice haunting the place from sheer spite. And my memories of my life with Thomas are pretty much haunting me too – I constantly remember a snatch of conversation here, a look, a word there, and I find it - not comforting as people would always have you believe - but very much the reverse. And now that the move is imminent, the haunting seems worse. I keep wondering if I'm making a terrible mistake. My emotions are yoyoing back and forth till I don't know where I am. Grief overwhelms me and I feel so empty and lost.

So on balance I think the place will give me the screaming meemies if I'm here alone with no furniture, even just for one night.

Speaking of screaming meemies, Monica is acting as if nothing happened last week, (which after all, maybe nothing did? I just don't know anymore) though at the same time I think she's also avoiding me. She's been busy, busy, busy. She hasn't said very much to me all the time she's been here, too busy ogling my Housekeeper's jailbird son or going just that little too far up a ladder and flashing her rather middle-aged thighs at him. When she has spoken to me she's been all conventional small talk (odd considering her almost hysterical behaviour of a couple of weeks ago, and her former, clingy, can't-bear-to-lose-me manner) and happy polite little smiles. But it's making me wonder if I really did just imagine the whole thing with the drink. I think I'm too highly strung. I need to get away from here. And the build-up to tonight hasn't done my nerves any good. I'm still not quite sure what to do about her. Perhaps I ought to just move away and let bygones be bygones? Just walk away?

It's not just a question of having the guts to go through with it. Really, I just haven't the energy to carry on this vendetta against her any longer. This house move is quite the most exhausting thing I've had to do in my entire life. They do say, don't they, the moving is the most stressful thing you can do apart from death and taxes. And I really am sick to death with people coming in and out and asking me endless questions and taking things away to pack. I feel like I've been gradually diminished by parts of me being taken away a little bit at a time and stuffed into boxes and sealed shut. The packing people have been excellent – even Mrs H has been pleased with them – but that doesn't change the fact that it's been very, very stressful. The whole thing's become a nightmare. I shall be so relieved to flop into a chair at The Beeches and start the Recovery Period.

So, yes, I haven't got the same urgent desire to see Monica dead as I had, and now part of me is thinking, actually, why bother? I'm moving away, starting afresh, so why take my old misery with me like so much broken furniture?

But then, alive, Monica may continue to be a thorn in my side, a pain in my bum, a millstone round my neck, I've just got this sneaking suspicion. At the end of the day, I may well find that Gloucestershire just isn't far away enough.

So.

Still can't decide about tonight.

To poison or not to poison?

Eeny meeny miny mo…

Fri 12 April - 10.45pm
Last night, it all came flooding back to me once the party got started. It was the music to begin with. The last time I heard that song, I was dancing with Thomas.

It was at a party last Easter in the home of one of his work colleagues. We never usually bothered to go, but for some reason we'd both just thought, why not? We were just both in the mood for a party. The music was perfect, and we just came together in the middle of the floor, both very slightly tipsy, and I remember clinging to him and as we moved, I remember thinking how perfect we were for one another and how we had a lifetime of years of dances stretching out warmly before us. And the music and the candlelight, and the scent of him, and his arms around me and everything – it was all perfect.

So at my party last night, memories seemed to surround me and as I drifted out of the way of the dancers to stand back in a corner, I just gave into the temptation (stupidly) to close my eyes for a few seconds and think back to that Easter evening, and I'm sure I got a whiff of his aftershave, could conjure up the feel of his jacket on my cheek, then I was trying to remember his voice and, like iced water suddenly splashed in the face, along came Monica screeching with laughter and very unsteady on her feet, slapping me on the back rather too heartily and making me spill lemonade all down my dress and the whole illusion was smashed to smithereens and suddenly it was all back again, all the old energy, the rage, the anger, the strength to take her scraggy neck between my hands and wring the fucking life out of it, I wanted to dig my fingernails into her flesh and see her bleed, hear her beg me with her last breath to forgive her and to be merciful.

I was shaking with fury and so after a none-too-gentle slap on her back and a forced hoot of laughter, I turned away, nauseous and He was standing there, watching me with that - that odd, speculative look he has sometimes. Matt Hopkins.

And there was no time to think about covering up my feelings, disguising my behaviour, putting on my party face. I was convinced I was going to be sick, and he (quite gallantly, actually) must have guessed how I was feeling for he shoved me firmly out through the french doors and into the cool of the garden, where suddenly all was peaceful and coldly beautiful in the moonlight.

He pulled me down to the end of the garden, away from the noise and heat of the party and plonked me down on the little wall there and told me to take deep breaths and pull myself together for a few minutes. And while I did that, I kept thinking to myself, any minute he's going to pounce and I was feeling so exposed. But he didn't. After a couple of minutes, he offered me a cigarette. When I shook my head, he asked if I minded, and I said I didn't, so he just stood there smoking quietly and I just sat there gazing at the ghostly grey flowers swaying in the breeze. Not that it was romantic or anything, just – peaceful.

Then quite suddenly he said, 'so how are you planning on doing it?' And I was so surprised I couldn't even pretend I didn't know what he meant, and I didn't want to insult him by not answering him truthfully, as he'd been so sweet and everything and suddenly he seemed to be my friend, so I told him about the ethylene glycol. He didn't seem surprised, he certainly wasn't shocked. He just nodded and murmured something like 'yes, that's a good one'.

And he sat down next to me, and we just stayed there, enjoying the quiet. From the house I could hear the strains of some romantic old song, and because it was only faint, it actually seemed even nicer. After a few minutes, don't know exactly how it happened, I was leaning against his shoulder, with his arm around me, and I held out my hand for his cigarette, took a couple of drags from it and felt very French as I handed it back again and he placed it between his lips.

'She killed your husband, Thomas?'

I nodded, my throat too tight to speak. My hair snagged a little bit on his chin stubble.

'But I killed hers first.' I confessed. I wanted him to know the truth. But he waved that away. Details, details.

'How're you planning on giving her the stuff?'

'In a cocktail.' I said after a few seconds to regain my composure. I felt like I was really just making a suggestion, he was the one making the decision. He nodded again. Thoughtful.

'Might work okay.' He said. I didn't bother to reply, just leant against him. He was warm and solid, and I realised I didn't dislike him so much anymore. And he didn't sound so – well, common – anymore. He actually seemed quite nice. One half of my brain was standing back looking at myself with him, saying in disbelief, just how much wine have I had?

'What were you in for?' I couldn't help blurting out. I hadn't intended to, but it had bugged me for weeks. Months, even.

He laughed, I felt him turn slightly in my direction, looking at me in the moonlight. He ground his cigarette out on my lawn. No. Not my lawn any more.

'Have a guess.'

'Murder? Armed robbery? GBH?'

He laughed again and stamped out his cigarette butt on the ground. Shook his head but didn't loosen his hold on me.

'Fraud.' He said.

'Fraud?' I repeated. I could hardly believe it. I felt a tiny bit cheated. Plus, you know, it's a bit middle class.

'I scammed some tourists out of some money.'

I hoped I didn't sound disappointed when I said, politely, 'Oh? How much?'

'Fifteen million dollars.'

'Fifteen…Oh My God!' I began to giggle hysterically. 'Is that all?' I asked him when I caught my breath.

'That's a lot of money where I come from.'

I gave a rather unladylike snort of laughter.

'That's a lot of money where anyone comes from! What did you do, sell them London Bridge?'

He shook his head. 'Kensington Palace. Told him that once the Queen Mum died, it was on the market, not needed see, as the rest of them all had their own places already.'

'It's genius. I'd have loved to see their faces.'

'Thanks.'

'Americans, I assume?'

'Japanese.'

'Oh.'

We fell silent again, leaning against one another and enjoying the night.

'I also sold The Angel of the North five years ago. Hong Kong businessman. Only got 1.2 mill for that.' He sounded a bit crestfallen. 'Didn't get caught, though. Nice little earner.' Then,

'What sort of cocktails?' He asked. It took me a minute to back-track though our conversation before I knew what he was referring to.

'Well der – blue ones of course! Anything with blue curacao in it. I was just going to mix it with vodka and maybe something else, lemonade or some juice or something.'

'Got any actual blue curacao in the house?' He asked. I had to admit I hadn't. He gave me a pitying look in the moonlight. Like I'd let him down just a little.

'What kind of party is this?' He asked. He got up, pulling me up with him. 'You put on your happy face and go and mingle, I'll be back in ten minutes or so. Go and have fun.' He led me back to the house, and promptly disappeared through to the kitchen.

I'm a bit surprised to realise he's nice. By the time I went back inside, I was feeling all warm and happy. Then, twenty minutes later…

'Cocktail, Cress?'

I jumped out of my skin, looking round to find Monica at my elbow. Mummy's Little Helper, she was holding a huge tray of glasses containing cocktails in various colours and shapes and sizes. Each one was complete with little umbrellas and chunks of melon or pineapple or whole strawberries in them. Two of the glasses contained very attractive–looking icy-blue liquid, each with a gold plastic stirrer, an umbrella and a wedge of sugared lime. To be honest, I wasn't really sure I wanted to run the risk of tasting any of them, but Monica looked so bright and keen, and I glanced over her shoulder to the other room, where Matt stood by the table, watching. He nodded and smiled at me so I thought it should be okay, after all.

I selected a glass containing a bright orange drink with a little umbrella and a paper parrot on a stick along with a big lump of ice and a wedge of watermelon and a cherry. God alone knew how I was going to get to the actual drink.

'Thanks, Mon,' I said brightly with a smile at my best pal. She beamed back at me.

'Great party,' she said, 'I'm so glad we did this.'

We? But I let it go. Not long now

'And a really great idea of yours to serve cocktails,' I purred. She beamed again and at the same time somehow contrived to smile over her shoulder at Matt who raised his glass in a salute. She turned to me with a coy look, bending closer as she lowered her voice to a mere bellow above the music and laughter.

'He's gorgeous, isn't he?' She said. 'Do you know if he's seeing any one at the moment? Or, no wait, don't tell me, I bet he's married. He is, isn't he?'

Was he? Mrs H had never referred to a daughter-in-law, or grandchildren. But I had never actually asked – until tonight he hadn't exactly been my favourite person, so he was a topic I had studiously avoided.

'I don't think he's married,' I said. 'But if you like, I can try to find out. Though I'm not sure I'd exactly describe him as gorgeous, but I suppose he's not terrible-looking and he does seem quite sweet.'

'Cress! Are you mad? He's definitely gorgeous! And all your girlfriends are flirting with him. Even the married ones.'

I glanced around the room to see a number of pairs of eyes staring in Matt's direction. One woman wiggled her fingers in a dainty hello at him.

'Hmm. I suppose.' To be honest, at that point I really wanted to not be talking about Matt Hopkins. I'd just discovered something and I wasn't very happy about it. I wanted to change the subject. Toot sweet.

'What's in this anyway?' I waved the glass at her. She took it off me and glugged a great gulp of it, handed it back with an exaggerated wriggle that went from her head down to her hips and back again.

'Everything, I should think! It's got a helluva kick to it! Nice, but really strong. Just like – what's his name again?'

'Matt.' I told her. But she was already walking away to join him, going into what I call her Jessica Rabbit walk as she got within eight or ten feet of him. I watched him closely as she came in to land.

'Matt, Sweetie, just what is in this cocktail anyway?' She batted huge black lashes at him and leaned far enough forward that he must have been able to see right down the front of her dress to her gold high-heels.

He gave her a huge sexy grin, and my heart did a stupid little flip thing.

Yes. She was right. He was gorgeous. Damn.

'Well, there's some pineapple juice,' he began slowly, and she was hanging on his every word like it was some sexy game she had just invented. He quirked an eyebrow at me, not that she noticed. I wanted to turn away but couldn't seem to make myself do the actual manoeuvre of turning.

'Ye – es.' She said, giggling.

'And some cream of coconut,' he said leaning a bit closer and making it sound much too naughty. She leaned towards him, her boobs practically tipping her off balance.

'Ye – es.' She giggled again and I finally turned away, unable to stand any more. I heard him do a little low chuckle, sexy as anything, and he said to her,

'And of course, lashings of rum with maybe just a little splash of vodka.'

She did a shriek of mock-outrage that nearly rent my eardrum.

'I think you're trying to get me a little bitsy tipsy!' She said again, hardly able to speak for giggling. He joined in the laughing,

'Is it working?' He asked, winking.

'Not yet,' she said, 'try me with a really big one.' And then I heard her hoot with laughter.

Oh God, I thought, she's not only drunk, she's an embarrassing cliché. It was all too much. I went out of the room.

It seemed like a lifetime later – though it was actually only three and a half hours – that I finally managed to shut the door on the last of my guests. I felt exhausted. My lips ached from smiling constantly and saying '…and I'm going to miss you, too! Yes, Darling! Of course we will keep in touch, Gloucestershire's no distance really!'

But it had been okay – no one had thrown up and no one had started a fight. In my book, that's a successful party.

Only one problem.

Monica was still here.

I didn't really bother to count her amongst the guests because she always used to come and go as she pleased in the old days of our friendship. She and Matt had disappeared for quite a long time after the 'what's in the cocktail' conversation, and now she was still slow-dancing with him in the middle of the room, her boobs squashed against his chest, her hips clamped way too firmly to his for my liking. If I heard Move Closer or Love Don't Live Here Anymore one more time I was going to put on some Sex Pistols or something else loud and strident just to kill the mood.

I wandered through to the kitchen where Sid was sitting at the table drinking cocoa and reading the paper, surrounded by leftovers on plates and in front of him, a massive plate of sausages and chips.

Lill was washing up a few last cocktail glasses. I felt despondent, the way you do when you're tired and some other woman (the one that murdered your husband) is slow-dancing with the man you've just realised against all good sense and your own better judgement you really fancy. I plonked myself down at the table, and nabbed a chip from Sid's plate without thinking about what I was doing.

I had bitten it in half before I came to my senses with a flood of mortification but he waved away my apology, pushing the plate towards me.

'Plenty of 'em, Duck. Dig in. Bad for me clesterol, anyway.'

I took another with a grateful smile. Mrs H turned towards us.

'Well it certainly went off with a bang. Your party,' she clarified at my blank expression. 'It went well.'

'Oh yes. Yes it did, and mainly due to all your hard work. Thank you, Mrs Hopkins.' She inclined her head graciously.

'It wasn't nuffink, I'm glad it went well for you. Nice to say a proper farewell to your pals.'

'Well, I really don't know what I'd do without you, you've been like a mother to me, you're a gem, Mrs Hopkins.' It must have been the alcohol making me sentimental. She blushed and giggled.

'Oh, now, it's a pleasure, really. And you and poor Mr Powell have been wonderful to us. What with us losing the house, and everything, and giving Sid here a job and giving our Matt somewhere to stay when he first,' but here she hastily caught herself and launched off in a different direction, 'well anyway - and I've told you already, call me Lill, please. It's much better than keep calling me Mrs Haitch all the time.'

I felt touched, and a little bit emotional. Like I said, too much booze. When I thanked her, it came out as a broken whisper, and there were tears in my eyes. We all beamed at each other with new warmth. Then Sid let out an almighty belch, and I bolted for the cloakroom and vomited horribly for about ten minutes. Thank God for toilet duck.

When I crawled up to my bed in my naked bedroom, there was a glass of iced water on the floor by my bed, and actually in the bed, a hot water bottle had been placed to provide comfort. I was too exhausted to write in my journal, which is why I'm doing it this morning.

When I came downstairs this morning, the last of the few bits and pieces were being loaded into the van. Lill gave me a tight goodbye hug as if we wouldn't see each other again for months, and then they were off, leaving me alone in this shell, wondering what on earth to do with myself until my train leaves tomorrow morning.

Feel a bit depressed and wish I could have seen Matt this morning, even though I know I look terrible and even though I've a horrid suspicion he's still tangled up with Monica's long but admittedly rather middle-aged legs, her newly bleached-blonde hair spraying across his chest. I'm sure they snuck off during the party, absolutely certain, I didn't see either of them for an age, but again, don't really want to think about it.

Feeling morose and full of self-pity, I grabbed my few last things together then went to take a last look around the house and the garden. But it was all oddly soulless, and now that it was empty, it seemed quite unlike the home I'd known all these years. It felt like a bit of a let-down – it was almost as if I was a prospective buyer, seeing a new and unfamiliar house for the first time. Even the garden held no pleasure for me, I felt only an odd sense of detachment when I looked around. The only thing that I felt sorry about was that I didn't catch a last glimpse of that little git-of-a-cat Twinkle. My new life was waiting. Time to go.

I was actually on my way to the front door to leave the house forever when there was a loud knock. I went to the door, puzzled, and opened it.

Matt smiled at me from the step.

'Depressed? Or just sentimental?'

'Both,' I said. He held out his hand for the keys, and as I joined him outside, he locked the door, and put the keys back in through the letter box as I had arranged with the agent. He turned and tucked my hand into the crook of his arm.

'Let's go and grab a sarnie,' he said, 'and then we're going to the zoo.'

'I'm not five,' I grumbled, pleased.

We had a lovely day.

It felt a bit odd, especially as he insisted on paying for everything, it felt almost like a teenagers' date, but although there were a couple of awkward moments, we had a fabulous day – I can't remember when I last went to the zoo, but he made it so much fun for me, and nothing was too much trouble for him – he made sure I didn't miss any of the feeding times, bought me an ice-cream (yum!), a hotdog (yuck!) and a cuddly tiger-cub, took photos of me with my head through one of those giant picture postcard cutouts, so that I looked like an eighteen-stone black woman in a tiny yellow bikini.

There were some absolutely gorgeous big cats – tigers, white and yellow, Siberian and – whatever else they come in, and lions, and even some little servals, looking sleek and content in the sunshine. I just adored them all, huge cousins of Tetley and Twinkle. Who knew that I of all people could become a cat lover?

It was when we were sitting having our hotdogs at one of the less crowded cafeterias, sitting at an outdoor table watching the antics of some truly stunning scarlet macaws, that I asked him if anything interesting had happened after I left him in charge of Monica and took myself off to bed (following a quick dash to the loo to yak up Sid's chips, but I didn't mention that, obviously).

I don't quite know what I expected – I kind of thought he and Monica might have spent the night together, and I was dreading hearing him confirm it, for some reason.

He admitted he took her home – she was too drunk to drive herself. It appeared (I was sad to discover) she had declined to try any of the cocktails he had tried to force on her, cleverly switching to vodka and lemonade – no chance of sneaking any anti-freeze into anything so clean and clear. And then, he said, once he got her home, she had made a clumsy pass at him before passing out cold, as per all the best fiction, while he was making her a mug of black coffee.

'So I got out of there with my honour intact,' he ended up, laughing, but his eyes were watchful as he took in my studiously indifferent 'oh?'

There was a long pause. Then he balled up his food wrapper and throwing it in the bin, and sending mine after it, he dragged me to my feet, and turning led the way out to the path, saying over his shoulder,

'There're some hippos around this corner, I want to see if they remind me of my Ex.'

As we set off, he murmured, 'shame about the anti-freeze, though. That would have been a nice one.' I had to agree.

After a pub dinner that evening he delivered me to my hotel room, didn't linger at all, just kissed me on the cheek and took his leave, calling over his shoulder,

'I'll be here at nine o'clock prompt to drive you down to your new home.' He waved his hand above his head as he walked away, not turning even once. And I didn't mind, didn't feel lonely, just felt relaxed and happy and that life was full of possibilities. With the added bonus that I was going to be chauffeur-driven to Gloucestershire!

I slept like a log.

Sun 14 April - 10.20pm
A surprisingly good run down this morning. I may have been a teensy bit late, and although he was a little irritated, I noticed he didn't dwell on it. By the time we'd been on the road for half an hour (eleven fifteen!) he was in a good mood again.

I know I shouldn't make comparisons, but Thomas could sulk for hours when he put his mind to it. Matt seems to just let things wash over him and roll off the other side. Of course Matt is six years younger, and has a bit more of a happy-go-lucky con-merchant sort of way with him. If Matt had a motto it would be something along the lines of 'you win some, you lose some'. He's a bit more laid back than Thomas, I suppose. Not that we're involved in any way, God no! But I was just thinking how interesting it is that people can be so different, people one likes, not just one's husband.

And I have been in such a good mood all day – couldn't wait to see the new house, and I felt so excited as we got nearer. And when we finally arrived (and Lill and Sid were there on the door step, beaming all over their faces! I was so happy I barely even noticed Sid's filthy vest.) I felt as if I had finally come home. There was such a feeling of recognition when we came into the drive. I was quite surprised how familiar the house seemed when we got there, on an emotional plane, I mean. It was the most wonderful feeling. I feel so full of optimism and hope for the future.

I'm astonished at how quickly Lill and Sid have got to grips with things – my bedroom and bathroom are immaculate, the main sitting-room downstairs is exactly right, and even the other rooms are already beginning to take shape. Immediately we arrived and had a bit of a chat and some lunch and a look round the place, Matt and his parents set straight to work once more.

At first I felt a bit awkward and on the edge of things, but once again, they were so good to me, they very craftily drew me in – first by popping out to the terrace to ask me how I wanted a particular chair, or where I wanted a certain picture, and soon I was inside, sleeves rolled up and getting on with it right there with them, showing them where I wanted everything put.

Now, it occurs to me for the first time that I am very much in danger of acquiring a family. These Hopkins' are so clever at managing me, I hardly know things are happening until it's all too late. Perhaps Jess was right after all? But no, I know they would never hurt me or take advantage in the way Jess was afraid they might. I mean, they might sneakily move half their relatives into my attic, but I know I can trust them.

Anyway, it's far too soon to be thinking along those lines, I'm just being silly. And Matt and I are just friends that's all, his parents work for me, he knows it's handy and useful to help me out and keep on my good side – after all he's got a roof over his head, hasn't he? I must remember not to let my imagination run away with me. Anyway, he's a working-class ex-con, for God's sake!

Decided I would go out for a while and leave them to it. I felt overwhelmed, it was all a bit too intimate somehow. Couldn't tell from their expressions how they felt about it, but it doesn't matter, I don't need their permission to go out, I'm allowed to get on with my life.

But later, I felt a bit guilty, so I brought back some wine and flowers. Lill had made a lovely, comforting stew, and warmed some rustic bread in the Aga, which she already seems to be completely at ease with. The house was full of tempting scents and I ate far more than I ought to have done. I'll soon be the size of those hippos we saw at the zoo if I'm not careful!

I spent a quiet evening on my own in my upstairs sitting room, putting books and CDs on shelves and generally relaxing, music playing in the background, and Tetley had somehow made it upstairs against my better judgement and was lying sound asleep on the newly-positioned sofa as if she'd been doing that for years. It was all very calm and pleasant.

I might redecorate my sitting room. I could see myself lounging here happily against a backdrop of lime green walls and brilliant white woodwork etc. All bright and fresh and clean. I'm a bit fed-up with so much delicate peach and sensible neutrals.

Same day - 1.55am

I'm downstairs, in Mrs H's kitchen, clasping a mug of chamomile tea as if I need to suck all the warmth out through the china and into my still-shivering body.

I woke up. Nothing weird about that. I didn't hear a noise or anything, I wasn't frightened, not then. I just – woke.

I'm almost afraid to think about what I thought.

But, it was just that - I had – forgotten.

So I turned to his side of the bed, and he wasn't there and for just that nanosecond, I thought, oh, he must be in the bathroom.

Then memory flooded in, ten seconds too late, taking my breath, my joy, my warmth and I remembered. He wasn't in the bathroom. And he wasn't coming back. Not ever.

And I feel so – betrayed – by my memory because the few seconds following that brief moment when I thought he was just 'in the bathroom' were far, far worse than any I have ever I had in my life. Because it was so ridiculous, so mundane. Insignificant. And it's been months now, and that's the first time something like that has happened,

And now I can't sleep. At least, I'm afraid to. Now it feels as though at any moment my memory might betray me again with that blissful forgetfulness followed by a gut-wrenching misery that makes me rush to the bathroom and vomit.

For one moment I thought he was still alive.

Tues 16 April - 00.40am
At about eleven o'clock, my phone rang. It was my mobile, not the house phone which, due to the utter incompetence of my telecoms provider, won't be up and running for three whole days! They just don't seem to realise some of us actually have a life! Anyway.

The screen showed 'unidentified caller' and as soon as I answered it – which wasn't very quickly as I dithered about a bit because I wasn't sure whether to answer it or not – the person at the other end hung up.

At least, after a moment they did. First there was a longish silence, like someone was listening at the other end, and like a complete moron I was saying 'Hello? Hello? Is anyone there?' Which I always think is a ridiculous thing to say. I mean, in movies, the woman always walks through the darkened house towards the strange noise and she always says something pointless and pathetic like 'hello, is anyone there?' thus giving any murderer worth their salt the opportunity to pinpoint her exact position, and when it's a dodgy phone call, they keep pressing the receiver rest down – we haven't had those kind of phones for sixty or seventy years, but people still do it – press, press, 'hello, hello?' press, press, press, 'hello, is anyone there?' I mean, what are they going to say at the other end? 'Oh hi, it's your killer speaking, just thought I'd give you a ring, let you know I'm hiding behind the sofa…'

Actually I've got a feeling there is a whole series of comic horror movies that take exactly that view.

So I felt utterly foolish, and a little frightened by the long silence and then the line just going dead like that, and I could hear the uncertainty in my voice as I said, 'is anyone there?' I felt like a child afraid of the dark calling for her Mummy. It was humiliating. And very unsettling.

I kept telling myself it was probably a simple wrong number or something. But I couldn't forget that long silence, and over and over in my head I kept hearing myself like a fool. 'Hello? Hello, is anyone there?' And that thread of fear in my voice.

I went to bed twice. The first time was at about ten past midnight. I read for a while but felt fidgety and irked, what with the odd phone call and everything, so I got up and went down to the kitchen for a hot drink.

Some of the first things Lill had very kindly unpacked a couple of days ago were my chamomile tea bags and my favourite little Spode teapot and the matching mug that I always love to drink my herbal tea from – it feels a bit more special, somehow. Ritual is so comforting, isn't it?

The kitchen was in darkness, though, as all the various Hopkinses had retired to bed, obviously, and I couldn't blame them as they really have done so much this last few days.

I fumbled for the light switch and pressed it and for a second or two it seemed like nothing was going to happen. I almost, being a bit tense already, I almost panicked, but then there it was and the room filled with lovely light, warm and reassuring, and I felt okay.

So I sat for a while thinking about how lucky I am. Especially to have the Hopkins' with me. They have been wonderful. As usual. I seem to have said that a lot lately. I hope they never decide to leave me and go somewhere else.

Five minutes later
Would it be weird if I got involved with the ex-con son of my housekeeper and chauffeur?

Ten minutes later
I suppose it would be if it all went sour. I might even have to find a new housekeeper. And I wouldn't want to have to do that, Mrs H – Lill – is wonderful. No man is worth having to break in a new housekeeper. And I've got a soft spot for Sid too, quite apart from how useful he is. Thing is, it could all go horribly wrong. And then things definitely would be a bit weird.

Fifteen minutes later
But he is gorgeous-ish. And so sweet. And he did take me to the zoo. And buy me an ice-cream. And a fluffy tiger. And it takes quite a clever chap to scam that much money out of tourists, even if he did get caught.

Sixteen minutes later
No, it would definitely be a bit odd. And what would my friends say? Or Jess? One can't get involved with the help! She even warned me, months back, that I was getting too intimate with them. And that was before Matt came along – so what would she say now? What would any of them say? What would Thomas have said if he had known?

Sixteen and a half minutes later
But I really like him!

Eighteen minutes later
I finished my drink and was feeling quite comfy and relaxed, so I wandered back upstairs. Got into bed, read a few pages of my book, felt tired and relaxed and so put the light out. Lay down to go to sleep.

Wed 17 April – 11.30am

Coming back to last night once more, so then of course, no sooner had I closed my eyes than I thought I heard a sound. I couldn't tell what it was, or even whether it came from inside or outside the house. It was just too faint, barely there on the fringes of my perception. Well, I told myself calmly. What do you expect? It's your first night in a new house, there are going to be all kinds of sweet little charming noises to get used to. A lovely new house, with a lovely new character to adapt to and get to know, delightfully unfamiliar and quirky on the first night.

I closed my eyes again and told myself I was going to sleep. A moment later, there was the softest of sounds downstairs somewhere and then suddenly I was falling out of bed with terror at the blaring of the burglar alarm, like a claxon, screeching out down in the hall below.

Fingers in my ears, I ran out onto the landing without pausing to grab my robe. Sid and Lill emerged on the landing above me, putting on the light (Sid in traditional 'Dad' pyjamas in navy and brown striped cotton on a white ground, struggling to meet around the middle, Lill surprisingly pretty and young-looking in pale peach satin), and right behind them, Matt just in black stretch-cotton shorts which even in that terrifying moment I found rather nice. (He's got a little patch of hair in the middle of his chest, and he's got MUSCLES!). After previous incidents, I was wearing my new up-to-the-neck-and-down-to-the-floor giant cotton pyjamas, and even in the confusion of the situation Matt found a spare millisecond to smirk at me about them. Git.

We were all confused and saying stupid things like 'how do you turn the bloody thing off?' and 'I didn't even know we had an alarm.' Sid and Matt charged downstairs to look around and to turn off the system and they tried to figure out if anyone had genuinely attempted to gain entry or if there was just a loose wire or something.

Lill and I stood close together on my landing, and she was asking me if the police would be called out automatically by the alarm being triggered, when suddenly the noise ceased and my response of 'buggered if I know!' was deafening in the clanging silence.

My nerves were now completely shredded. Once Sid had called up to say all the doors and windows seemed to be locked securely and there wasn't anything obviously wrong, Lill and I went downstairs to the kitchen where she put the kettle on to make drinks yet again. Matt dialled the number to report the false alarm to the security company. He asked them to send someone over in the morning to check the system.

By then it was twenty to two in the morning. I felt exhausted but too edgy. The Hopkins trio sat at the kitchen table and chatted happily over their cups of tea whilst I sat a little apart, hunched over mine, staring at invisible ghosts and trying to force myself to relax. I kept telling myself it was just the kind of annoying little trifle that occurs in a new house from time to time. But I just couldn't seem to calm down.

Matt went back up to bed. Then Lill. Finally I felt I might as well go upstairs as sit in the kitchen worrying, and so once again I went upstairs and left Sid to check the doors and windows once more.

I reached my room as the little sitting room clock chimed two o'clock. I paused momentarily in the doorway. The room was in darkness, but something was wrong. I immediately sensed something was definitely wrong, but couldn't quite think what it might be.

I stepped over the threshold and the door closed softly behind me. Just like in the films, but hilariously unfunny, something cold and hard jabbed my neck. A soft voice broke the silence.

'Come in, Cressida. Don't make a sound, will you, or I'll have to blow your head off, just like I did to poor old Thomas.' Monica said.

I hardly dared to move. I felt her free hand hard and rough on my arm as she pulled me into the middle of the room, pinching my flesh through the sleeve of my pyjama top. I still couldn't see her properly, she was just a darker shadow in an as yet unfamiliar room full of shadows. But I could see the soft glint of the gun she held in front of her, and I had no doubt she would use it. I wondered vaguely which particular pub she had gone to in order to obtain it, and what calibre it was and how much she'd had to pay for it.

I felt I had to speak, to say something, anything, to try to keep the communication channels open and give myself time to think of some way out of this situation. Not surprisingly I wanted to delay the apparently inevitable outcome as long as possible. I seized on the first thing that came into my head. It wasn't very profound.

'How did you get in, Monica?'

She laughed softly. Her old laugh, familiar but it made me cold.

'It was child's play.' She said and then stopped. 'But this isn't one of those old movies where the heroine keeps the villain talking until help arrives or the heroine manages to catch the villain off guard. No one is going to find you until the morning, and obviously by then, it'll be a wee bit too late. And, FYI, you're the villain, not me. I'm the avenging angel. I'm the heroine, the victim of the piece. You're just some calculating bitch who killed my husband.'

There was another short silence, and I was wondering what to say, if anything. My mind seemed to have frozen. Why was she just standing there, watching me? I knew I had to say something, anything, but I couldn't think. Then I felt her do a little shrug movement and she said in an indulgent voice, warm and breathy, as if she was smiling in the darkness.

'Oh all right then, I'll tell you. What harm can it do? Though I think you'll be a bit disappointed at how ordinary it was. I took a key labelled 'new house back door' from your housekeeper's handbag in the kitchen when I was there the other day, took it away, got a copy made quite quickly and cheaply in a place not far from your old house – you should be pleased, I know how you love to support independent local businesses. Then it was absolutely a doddle to slip the original back into her bag on the night of the party. Wasn't quite as drunk as you'd hoped, was I? And obviously I'd already seen the listing from the agent – I simply grabbed it, toddled off to the loo, took a photo of the address with my phone and slipped it back later. Then, when I got home, I did an internet search. Great location. Easy to find. Nice area. Quite the bargain. Lucky old you.'

'So how did you come to set off the burglar alarm?' I asked. She tsked. I felt her shake her head impatiently.

'Oh that was just your stupid system – I didn't realise it was one of those where you have to key in a code within twenty seconds of unlocking the door or the alarm goes off. And of course, I didn't know the code. All I could do was to dive into the cloakroom and wait until I heard the alarm turned off and everyone trundle into the kitchen for a cosy little chat and a nice cuppa. By the way, you are getting rather intimate with the help, aren't you? I suppose it's because you fancy the son. And in all honesty, Darling, I can see the appeal, I rather fancied him myself, but really Cress, they are the Staff! I mean, he's been in prison, for God's sake! Have you no self-respect? I bet Thomas is turning in his grave right this minute at the very notion of you slumming it! And him only dead for eight short months! But I digress.

'Anyway, so then I nipped upstairs and waited for you. And now here we are. Best Friends Forever and all that crap. I must say, Cress, this really is the most lovely home. I can't wait to have a proper look round.' Her bleached teeth flashed white in the gloom as she smiled.

'I suppose I don't need to ask why you're here.' I said, still trying to remain calm, still frantically trying to keep her talking until I thought of something more effective. She didn't notice I was no longer keeping my voice down. She snorted.

'I should bloody well say not!' She said, not so quietly this time, but immediately lowered her voice to a hiss. 'You killed my husband! Did you really think you were going to get away with that? I want you dead, you evil bitch, I'm not going to let you just go wandering happily into the sunset to your lovely new life in your lovely new house with your lovely new bit of rough after what you did!'

'I've told you before, I thought it was what you wanted!' I protested. And I have to admit, even to me it sounded a bit lame. She shushed me hastily and pressed the gun a bit closer to my chest. But I was indignant, I wanted this misunderstanding cleared up once and for all so I continued in the loudest whisper I could muster, 'we've talked about this, I thought we'd moved past it. I thought you'd let it go.'

She was enraged.

'No! No no no no Cressida! I have not let it go!' She snarled, 'we have not moved past this – most definitely not! How could we? How could you even think that we could ever put something like you killing my husband behind us?'

'I did.' I lied. 'You killed Thomas. He meant more to me than my own life. But I've tried to move on, be your friend again, forgive you. Put it all behind me, rebuild my life.'

'Well I guess you're just a better person than me, aren't you?' She snapped, sarcasm making her voice louder and more carrying than she was probably aware.

All I could hope for was that one of the Hopkins would hear our voices and come to my rescue, but deep down I had a horrid floppy feeling in my stomach that Monica was just going to shoot me and walk away, stepping over my body like something nasty on a pavement and be gone again into the night before anyone even noticed anything was wrong. And I hadn't even made out a new will.

'But I thought that made us even and that we were friends again!' I said and this time I managed a bit of a sob. I suppose I wasn't really acting at this point, I really was terrified, trembling, and it was entirely possible I might wet myself at any moment.

She shook her head, as if she couldn't believe I was so stupid, and with more than a touch of exasperation said,

'God, Cress! That was what I wanted you to think! I wanted to get close enough to catch you off your guard. God, you're so stupid! And I know you put something in my cocktails – or if not you, it was your below-stairs screw. I had to switch to vodka and you know I can't mix my drinks. I was as sick as a dog the next morning.'

I was vaguely aware that I could see her more clearly now. For a second or two, I thought it was just that my eyes were adjusting to the low level of light in my room, but I then realised that while we were talking, we had moved slightly and now it was she who had her back to the door, and so she wasn't aware that behind her, the door was very slowly opening.

But even as I became aware of this, she seemed to sense something. And almost in slow-motion she began to turn her head and shoulder to glance behind her, and although there was no time for sound, there was a feeling, a rushing sensation, as if a sudden wind blew across the room, and Monica was making a grunting sound as all the air went out of her and she began to sag forward At the same time, I snatched up my heavy Art-Deco bedside lamp and swinging it hard, I flailed at her with all my might, aiming for her head, but she somehow twisted and avoided the blow and was forcing her way back through the door, taking the others completely off guard so that she was already halfway down the stairs before Sid and Matt had even begun to move.

Matt shoved his father out of the way, and taking the stairs three and four at a time, he tore after her, but didn't reach the front door until she had already wrenched it open and was throwing herself out into the night leaving him holding a piece of her blouse and I could still hear the sound of ripping fabric even though there was nothing but inky night filling the doorway and no sign of her. My best pal.

Then they all rushed around me, fussing and worrying, and I was astonished to realise that I was fine, not upset, just very slightly shaken but feeling – I don't know, somehow empowered - a wonderful sense of release washing over me. I was, after all, alive. Lill wanted to make me yet another of her hot drinks but I just dropped a kiss on her cheek and said,

'It's all right, thank you, I think I'll just read for a little while before I go to sleep. See you all in the morning.'

And I traipsed upstairs for the umpteenth time, and did as I said, I climbed into bed, leaving all my lights blazing, read a bit of Northanger Abbey, then after about ten minutes or so, I was relaxed and ready to sleep. I put out all the lights, lay down and the next thing I knew it was a bright, sunny morning. I wasn't being brave, I just knew she wouldn't be back that same night, and now – I'm not certain, but I don't think she'll be back at all. It is – it's finally over. Done and dusted.

But just to be sure, this afternoon, I'm having all the locks changed, and a new security camera on front and back entrances. One can't be too careful, there are so many dodgy people about.

Same day – 7.45 pm
Am absolutely dreading tomorrow, btw. But as I keep telling myself, it's another milestone reached and survived. Once I've got past tomorrow that will be another step in the right direction. Every day things get a tiny bit easier.

I'm getting more used to being alone – and although I do have days when all I want to do is cry or hide away, they're not as frequent as they used to be. And much as I miss him, I don't hate myself for being alive any more. One more step on the way – I'm like a recovering addict!

Thurs 18 April - 10 pm
It would have been Thomas's birthday today – he would have been – should have been – 37 years old today.

I can remember his last birthday so clearly. We had a wonderful candlelit dinner at La Maison des Saisons, we stayed for hours, just chatting, the long gaps between the courses melting away in the dancing light of the flames. Our eyes met across the table. The white linen, the gleaming glassware reflected the flickering candles. Everything had seemed either to be a mirror or a shadow, and it was all so tranquil, so intimate, like a tiny oasis that was ours alone.

So much has happened since then – so many unbelievable things. And most unbelievable of all, Thomas is gone.

And now it's difficult to remember his face. If I want to see his face, I have to get out the photo albums. I keep them on a chair by my bed, there's no point in putting them away, I need to refer to them so often. I can almost hear his voice on the edge of my consciousness, if I concentrate. But I no longer see his face, except in my dreams. Then I awake and it's as if he has left me all over again.

It's been a quiet, melancholy sort of day. I feel so guilty to be relieved it's almost over.

Lill remembered what day it was. She made one of her hearty stews and I ate with them in the kitchen.

I asked her,

'Was it ridiculous to buy this great big house? Perhaps I should have bought a little flat, something just big enough for one?'

She seemed surprised. Sid stopped eating, a drip of his stew meandering down through his grey goatee. Matt was looking at me with watchful eyes, his hands still.

'Aren't you happy here?' Lill asked me. I shook my head.

'Not today.' I stood up, pushing back my chair. 'Excuse me please. Dinner was lovely but...'

And I had to leave the room. I've been sitting looking out at the garden, Tetley curled up on the cushion of the window seat next to me, and she purrs whenever I scratch her cheeks or plump sides. She really is a dear little thing. I feel so awful about the other two. How callous I was. How uncaring. In some ways I'm glad I've changed.

Sun 21 April – 9.35 am
I can't believe it Why can I not just be left alone to get on with my life without **People** pissing me off with their interference?

Every time I feel like I'm at last getting a bit of peace and quiet, some moron decides to come and make a nuisance of themselves. I've just had a text from my mother, announcing she is arriving tomorrow. No 'do you mind?' or 'is it convenient? Just a text saying 'arriving Heathrow 1.30 Monday, send car, expect to stay three weeks or so Mother'.

God, I'm so furious. And what is she going to say about the Hopkins? No doubt she'll 1) disapprove of them, or rather my friendship with them and 2) upset them almost immediately by being as obnoxious as usual and 3) ruin my life and 4) try to make me marry some fat old bald millionaire with a dodgy heart just to appease her conscience and bolster her bank balance. (I think she gets a finder's fee.)

And she'll drink the place dry. And she hasn't said who she's bringing with her, but I mean, it's my mother, she can't possibly be travelling alone. She never does. She'll have some anaemic, terrified secretary with her, and her latest husband (can't even remember his name), and any variety of minions, step-children and Chihuahuas in handbags.

Why can't she stay in Guildford with my sister?

This is ridiculous. I won't go. If we don't pick her up, then she can't come here. It's as simple as that.

Except that she'd probably track me by satellite through my mobile. She's probably slept with the bloke that is in charge of stuff like that. And she's perfectly capable of contacting Scotland Yard if she thinks they will help her. Or Downing Street. Even the Royal family wouldn't be safe if she got it into her head they could do anything useful for her.

It's crazy. After all the effort I went through to get rid of Clarice, then Huw and what's-her-face, and Cess and thingy…and now I'm being terrorised by yet more relatives. After all the trauma I've been through! It's a wonder I'm not in therapy. Surely there's something I can do?

Mon 22 April - 8.30 am
I've been thinking about the Unwanteds and their impending descent. I think it's time to fall back on an old – but untried – favourite. Ethylene Glycol. Pale blue heaven in a bottle. I can't remember how much to use and there's no time to look it up now, we've got to leave shortly. But once we're on our way, I'm going to ask Mr Google on my phone and find out everything I need to know. I believe we may still have a little left in a tin can in the garage workshop?

In fifteen minutes Sid is driving me to the airport to meet my mother's plane. But before we leave I just wanted to let off a bit of steam. My life is an even huger disaster than I have so far confessed!

Matt and I are not on speaking terms at the moment. Yesterday afternoon I mentioned that my mother and all her hangers-on were about to descend and it was clear I wasn't pleased about it. Lill said they would rally round to help. Yes, Sid added, we've got your back. Bless them.

A few minutes later, from absolutely out of nowhere, without any further comments from me, their little Bundle of Joy said,

'Why do you always solve your problems by killing people?'

I gaped at him. Had he really just said that? Could he read minds now? Sid pushed back his chair from the table, as if trying to avoid getting splashed with blood, and Lill gave a horrified little gasp and spilt her tea.

How could he? What a thing to say. And anyway, so not true. I've faced up to and dealt with loads of problems. Like – like – well, I have! And anyway, I haven't killed that many people – it's only been – er – four. I didn't kill Clarice, did I? So obviously that wasn't my fault.

Anyway.

So I just got up and went to the door and walked out. I grabbed my car keys and my new favourite bag and drove into town for a sulk around the shops.

It's taken me until now to think of a witty comeback. I should have stood my ground and said,

'Probably for the same reason you deal with your problems by conning tourists out of large sums of money!'

Well, okay, it's not exactly the witty comeback of my dreams, but that doesn't make it any less to the point! He's not one to point the finger. But it's too late to be clever now. Hence the angry silences on both sides. Sid and Lill have tried to apologise, to reconcile the two of us, and I told them not to worry, it's not their fault. (Which of course it is, because a) he's their son and they should have brought him up not to say things like that, and b) they brought him into my home when he was released from prison and here he has remained.)

Am half-inclined to write to the Department of Prosecutions and grass him up for the Angel of the North thingy. That would teach the smug bastard a lesson.

Wed 24 April – 11.30 pm

Am practically a prisoner in my own home. Have fled to bedroom for privacy and solace but even here I'm not guaranteed to be left in peace!

My mother has arrived sans entourage but avec a step-child – to whit one sulky sixteen year-old. Not sure which of the exes is the girl's father – if anyone even knows. She is dressed exactly like my mother - a teenage Mini-Me – except that her red hair and prominent eyes don't do the little madam any favours. She looks a bit like a Muppet. Her real name is Whisper! I asked my mother what had happened to the nine-year-old boy I saw last time. She just shrugged.

Anyway, the house is all wrong – obviously! The area is wrong, my 'staff', me, everything – everything is all wrong and Mother is draped about the drawing room – as she insists on calling it – sunk deep in a slough of despond.

Surprise, surprise, she has already suggested I go back with her as she knows a lonely 'older gentleman' with a dodgy heart, a man who would appreciate a 'not-unattractive' girl past the first flush of youth. God!

And!!!

They've been here five minutes and already Sid has shut himself away in his workshop and Lill is banging pots and pans in the kitchen, her mouth a tight, straight line.

There have been a number of demands for special diet items – sushi, wheatgrass and tofu smoothies, weird barley-based hot beverages. Apparently Mother no longer drinks like a fish and is on some kind of health kick. And there have been quite a few comments about the meals coming from my kitchen being 'old-fashioned home cooking', being 'good, solid, plain fare', perfectly suited to 'farm workers and labourers'. I think if we had still been on the old employer/employee footing, Lill would have given notice.

Plus, from the second they arrived, Mother and The Muppet have wanted to go out. The Muppet seems to require constant entertainment, she can't do a thing for herself or by herself. We've dragged them out to a couple of local crags and monuments. The Muppet has barely looked up from her phone to say more than 'is that it?' Mother just kept complaining that everything was either too remote, not remote enough, not enough like LA or not enough like ye olde Englande. And then she kept stifling a yawn as if a) she was being bored to death or b) she was terribly frail and weary and I was dragging her all over the place against her will.

Want to strangle them both.

Fortunately they are both late risers so I had a peaceful and pleasant breakfast in the kitchen, and Lill has had a chance to let off steam to me.

But!!!

Again!!!

That stupid man! When I began to complain about my mother's behaviour, well not just hers, The Muppet's too, once again Matt just snapped at me,

'So tell them to go. Stop whining and tell them they've got to leave. It's your house, you don't have to put up with them if you don't want to.'

We had a bit of a tiff about that. Stupid man, does he really think it's that easy to get rid of unwanted guests? If it was, he wouldn't still be here!

Smartarse!

But have had a chance to think about it – and I suppose he could be a little bit right – I am the only one who can put an end to all this misery. And it's not fair Lill has to put up with all the extra hassle and the rudeness.

Stupid man. He's always right. I hate him.

Thurs 25 April - 11.25 am
My mother is driving me crazy. From the moment they set foot in – well, no actually it began about a minute after we left the airport – why hadn't we got them two luggage trollies – why had we parked so far away – why was it so bloody cold and miserable (like that was our fault – it's Britain - it's always cold and miserable, except when it's not hot and miserable, that is – and that's the way we Brits like it. You can't be always moaning about the weather if it's nice.)

Then when we were on our way back to the house it was 'why did I have to live so far away?' All they wanted, Mother said, was to get home and rest after their ordeal.

Then – why hadn't Sid carried their luggage upstairs - he had been about to do just that, once he'd located young Matthew, no point in having a young dog and barking yourself, after all – why was the house so small – why didn't all the bedrooms have an ensuite – when they stayed in Marrakech they had gorgeous bathrooms! I pointed out somewhat crisply that that had been in a five star hotel – this was a private residence. It made not a jot of difference. I'm certain she expected to find a bell-pull in her room.

Next it was – surely they weren't expected to unpack their own luggage? (Three cases each) Surely – my mother opined in a hurt voice – surely it wasn't too much to expect that SOMEONE could have spared a few moments to unpack for her? It wasn't as if she ever expected anyone to go to any trouble on her behalf. Why oh why oh why did I not have a proper, professional staff? My very standing in the community demanded it!

All this in the hearing of the kitchen – Mother never troubles herself to lower her voice or show any tact or delicacy. Have horrid sense of doom. Even more horrider than Sunday's sense of doom!

Same day – 4.15 pm
I made the mistake of mentioning my misery about my mother to the Hs again over an afternoon cuppa whilst Mother was 'resting'. (I have no idea what The Muppet was doing, locked away in the guest room reading erotica on her phone I should think.) Matt was there. It's my own fault, I should have known better than to say anything – he immediately said the same as he said yesterday, only even more forcefully:

'Just tell them to get out!' He said. I floundered. I tried to think of excuses. He just growled at me,

'For crap's sake, Cressida, strap on a pair for once in your life!'

Needless to say, we haven't spoken since then.

Doomier and Doomier.

Fri 26 April – 12.45pm
With what Matt-the-beast-Hopkins said still practically ringing in my ears, I sought out Mother after breakfast. She was lying on the swooning couch (my favourite spot – how dare she!) like a beached humpback, watching the television. Yes, she had even turned the couch away from the garden towards the goggle-box, I ask you! She had the TV tuned to ***Escape to a New Countryside Location by the Sea***, which was ridiculous because there was all that lovely greenery right behind her and birds singing their little heads off and there she was avidly gaping at the telly.

'Mother,' I said, 'I need to tell you something.'

She rolled her eyes just like The Muppet and with a big put-out sigh, muted the television.

'What is it now?' She asked. 'I'm trying to relax for once, and enjoy a little bit of television. It's so dull here. There's absolutely nothing to do, I can't think how you bear it!' She sounded just how I would have sounded at about 14, or in fact, just how The Muppet would have sounded if they had exchanged places. But The Muppet is still a child. Mother merely acts like one.

'I'm going to the Seychelles tomorrow.' I told her, mentally reminding myself to check Google to find out where it or they is or are. Just in case she cross-examined me about it later. She looked at me as if I'd just announced I was joining the NASA space programme.

'But why haven't you mentioned this before?'

'Well, I…' I faltered. Even though it was true, I didn't really like to say 'because you turned up here unannounced and uninvited and have been complaining and bulldozing me ever since', so I had to just say, rather lamely, 'Oh – er – I'm afraid I forgot.'

She would have frowned at me if she could, but instead settled for narrowing her eyes at me menacingly and cracking her foundation. I wondered if Sid could spare her some Polyfilla. I wonder if you can get it in Tangerine?

'You forgot?'

There was so much – I don't know - venom seems to be the most accurate word – in her voice. She seemed angry, disbelieving, and the look in her eyes. I just don't really know what I saw, I really don't. It was – evil. I was taken aback by her reaction, but it was too late to get out of it now. And I could hardly explain that it was the only way she would survive before I felt I needed recourse to the blue stuff in my bag.

I shrugged my shoulders. 'You know how the days run into one another. I just sort of lost track.'

'Well I don't see why we can't stay here if you really are going to the Seychelles. After all we'll have your staff to look after us. They're better than nothing.'

My Staff! I wanted to scream that they weren't my staff but my family. More than she has ever been to me. Where had my mother been when Thomas died? She had sent an elaborate bouquet of lilies and a card. Lill had held me in her arms as I sobbed snotty tears on her shoulder. Sid had driven me to my husband's funeral, he held my arm as I walked from the car to the crematorium on wobbly legs, and he gave me his huge hanky on the way home. My voice was cool as I said,

'I'm afraid I've given them some time off whilst I'm away, the house will be closed in order to have the electrics and plumbing updated. So I'm afraid you'll have to move into a hotel.'

'But how long are you going to be away?'

'Three months,' I said, off the top of my head, 'longer if I find I like it.'

'We can come with you!' She said, as if suddenly inspired.

I hadn't bargained for that. I couldn't think of anything to say. Suddenly exhausted, I couldn't be bothered to argue about it any longer. If she and The Muppet decided to join me there, then I would simply come back here.

'As you wish.' I said. I went to the door.

She gave me another one of those looks. At least, she tried to, but Botox is simply wonderful for preventing a petulant frown.

'You don't want us here, do you?'

'No,' I said. And I turned and left the room.

I headed for the kitchen and slumped down at the table with Sid and his racing pages and a large plate of chocolate digestives.

'I've told her to leave.' I announced. They exchanged a look and Lill dropped her cloth and rushed over to kiss my cheek,

'Oh that is good news!'

I gave them the gist of the conversation, if it could be called that, and ended with,

'So I hope I won't actually have to go to the Seychelles, however nice they are. And I also hope neither of you will need to move out either.'

Lill looked anxiously at Sid and then back at me. As usual Matt was off God alone knew where doing God alone knew what.

'What's the matter?' I asked her.

'We can't go away now,' Lill said, flustered.

'It's only a possibility, I'm hoping it won't actually come to that...'

'We've got some news. Good thing you're already sitting down.' I gaped at her, holding my breath. What fresh new hell was about to befall me? I held on to the edge of the table, my knuckles white.

'Tetley's expecting!' Lill announced proudly. I digested this revelation for a moment. The cat. That bloody cat! I looked over to the cosy cat bed in the corner. There appeared to be a small tabby elephant-seal curled up on a massive cushion made from some of Liberty's finest fabric. I sighed.

'I suppose that explains why she's a little – er – plumper than – er usual...'

'Exactly. The vet's had a look at her,' Lill was warming to her favourite topic now, and pulled up a chair to perch next to me, all the better to give me a full outline of the case history. She was doing 'everything's okay' gestures to me, both hands palm down. As if I was the hysterical one. 'He says she's fine, everything should be perfectly straightforward.'

'When?' I asked weakly, trying not to catch Sid's eye, trying to remain composed.

'About another two weeks.' Lill said. 'I've arranged a nice healthy diet for her and the vet is going to pop in a couple of times a week, and we can call him anytime, day or night, if we've got any worries whatsoever. Only, of course, it does mean no disruption of routine or nasty shocks.'

I nodded. If she'd told me the cat was checking into a private clinic for the duration, I would not have been surprised.

'Well, let's see what happens over the next day or two, shall we, and hope for the best?'

Same day - 6.15pm

Visitors gone by teatime, hooray! And – I hope Matt is happy – I haven't killed a single person!

Clearly I'm growing as an individual. I mean, no one knows how difficult these last few days have been for me, and yet I have managed to deal with my problems in a mature and non-violent manner. I deffo deserve a Nobel peace prize – I'm practically a humanitarian! Especially when you consider what I'm paying in vet's fees!

Sat 11 May - 1.55pm
OMG!!!! I can't believe it! I just can't believe I could be this low, this shallow, this selfish, this disgusting, this…this…well I can't think of enough words to say what I want to, but I hate myself – and him! Especially him! It's his fault too. In fact it's all his fault!

    I took myself off upstairs because I was upset about the kitten that died. I know it's really stupid, I know it's just an insignificant little scrap of life, but it really upset me for some reason – I mean it should have been something that would (eventually) grow into something tiny and fluffy and adorable but instead it was damp and limp and pathetic and the horrid little noises Tetley made, as if she knew, and so it was all too much and I fled upstairs like the coward I am, intending to just take a few moments to collect myself.

    And then he came up. Was I okay, that sort of thing. Hateful man. How dare he! How dare he be so tender, so gentle yet somehow so persistent. It's almost as if he planned it. I feel so – not just used but manipulated. I feel as though I've been studied like a rat in a lab and then put into a maze where every turn I made was calculated to bring me to one single point and place. He knows my behaviour, anticipates my emotional responses, he knows exactly how to draw me in.

    So he sat next to me on the edge of the bed and put his arm round me, which made me go all weak and weepy and clingy. (I hate myself and as I remember this, my face is absolutely burning with shame!) And then he was kissing my neck and it just sort of happened. He nuzzled my neck and was saying soft words against my skin and suddenly we were literally tearing each other's clothes off and – well – oh dear…

I'm weeping again. But it's not just shame or anger – my guilt goes deeper. I have betrayed Thomas! I can't understand how something so devastating could grow out of an apparently ordinary situation. I feel like I'm lost. Now I will never find my way back to the right path again. How can I ever redeem myself so I can look my husband's memory in the eye again?

And I'm almost afraid to go downstairs. I'm dreading looking into his eyes and seeing that amused, knowing look, that smug, all-conquering expression – my downfall part of his entertainment for the week.

And what if Sid and Lill know? What will they think, say? Will they be horrified, disgusted? Or is this what they've all been planning all this time, to get me in a position of vulnerability?

But no, I don't really think…

Oh, God! I just don't know what to think…

And of course, afterwards, I just sort of mumbled something and grabbed my clothes and raced for my bathroom and locked myself in. I ran a bath to cover the sound of my hysterics and after about ten minutes or so, when I was calmer, I heard him leave.

If only I'd shouted at him. Or mustered my tattered dignity and told him to get out. But because I ran, I lost the advantage, lost the chance of taking charge of the situation and knowing exactly how things stood.

Why am I such a moron?

Oh holy shit what am I going to do?

Later – 2.45 pm
I've been sitting up here for nearly two hours, too scared to go downstairs. But it's my house after all, and obviously I can't stay up here forever.

So I've mustered the tatters of my dignity etc etc and done my face and my hair and changed into a really super new outfit. I look as cool, calm and collected as it's possible to look when one feels like wetting oneself in terror.

Right then. I'm going to go downstairs and generally stalk about a bit being confident and unruffled, then I'm going shopping. Wish me luck!

Later still – 9.30pm
So I went down and after a bit of pointless and unnoticed stalking and unrufflage, I finally tracked Lill down to the utility room where she was tucking in Tetley's blanket around a few semi-furred, tiny bodies suckling happily at her enormous undercarriage (Tetley's not Lill's!)

Lill turned and beamed at me in teary happiness, her mind wrapped around just one concern.

'Just the four then,' she said, 'but the vet's been and checked Tetley and the babies over and said they're all fine. Two girls and two boys. The two tabbies are a boy and a girl and the tortie, obviously, is a girl and the ginger one, as I'm sure you realise, is the other boy. And the vet took away the poor little chap what didn't make it.' Her voice quavered, and before my own precarious composure crumpled, I pointed to the ginger kitten.

'Looks a bit like Twinkle, doesn't it?'

'Hmm well, I suppose sometimes even a lady goes for that rough, dangerous type.'

I looked at her sharply but there didn't seem to be anything behind what she'd said. So I asked,

'Have you thought of any names for them yet?'

'Thought I'd wait and see if you had any suggestions, Cressida.'

'That's all right, you can name them. But don't forget, we will have to give them away to new homes, we can't possibly have five cats around the house.'

She laughed merrily. And changed the subject by asking if I was going out. I said I was. She said something about everyone going out and leaving her to her babies. I said,

'Are the boys out too, then?' 'The boys' meaning Sid and Matt-the-Vile-Seducer. Of course, she, being blind to their faults, referred to them simply as 'the boys', and I had begun to do the same. She nodded.

'Gone down the pub.'

I said a hasty goodbye and left.

OMG! That means Matt will be sharing bedroom secrets (my bedroom! Eek!) over a pint with his father! OMG I am never going to be able to show my face again.

Quick, I thought, I need therapy, and was driving down the road to Gloucester in twenty seconds flat.

For the first time in ages, I wished Monica and I were still friends. I really needed her advice and sympathy right now. I missed having someone to hang out with.

Desperate, but knowing I was letting myself in for an I-told-you-so lecture I rang Jess in Scotland once I got to the nearest coffee shop, and I poured out the whole story to her, horribly aware that a woman sitting at an adjacent table was unashamedly eavesdropping.

After Jess had worn out all her I-told-you-so remarks and simmered down, I said,

'Yes, yes, you're a bloody genius, now stop telling me off and tell me what I can do to make this all okay.'

'Do you think he was just using you?' She asked. I laughed, angry. What was she talking about?

'Of course he was just using me! What else would he have been doing?' I said with as much scorn as I could load into those few words. I mean, I love her to bits, but really!

'You could sack him, if only he actually worked for you. I suppose you could sack his parents…'

'That's just not an option,' I snapped, envisioning Lill suing me for custody of the kittens.

'But as I was about to say when you so rudely interrupted, that's not going to happen, so you'd be better off just having a chat with him, grab the bull by the horns and say that it was all a terrible mistake and you would like to forget all about it, and then you will just have to make an effort to get on with your life. Hopefully lesson learned.' When I didn't say anything she added, more gently, 'it will get easier, Cress.'

I nodded then realise this wasn't radio and said thank you.

'And now, my Darling, I'm sorry,' she said, 'but I've got to go, we've got Americans.'

I sighed and put my phone away. The woman at the next table was still watching me and I toyed with the idea of saying something simply horrid just to make her leave me alone. She leaned forward and whispered loudly,

'I'm terribly sorry to intrude, but I couldn't help overhearing. Something similar happened to me a couple of years ago.'

She was well dressed and wearing gorgeous shoes and so I patted the seat of the chair next to me in invitation and she and her cappuccino scooted across.

'Vivienne Spartan-Martin,' she said. She held out a dainty little beringed hand and I shook it.

'Cressida Barker-Powell.'

She took up her teaspoon and began to swirl her foam with it.

'I take it you've slept with your hired chappie, and regretted it in the morning?'

I admitted it was something along those lines.

'Well,' she said, and leaning closer she began to carefully and embarrassingly lick the foam from her spoon. 'You might find that a more regular arrangement is satisfactory to all concerned. I decided to allocate funds to my chappie, to make it an official and prearranged thing. After all,' she took another dainty lick with the hot-pink tip of her tongue, eyes half-closed in pleasure, 'we women have our needs.'

Oh God, I was thinking, what new nightmare is this? Outwardly I sipped my coffee nicely, patting my mouth with my napkin now and again. I said,

'I don't think that would really be quite 'me'. But it's an interesting idea.'

She didn't seem offended. She gave a little shrug.

'Well in that case, you will just have to apologise for the lapse and ask for his discretion. Presumably, if he's in your house, you trust him? I mean, there's not really anything else you can do.'

She was right. Jess was right. Time to stop panicking and just hope I could trust him, hope we could move on.

'You haven't done anything wrong,' she added, 'and you are only human.'

I nodded. True. All too, too true. Unfortunately.

'Was he any good?' She asked. I couldn't help a rueful smile. Now I stirred my coffee.

'Oh yes.' I said.

I mooched around the shops with my new friend. We exchanged phone numbers and email addresses. Possibly we might meet up again some time, she seems all right, if a bit, well, you know, unusual.

Mon 20 May - 4.10pm
I managed to corner Matt in the front hall when he was doing something with a screwdriver and a shelf bracket and, seizing the moment, I said in a rather rushed voice,

'With regard to what happened between us the other day, I would like to apologise for my regrettable behaviour and to assure you that I will in future always maintain my composure and of course, my distance, at all times and without exception, so you may rest assured there will be no further unpleasantness in that regard. Good afternoon.'

He looked first surprised, then even more surprised, then distinctly annoyed. I do not understand that man. But at least he now knows where he – and I – stand on this rather tricky issue. Hopefully that's the end of it.

It is too late to get my perfect life back. I see that now.

I used to think all I wanted was a) a baby and b) for Clarice to leave us alone. And now, I will not have the baby, and even though Clarice is dead, I will never enjoy a long and happy life with Thomas, so her death has made no difference to my life one way or the other. It was all completely pointless.

I've realised now all I long for is for things to be how they were then, at the beginning of this mess. I want to go back to how things were at the start of this journal, on page one, the day of my birthday, when Clarice's lack of consideration was really all that was troubling me in the rosy little garden that was my life.

Thurs 23 May - 8.45pm

I wrote a few days ago that all I wanted was to go back to that time last year before everything changed.

But obviously I can't go back in time. So I have to look forward, no real choice about that. I've thought of suicide a few times, but I'm too gutless to do anything so drastic, and therefore, as a human being I have no choice about going onwards into the future. I can't remain in the 'now', let alone return to the 'then'.

So what do I want out of life now?

Well, I still want to be left alone. I hate it when people phone up, text me, email me (actually this one isn't too bad, it's nice and remote and impersonal, I can open the email or not open it, as I prefer, when I choose). I hate actual, physical visitors even more.

So how do I get what I want?

I could join a monastery. Or well, no, I mean a nunnery. But I don't think I'd like getting up in the middle of the night to pray and besides I'm still very cross with God for letting Thomas die.

Monica might be the only thing that is standing in the way of my peace and quiet. I mean, I know I'm not keen on chatting on the phone or having people over – or – even worse – going to the homes of other people for dinner or what-have-you, but in the main it's because Monica is the one person I dread to hear, to see, to meet. She has become The New Clarice.

But on the upside, I now have no one left whom I would dread to lose. So.

I have made a decision.

In a way, I've re-made an old decision.

But now it's time to get on with it. I've wasted far too much time already.

As an early birthday present to myself, and to greatly enhance the quality of my life, I'm going to kill Monica. Let's get this over with once and for all. I need closure.

Sat 25 May – 9.25pm
Just had the most bizarre text from Mother. And now I feel just terrible after the way I behaved. Goaded on by Matt of course, (who has not spoken to me for almost a week and seems to be sulking about something) and out of concern for Lill and Sid, but that doesn't make it any easier. Here's the text she sent, word for word, with her own special text-speak.

'Darling, plse forgive sudden invasion. Didn't stp to thnk. Soz sweetheart I know we were bit difcult. But smthng happnd and had to get out. Cn u believe that horrid man has actlly been forcing hmslf on Whsper. She finlly told me in fluds of tears and my only thght was to get hr awa. Now in hotel in snny Med. Will be in touch. Take care Darling luv mummy. xxxx'

I feel absolutely terrible. If it's true. And why would she make something like that up? I mean she's many things, my mother, but a liar she is not! That poor, sweet young girl. Have tried to think of something to say but can't quite think how to put it into words and not sound totally inane. And – can't remember 'his' name. Boris? Morris? And can't even remember if he's Whisper's father or a 'step'.

She's never called me Darling like that before. As if she meant it.

Same day – 10.40pm

As I was cobbling together some clumsy response, Mother rang. I think that's the first time she and I have ever had what I would call a rational talk. She was like a completely different person! It was – nice! She had a little cry, said she blamed herself for her poor judgement over this chappie, husband number five, whose name apparently is Desmond (nothing even slightly similar to Boris!)

She said she was so upset last time things fell apart over the loss of her little step-son Clement, (the nine year old I asked her about – she said she'd found it too painful to talk about that situation!) that this time she pulled out all the stops and got custody of Whisper from her drunk father and his barmaid-mistress. Then of course, Mother met Boris, I mean Desmond and now it turns out that Desmond has been doing horrid, horrid things to poor little Whisper – no wonder she's such a sulky little brat. So Mother had to leave Desmond and take Whisper with her. She said she just didn't know where else to go, and she hoped that, being a bit closer to Whisper's age, I'd know what to do and say.

Oh God! They sought refuge with me and look how I betrayed them! I threw them out! I've told them to come back, but Mother says it's all right, she has arranged a trip to Switzerland once they have topped up their tans, to give Whisper a bit of a break, but they might pop back here in a couple of months. Will set some sensible ground rules then, and hopefully we'll all have a nice time. She said she just doesn't know what to do about Desmond – I mean, she doesn't want to live with him after what's happened as he is now officially scum, but apparently her money is running out rather rapidly and she's worried if she doesn't hook herself another millionaire quite quickly, she will be left high and dry.

    Am wondering if there is anything useful I can do about Desmond. I mean, if he did that to Whisper, what are the chances there have been – and might continue to be – other young victims? He's a menace to society!

    Hmm.

    Ponder. Ponder.

Wed 29 May - 11.30am
Okay, so there's the perfect little retreat I've just found on the Interweb. It's not as grand as Chapley's, nor does it offer quite the same range of activities and therapies. But it does have two distinct advantages: 1) They can fit me in next week and 2) They're only twelve miles from Monica's.

This new place is called Lavender Hall Health Spa. Bit uninspiring to be honest. Still, how bad can it be? I'm getting déjà vu just thinking about it. It's Chapley's all over again. Not quite sure about the details yet but I'll think of something, I know it. I've just made the booking – four nights (so there's time for some actual relaxation slash therapy!). And obviously I'll drive myself, so that will give me plenty of flexibility.

I asked for a room on the ground floor, told them I was nervous of fires. Hopefully they've still got the same windows I saw in the website photos of their guest rooms, I'm absolutely convinced I'll be able to just hop out the window to go to Monica's, and no one any the wiser! Still, I might need to think of a back-up plan in case they've done something ridiculous like replace all their windows in a hysterical refurbishment programme (and to be honest, it does look a teeny bit in need of a little refurb.)

It's astonishing. I can feel all the old excitement of last year's first trip to Chapley's. Am humming 'Like a Virgin' as I look out of the window and find inspiration to finally deal with this ultimate pain in my perfect little bum.

Soon Monica will be no more. Must start practising tribute phrases so I can say them on the day without giggling.

'Much missed'
'Beloved Friend'
'Sadly taken in her prime'
'Senseless waste'.
Yay! ;)

Same day - 1.00pm
I think I will take all my old Clarice-killing gear, as I haven't firmed up my plans yet.
So here's my list:
Leotard x 2
Yoga pants & vest x 2
Zippy jacket (in case weather is beastly)
Trainers
Nice top and skirt/trousers for evenings
Nice wrap in case a bit chilly after dinner
Little heels and bigger heels
Jeans and nice blouse/t-shirt
Sports bra (in case I need to run – and because of yoga and other assorted keep-fittery)
Balaclava
Black sneakers
Black sweater and black leggings
Gloves
Small handgun or knife? Hmm not sure about the knife – don't want to get icky)
(I wonder if Matt knows anyone who can get me a gun on the QT? Surely he has oodles of dodgy ex-con mates?)
Ooh – almost forgot - extra-gentle moist cleansing tissues

Same day – 1.45pm
No.
I've got it now. Ethylene Glycol. After all I've waited so long, and so patiently to use it. So, so long. So, so patiently. It's time. I will slip in and put it in – well, something, not sure what. I'm sure to happen on something as I rummage around her kitchen. Then I'll leave. By the time it finally happens, I'll be miles away. With luck, it should be chalked up to food poisoning or even suicide – after all, it's well-documented that she has suffered from mental illness in the last year.

So I will add to my list 'a tiny bottle of my favourite stuff'.

I'm flooded both by a sense of relief and a sense of fulfilment. This is what I should have done a long time ago. At last I'm going to be free of that selfish bitch and Thomas can really rest in peace, atoned for, avenged, appeased.

It's all so wonderful, I feel all teary.

Thurs 6 June – 6.15pm
Arrived in good time for afternoonsies. Gorgeous Pimms, best I've ever had. It is a small place, as I suspected but so good – really personal service and very discerning clients, the few I've met so far. Apparently Lavender Hall is something of an open secret (probably the twee name alone puts people off) and much treasured by its clients who seem to all be regulars. One lady said this was her thirtieth year of coming here. Didn't like to point out that it didn't appear to be doing her much good – terrible skin, dreadfully arthritic, short-sighted, in fact I'm not sure any part of her was working properly apart from her snobbery. She was all right with me once I opened my mouth and she heard the finishing-school accent, but the comments she made about a couple of other ladies – games mistresses by the look of them, here for a dirty weekend.

My room's nice enough. A bit small, especially when compared to Chapley's more generous proportions, fairly plain, but actually I quite like it. One can have too much luxury. Windows even better than I could have hoped – they are mini French windows, opening onto the garden at the rear of the Spa, quite close to the car park (convenient for sneaking out!) but not so close as to endanger one's healthy spa-experience with noise pollution.

Getting ready for dinner in a mo, should be interesting to see how their food compares with Chapley's. Then I might have a little potter around the grounds, followed by an early night (ready for a good day of therapy tomorrow) and if I chance to have a little wander in the garden late this evening, before retiring for the night, and if my little walk should happen to take me to my car and thence to Monica's, well, I really don't think anyone is going to notice.

What a nice place this is.

Must recommend it to all my new friends.

Same day – 9.20pm

Absolutely exquisite dinner – the chef here really knows his stuff! And I've made an utter pig of myself – don't know if can even move, let alone have a quick walk round the gardens and then go to Monica's.

Perhaps a little sit in the bar with a couple of new pals? Got to let my dinner go down, obviously, as don't want to get indigestion, and after all this is supposed to be a health spa – obviously one's digestion is treated with more than the usual respect here.

Haven't heard anything from Mother since the other day. I do hope Whisper is all right. Perhaps she'll relax a bit in Switzerland and will be able to recover a bit from all that's happened. And hopefully Mother will meet a nice elderly Swiss chappie who has no interest in young girls. Of course, he'll have to have pots of cash and a dodgy heart. But where better to find someone like that than at a Spa in Switzerland?

I'm still wondering if perhaps Desmond should go the same way as Monica is about to. I think I will have to take some 'affirmative action'!

Fri 7 June – 10.10am
Why on earth she needs such a massive house, I'll never know. After all she has no one to share it with – not a boyfriend, a cleaning lady or even a cat. (I wonder how Tetley and the babies are, must text Lill in a mo.)

    I arrived last night in time to see Monica's lights glowing behind upstairs curtains – she must have been in bed. The rest of the house was in darkness so it was easy to nip in the gate and stand in the shadows of the little shrubbery by the front door, taking it all in and waiting for the right moment. I put my gloves on.

    I waited. The drizzle was cool and pleasant on my face, the night full of the soft noises of the evening. I could hear the murmur of her TV as I made my way through the negligently unsecured side gate and along a rather nice undulating walk to the rear of the house and the kitchen door.

    I was going to whack the glass in the window next to the door with my torch. But on an impulse I tried the door and that too was unlocked! Honestly, single women living alone ought to have a bit more sense, I mean, anyone could just walk right in, and that is exactly what I did.

    I was in a darkened room. I risked a quick flash of my torch, curtained by my fingers, and holding it below the level of the window. I was in a utility area.

    Ahead of me, an open door revealed the dim interior of the kitchen – the red eyes of the microwave and cooker glowing softly. A humming nearby told me I was by the fridge.

    I opened the fridge and peeked in, dazzled by the sudden brightness. From somewhere above my head I heard a soft movement and I held my breath, letting the fridge door close. There was the sound of a door closing and a bolt being drawn across. I could hear someone – presumably Monica – peeing and then a couple of unladylike farts. Really, I thought, then remembered that of course she thought she was alone.

I looked in the fridge again. And found an opened bottle of Sangria, still half full (optimist that I am), so I decanted some of my precious cargo into that. The remaining anti-freeze I poured into the last quarter of a carton of orange juice. I felt that I had covered all bases.

Mission accomplished I closed the fridge and waited for a few seconds for my eyes to readjust to the darkness.

Upstairs, the toilet flushed and water ran in a basin, and a moment later the door opened and was followed by a soft sound that told me she had gone back to bed.

I waited another minute for her to get settled then quickly flashed my torch in the direction of the rubbish bin.

In the bin I found an empty water bottle. This was perfect for my plan, and served her right for not recycling. The woman clearly had no social conscience at all. I imagined my suicidal friend, trotting out to the garage, tipping some of her antifreeze into a handy little mineral water bottle, taking it back into the kitchen, doctoring her fave tipple and her healthy breakfast drink, then binning the empty(ish) water bottle. It was perfect!

I emptied the dregs from my bottle into Monica's discarded one, being very, very careful not to touch it more than I had to, and only gripping it by the screw top – didn't want to run the risk of spoiling her depressed little fingerprints. A quick swish and then I put the bottle back in the bin.

Two minutes later and I was back in my car. Fifteen minutes after that, I was back at Lavender Hall tucked up in bed with a nice book.

Slept wonderfully last night. I feel so full of hope, of confidence. Life seems once again full of possibilities. Hurrah!

Sun 9 June - 5.35pm

Hmm. Must admit to feeling a vague sense of anti-climax. Have heard of no calamities relating to a single lonely, mentally unstable woman killing herself with anti-freeze in either sangria or orange juice. I've listened to the radio news and the television news, and scanned local and national papers. But not a sniff of a police person laden with sad news in the village. How disappointing!

Not quite sure what to do. I mean, I can hardly ring Monica and ask her why she's not dead yet. And I don't really know anyone that is still in touch with her. It's all a bit of a predicament.

And I'm finding it very hard to properly enjoy all the pampering and the therapy with all this uncertainty hanging over me. Greta, the masseuse, says I'm really very tense and knotted up. 'Relax!' She keeps telling me. 'About what do you have to worry? You here to relax, Mrs Cressida, so do that!' Nice lady, a bit butch.

Did think about casually driving passed a few times in the hope of catching sight of her – thus alive – or seeing the house engulfed in crime-scene tape – thus dead. But obviously I can't exactly frequent the vicinity in case I arouse any suspicions.

What to do?

Sun 16 June – 3.45pm
It's been a little over a week since I popped round to Monica's, and I'm falling apart.
I can't stand the tension. I mean, I know I don't need to go over there, because I know that she's still alive, because if she was dead, by now I would have heard something one way or another. But not a dickey-bird. And the urge to go and check for myself is almost overwhelming. I just don't know what to do. And all that good work at Lavender Hall has been undone.

And as if things couldn't get any worse – must pause to detach a rotund tabby kitten from my bedroom curtains – as if things couldn't get any worse I am now completely and utterly certain that I'm pregnant!!!!!

I've peed on three sticks in the last three days, and the same result each time. There's no doubt whatsoever. Plus my tummy feels tender, my boobs are sore and I feel very slightly queasy most of the time.

My feelings are an utter mess of contradictions. I mean, first of all, obviously, it's Matt's baby, and I could write about 1000 pages on that problem alone. BTW he's seems to still be sulking over my apology for seducing him.

Secondly, when I think of how much Thomas and I wanted a baby, and it never happened, and I think of how many doctors we saw, how many tests we underwent, of the hormone treatments, the poking, the prodding, the anguish of failure of each passing month – and now, completely by accident, unplanned, with no difficulties, no intervention, no treatment, here I am, up the duff! Bloody robust working class genes.

What the hell am I going to say to Matt? And how the hell are we going to break the news to Lill, and to Sid???? OMG!!!!!!

God, that bloody little cat again, I'm sure it's Bingley, it's the tabby one. He's such a little rogue. My curtains will be completely shredded by the time he goes to his new home. Must find out from Lill how soon that is likely to be.

Anyway, so I'm completely freaking out – I don't know what the hell I'm going to do, and I've got no one I can talk to about it. I mean, this is DEFINITELY not one for Jess.

I mean, if it was just me, I'd be thrilled, and whenever I stop panicking and just enjoy the enormous secret, I'm so excited and happy.

I'm pretty sure Lill will be over the moon, to use her own favourite phrase. And I think Sid will be too. And I know they will fuss over me and take care of me. I mean, just look at the way our vet – before he retired to Antigua – look at the way he was called out morning, noon and night just for a bloody cat.

Though come to think of it, cats probably rate a lot higher with Lill than humans, but even so – her own grandbaby. And Sid will just keep shaking my hand and telling me that he is chuffed. He is a brick, and I've got no qualms there.

But how will Matt react? Will he be angry? Will he try to make me get rid of it? What if he hates the idea? What if he thinks I somehow tried to trap him into this?

OMG my thoughts are just such a whirl of confusion – I'm just not getting anywhere!

Mon 17 June – 3.30pm
Had a quick chat with Lill this morning re the kittens.

Theoretically they should be going to new homes quite soon. In practice, I suspect she is trying to wangle them a longer stay with us. Bingley and Darcy are a pair of little fiends, into everything and I've lost count of the number of time I've had to rescue them from difficulties. They're always balancing precariously on top of a bush or halfway up a curtain or stranded on a high shelf with no visible means of how they got there to begin with. Never knew cats could be such fun. That Darcy is the image of Twinkle – so I suppose with hindsight I realise that the fight in the shrubbery that day was not exactly that, after all!

On the other hand, Jane is a boring, well-behaved, cautious little thing, always perfectly clean and tidy and just where you left her. Lizzie isn't much better – she is something of a tomboy, getting into small amounts of mischief, chiefly things like running up the nearest human leg and using the resultant human shoulder as a launch pad to higher things. But her mischief is nothing to that of the boys!

But although Lill has her contact in the village post office who has promised to broker a deal between us and a farmer's wife in respect of Jane and Lizzie, there appears to have been no success whatever in getting Bingley and Darcy adopted.

I am convinced Lill has no intention of letting them go, and she is probably making no attempt whatsoever to find them new homes – in fact I would not be the slightest bit surprised to find that she is making sure all offers for them never reach my ears.

And even Sid and Matt are smitten with the furry little gits; I'm always happening upon one or other of 'the boys' scratching and tickling and playing with one or other of the 'babies'. And most sickening of all is the way they talk baby talk to them if they think no one else is around!

Can't help wondering how everyone is going to react when I make my announcement.

Have decided I've no choice but to face up to the situation – or at least, start to face up to the situation. I've got a doctor's appointment tomorrow. This is not likely to go unremarked, as I'm not the sort of person to be constantly at the doctor's.

Quite scared about the fact that soon I'm going to have to tell the Hopkins'. But, however much I try to pretend, this is not something that is going to go away.

Had a call from Jess and Murdo, was I planning on coming up this August 12th? She phrased it a lot more delicately than that. But she wasn't surprised when I declined. Have promised to go up at the end of September – it'll be all nice and autumnal, and I won't be there like Banquo's ghost, ruining the shooting party for them. I think she was quite happy with that. Feel a bit bad not telling her my news, but frankly, I'm dreading her reaction. Anyway, I can't tell her before I've told Matt.

Also, in my mind, getting past that terrible date is key to getting over losing Thomas. It's the anniversary, looming like a horrid black deadline on the horizon, and I feel that once I get past that date, things will be a bit easier, like getting past

Christmas, and Thomas' birthday. It's taken me a while to allow myself the possibility of having a life without feeling guilty and treacherous. I mean, it's not like I've stopped missing him – that couldn't happen. But I've got used to the fact that he is gone and it's okay for me to carry on, and now I realise I can do things differently if I wish, I don't have to confine myself to doing what Thomas would have wanted to do. Just as well, really, considering this thing with Matt and the baby and everything. I tell myself Thomas would have been pleased for me. He might not approve of my choice, but he would have wanted me to be happy. So happiness is what I'm going to try to aim for.

It feels a bit weird to say that. It feels a bit awful too. But my mind keeps telling me this is the right way to deal with everything. Because now there's a baby to think about, and there's Matt – well, there's sort of Matt.

Which brings me back to what I was talking about earlier – OMG what am I going to do? Is it best just to blurt it out over dinner, tell them all together, get it over with? Or should I take him to one side with a quick 'could I have a moment with you in private?' Which will raise expectations and eyebrows and ensure everyone's attention is firmly focussed in my direction.

Huff. Just don't know what to do. Maybe he'll just somehow be around, and I'll be around, and no one else will be around and so I can nab him and quickly get it off my chest????

Then wait for the fireworks, I imagine.

Oh God, what if he hates me? Suppose it's a total disaster. What if he, and Lill and Sid, and Tetley and Bingley and Darcy all up and leave me, and it's just me and my poor little baby all alone in this big house like Lady Catherine de Bourgh and her useless daughter?

Same day – 6pm
I can't believe it. After all my anxiety about how to broach the subject, how he'd react, how Lill and Sid would react…

I went into the kitchen at about four o'clock in search of an afternoon cuppa. And there he was, my knight in stolen armour, clearing up cat sick from under the table, bum uppermost, and he didn't hear me come in, and jumped half out of his skin when I spoke and banged his head on the table, dropping the cloth and kneeling on it at the same time, all in one smooth move.

What a guy!

Obviously the language that accompanied this event was not exactly Shakespeare.

He got up, rubbed ineffectually at the sicky-damp patch on his jeans and glared at me.

'What the hell are you trying to do?' He snarled.

'I'm pregnant.' I said, and burst into tears. And at that moment Lill and Sid walked in from the garden carrying siege-quantities of cat food.

'What?' He looked at me. Sid and Lill looked at both of us.

'I'm pregnant.' I said again, but now it wasn't exactly the perfect moment I had been waiting for.

Lill gasped, dropped her bag of Kitty Snax and clapped her hands to her mouth in shock. Sid said something colourful along the lines of 'fuck me!' then apologised profusely.

And Matt swept me into his arms.

This was a huge relief. He seemed to be pleased. I thought he was pleased. Was he pleased? Just to be certain I said,

'You are pleased, aren't you?'

He looked at me and I could see his eyes were full of tears. He nodded and gripping me close to him in his arms he grumbled,

'Yes, Cressida, of course I'm fucking pleased.'

And he buried his face in my hair and held me, saying nothing more.

Of course it was next to impossible to have a proper discussion about it with Lill all teary and happy, and she kept hugging me and saying things like 'bless you, dear' and 'oh thank you, thank you.'

It was all very moving but more than I could cope with and I had the urge to get away so I said I was a bit tired – that useful catch-all stand-by for the pregnant woman – and went back upstairs.

And now I've got to get ready to go for dinner with some people in the village – newly met – the Maxwell-Billings – and even though it isn't very far, Sid insists on driving me.

Tues 18 June – 10.45am
'Goodnight, Gorgeous.'
That was what he said to me outside the front door last night.
He came in Sid's place to collect me from the Maxwell-Billings. I was tempted to sit in the back and let him be the chauffeur proper, but in the end I schmoozed into the front seat next to him. He drove slowly, then when we got back to the house, we sat in the car for a good hour, although in fact we said very little.

I said something needy and pathetic like,
'So you're okay about the baby, then?' At the same time he said,
'So how was your dinner?'
I told him dinner had been fine, the M-Bs seem very nice. And then he said,
'Yes, Cressida, I'm 'okay' about the baby. More than okay as a matter of fact. But, where does that leave us?'
I said I didn't know. Suddenly I felt very small and miserable. His hand came out and covered mine, and it was warm and reassuring. He asked a few things like due dates and so on, and I told him I wasn't seeing the doctor until this afternoon but that I think the baby will be due about end of Jan, beginning of Feb. I think he's a bit worried I'm just imagining it all now he knows I haven't yet got any medical backing for my outrageous claim. Never mind.

And whilst we sat there, I expected we would have a long conversation about our feelings for one another and our relationship and everything, but in the end he simply said,
'Did you see anything of Monica while you were away?'

It caught me off guard. Surely he didn't still have feelings for her?

'Just wondered if you'd decided against bumping her off, that's all.' He added.

Ah.

I told him about my little field trip to her house late at night, and about the ethylene glycol and the lack of events resulting from its deployment. He nodded in the dark.

'Ah well, disappointing.' He said. And that was it. He kissed me on the cheek and dashed round to open the door for me. Conversation terminated at 00.26hrs.

'I'll get the car put away for the night then. Goodnight Gorgeous.'

That was it.

After a few seconds of standing on the drive like the last kipper at breakfast, I went in and went to bed.

That man is a moron.

Same day – 4.15pm
Just got back from the doctor – I was booked straight in to the ante-natal clinic – I assumed they would want to do their own pregnancy test, but apparently there's no need – she said the tests you can buy in the chemist are every bit as reliable as their clinic's own. Anyway, nice chat etc all okay now have a schedule of visits and appointments to make and will be hearing shortly from the rather nice private hospital where I have elected to have the baby. So feel like I've got an 'official' seal of pregnancy which will no doubt please 'Himself' who clearly thinks I am not capable of knowing whether or not I'm pregnant. Must write my due-date on the calendar – Sunday 2nd February 2014. Plus or minus two weeks, apparently.

Same day – 9.45pm
Today has simply dragged by. And talk about a let-down. Lill has been busy all day with cleaning and cat-sitting, and she's been on the phone to prospective adopters.

Sid and Matt have been out all day. I've been on my own virtually the whole day. Feel a bit neglected and sorry for myself. And bored.

Got a postcard today from Mother in Switzerland. No indication she's has met a poorly millionaire, but you never know. Just a quick note about how nice it was to have a proper chat and that they were having a nice quiet time, and she would phone me again soon.

Speaking of phoning, I phoned Madison Maxwell-Billings to say thank you for the lovely dinner, and we had a nice chat. She's very pleasant but we're just not on quite the same wavelength. I think we will be friends but never exactly bosom-buddies. And she's all for doing the church flowers and holding charity lunches. That's just not me.

I wandered down to the village church on the way home from the doctor's this afternoon. It's quite pretty, and old, one of those typical village churches built about 800 years ago and patched up once Henry VIII was safely dead and not likely to bash it about again. It might do for our baby's christening next year.

Sat 22 June – 9.30am
I don't know why I'm surprised.
Have just come back from the kitchen. Lill is in floods of tears due to Jane and Lizzie being adopted today by a friend of the farmer's wife. Bingley and Darcy are wandering around in a pathetic little daze mewing for their siblings, and Tetley is prowling the house and gardens in search of her lost babies. It's just like a crisis centre for the homeless.

I'm still not too sure that it wasn't all an elaborate plot to weaken my resolve. No sooner had I said the words, 'perhaps we ought not worry about finding homes for Bingley and his little bro…' than Lill was out of her seat like a greyhound out of the stalls and enveloping me in one of her surprisingly strong housekeeper's hugs.

'Oh thank you, thank you! I was so hoping you'd say that. It's almost too good to be true. With the baby as well,' she added, as an after-thought.

Oh God, now what have I done?

But it has been another dull day. Must try to think of something to do to make the time go by more quickly. But somehow I had foolishly imagined I would see something of the father of my child, that somehow we'd be able to develop a relationship.

But as always, he's been out all day. Where the hell does he go?

Same day - later – 4.45pm
I wandered into the kitchen earlier for a cuppa. Sid was outside doing something manly with a hammer and some wood. Lill was busy getting together her baking bits and pieces – she's making me a birthday cake! But she sat down with me at the kitchen table. Bingley was trying to eat the leg of my chair and Darcy was asleep in the middle of the table. I made some remark to Lill about Matt's strange absences. She gave me one of those knowing looks, and then cleared her throat as if she'd made up her mind to tell me something. Felt a vague sense of dread.

'He visits his son.' She said. I gaped at her, goosebumps coming out all over my arms. 'I told him he should tell you – you've got a right to know. Now you're – you know,' she nodded towards me.

'Pregnant?'

'Involved, I was going to say.' She sipped her tea and I stared at the floor, the tiles swimming before my eyes. She patted my hand.

'It's all right, Cressida, there's nothing going on with him and his Ex. He hates her. But he loves the little boy, obviously, and that's why he's spending time with the little chap when she's at work, and he's doing everything he can to keep out of trouble and sort himself out. He wants to get custody of the little boy. Her new fella's not a very nice bloke from the sound of it. Matt says little Patrick's not being looked after proper, but these things take time, and the little one's not in any actual danger, Matt doesn't think.' She looked down at her skirt, biting her trembling lip. 'He's a lovely little boy,' she said. 'He's not quite four and he can write his letters and count and all sorts.

And his lovely blond hair, he's the spit of Matt when he was little.'

And on she talked. She found a few photos and showed me them he did look like a little sweetie, if a bit pinched-looking in the face, and a bit small for his age. Didn't have the happy, well-cared for look of a normal pre-schooler. I felt a surge of maternal dismay when I saw how thin he was. I groaned inwardly. Another one or possibly two to go on my new hit-list. First Desmond, and now this 'Ex' of Matt's, Tracey. And in all probability her new 'Fella' too. Not only that, but continuing the trend that began first with Sid, then the cat, then Matt, it sounded as if once again my household was about to expand. It sounded as if little Patrick should be brought home to us as soon as possible. Once again, my mind is a whirl of thoughts and feelings and images.

As I got up from the table, I patted her hand.

'Don't worry,' I said. 'There's plenty of room here for one more. I'll talk to Matt.'

For once Lill had nothing to say, but it was all there in her glistening eyes. She reached for her phone and began to text.

Sun 23 June – 10.30pm
Just got the strangest text from Matt. All it said was,
'Criss Cross Cress.' And two kisses.
Does this mean what I think it means? I mean, we've talked about it. And he knows what I want to do, what I'm thinking and what I've been planning for my 'best pal'. He knows this is the same message, or near enough, that Monica sent to me. So I can only think it means…He must have done it! He knew it would make my day, that it would be the perfect birthday gift, and he no doubt wanted to prove his love to me. What a wonderful man! Oh the relief – to think she's actually gone from my life. It's all over. I can't get over it, it's just wonderful!

Mon 24 June – 2.20pm
Thirty-three today. And I thought thirty-two felt old! Have received some lovely cards and presents from a few people – Jess and Murdo, obviously, even Mother and The Muppet managed to send an eCard with a cuckoo-clock on the front, and a card from the Hopkins', very sweet of them to remember. And a small package from Matt that I guessed even before I opened it was a new journal.

But in spite of all this kindness I'm still a bit blue today.

I looked back to the very first page of this journal, to that lovely little note from Thomas. And now the page is blurry from splashes of tears. His lovely neat, loopy script, in its purple ink from a 'proper' pen, it's a bit blotchy now. But still comforting, still familiar.

I can recall last year's birthday so clearly – the excitement of waking up and remembering it was my birthday. I was like a child! And Thomas, laughing, the little crows-feet in the corners of his eyes crinkling as he laughed, the white even teeth, the sound of his laugh in my ear - a sudden, loud bark of laughter. The two of us had made plans which Clarice then proceeded to destroy.

But Thomas is gone and now my life is shared with this bunch of eccentric people, and this baby who is growing day by day inside me. Oh dear, birthdays make one so introspective! Will wander back down to the kitchen and see if I can scrounge a cup of tea.

Matt has been odd today, very weird and smug. He keeps doing his 'alright Darlin' smirk at me – he really thinks he is God's gift to us poor womenfolk. I haven't had a chance to talk to him about his little boy in London, or to thank him for his other little 'surprise gift' – still no news as yet on that front, but fingers crossed, it's still early days. Mainly because he's being too annoying. How on earth am I going to get him to toe the line?

I suppose he'll think he has the right to sleep with me soon, as he is now more or less my partner.

At least, I hope he'll think he has the right to sleep with me. He keeps smirking at me, as if he's got an exciting secret only he knows about. I've read that men feel more potent when they become – or are about to become – fathers, due to the baby being evidence of their virility. Essentially I am now a referee as to his manliness – all his future conquests will be referred to me for confirmation that he is a fully-functional male.

Feel bad-tempered now. Hope that's just a symptom of being pregnant and not just me being my normal grouchy self.

Lill is sweetness itself though, treating me like a queen. She is decorating a little cake for me.

Sid is all sentimental too, and typically male, he is trying to act as if nothing has changed but all the while he looks as though he would like to high-five his son and shout 'Yes!' Anyone would think Matt had scored a winning goal for England.

Ooh phone call for me.

Same day – 4.15pm
OMG!!!! OMG!!!! OMG!!!!
That was Nadina. She had the most amazing news. I'm so excited. It's all true!
Apparently late last night, Monica 'fell' down her stairs and died.
Of course I had to pretend to be distraught and numb with grief and shock, but as soon as I'd said goodbye, I did a little dance around the sitting room. It's too wonderful, I can hardly believe it. I must find Matt and thank him properly. Nadina says Monica had been drunk – well, no surprise there! She was found this morning by her cleaning lady who called the emergency services but it was all too late.

Wow.

It's really over. Must take a moment to let that sink in.

Can't write any more – I really must go and find Matt. What a lovely, adorable and clever man he is.

<u>THE END</u>

Caron Allan lives in Derbyshire, Great Britain with her husband and two grown-up children, and two cats. She mainly writes mystery and crime fiction but has occasional forays into fantasy fiction.

Criss Cross is the first book published by Caron Allan, and a sequel is in the pipeline, hopefully to be unleashed on the public in the Autumn of 2013. Caron is also hoping shortly to publish a ghost story, The Silent Woman as a Kindle eBook.

If you liked this book, please consider reviewing it on Amazon, and catch up with Caron Allan on Facebook where you will find further and exclusive fiction as well as news and views.

Thank you.

Printed in Germany
by Amazon Distribution
GmbH, Leipzig